DARK WIDOW'S SECRET

THE CHILDREN OF THE GODS BOOK 23

I. T. LUCAS

VIVIAN

One month ago.

"*I*sn't it amazing?" the woman sitting next to Vivian whispered loudly. "Who knew colors have such a strong influence on the psyche. Just this one class is worth the price of admission."

"Uh-huh." Vivian nodded.

Money-wise, maybe; time-wise, not so much. Getting a one-day pass to the convention wasn't a big deal, but wasting the Sunday she could've been spending with her kids was.

It seemed that psychic conventions had very little to do with actually being psychic—or telepathic, as in Vivian and Ella's case.

There had been one lecture on communicating with the spirits of loved ones who'd passed away, but nothing about conversing telepathically with loved ones who, thank God, were very much alive.

Evidently, what she and her daughter could do was unheard of. They were indeed the anomalies Vivian had always suspected they were, or freaks of nature as Ella referred to their special abilities.

At least they were lucky enough to be born in a supposedly enlightened era. During the witch hunts, those abilities would have branded them as witches, and the two of them would've ended up burning at the stake.

Vivian shivered. It was such a brutal world, and witch hunts of one kind or another still haunted societies that believed themselves to be ruled by logic and science and not by superstition. It always shocked her how easily people could be convinced of nonsense and then commit atrocities in its name.

How are you guys doing? she sent to Ella, then waited for a response.

If Ella closed the channel, Vivian couldn't open it from her side. Ella, on the other hand, had no such limitations. Whenever she sent a telepathic communication to Vivian, it got through whether it was convenient at the moment or not.

I'm at work, Ella answered. *Sally called in sick, and Ronda asked me if I can cover her shift. I dropped Parker at Ethan's.*

Vivian rolled her eyes. It was amazing what that girl would do to get out of babysitting her brother, going as far as taking on an extra shift at the diner instead of spending time with her friends.

I told you that he has a history project to finish.

He said he is going to work on it with Ethan.

They are just going to play video games.

His problem. Not mine.

When are you picking him up?

After my shift. How is the convention? Did you get to meet any interesting freaks? I mean like us. Not the turban-wearing fakes with crystal balls.

No. So far it's been a colossal waste of time.

I told you so.

Yes, you did.

I have to go, Mom. People are looking at me funny. See you at home. The barrier slammed into place, disconnecting the mental line as if it was an ordinary phone line.

Unlike Vivian, Ella had complete control over the telepathic communication. The girl could close the channel and block Vivian out when she didn't want to talk to her. And since she'd reached puberty, Ella could also limit the communication to what she was actively sending and not her other thoughts.

Vivian could only do the latter but not the former. But then her daughter had been born with the ability. Vivian hadn't.

When her baby had first started sending images into her mind, Viv had been sure she was going crazy. But when the pictures had turned into fully verbal conversations, she could no longer deny that the communication was real.

The instructor held up a thin paperback. "This is your chance to buy a signed copy of my book, *Living in Color.* Come and get it, people!"

As her classmates rushed to the front of the lecture hall, Vivian grabbed her purse and hurried the other way. Out in the corridor, she stopped and pulled out the syllabus. With both Ella and Parker doing their own thing, she might as well check out some of the other classes.

"You should try the one on the healing energies of gemstones," a pleasant male voice said from behind her. "Research shows that there actually might be something to it."

With an inward smile, Vivian looked over her shoulder, and then was taken aback. The young man was gorgeous, and she'd only gotten as far as his face.

Smiling blue eyes, chin-length light brown hair, and lips

3

that were made for kisses. And what's more, his breath smelled good, all fresh and minty. As a dental hygienist, Vivian appreciated people who took good care of their teeth.

Ella would've gone gaga over the guy, and Vivian would've approved.

The problem was that he was hitting on the wrong woman, one who was too old for him and had sworn off men after killing a husband and two boyfriends. Well, not actively, only by association, but still. Vivian did not want a fourth on her conscience.

Besides, it was better to be alone than to suffer through another tragedy. Her heart could only take so much.

Fortunately, she was adept at getting rid of unwanted attention. "Really? Did you read it in a medical journal?"

He moved in front of her and offered his hand. "In fact, I did. Dr. Julian Ward at your service."

He looked like no doctor she'd ever seen.

Over six feet tall, athletically built, and a face that should be on the front of magazines, or medical journals, if he was telling her the truth. Some guys went to extreme lengths to impress a woman.

With a smirk, she shook his hand and introduced herself. "Mrs. Vivian Takala."

Glancing at her ringless fingers, he arched a brow.

Damn, she'd forgotten to put on her wedding ring. Having a job that necessitated wearing disposable gloves meant that she couldn't put on rings, and she never wore them at home. They were reserved for situations like this, when a guy was hitting on her and she needed to refuse without hurting his feelings.

For some reason, though, Vivian felt bad about perpetrating the lie. "I'm a widow." God, how she hated that word. It never failed to give her heart a painful squeeze.

Seeming genuinely saddened, Julian winced. "I'm sorry for your loss."

What a nice guy. Maybe he really is a doctor?

She should give him the benefit of the doubt. If she spent some time talking to him, she could get him to give Ella a call.

He might not be interested in an eighteen-year-old girl, but that would change once he saw Ella's picture. No man was immune to that kind of beauty, and in a few years, the age difference would become irrelevant.

Viv and Josh had married by the end of their senior year of high school, but that was because she'd gotten pregnant with Ella. They had been in love, but it hadn't been easy for them. Both had to give up dreams of attending college, and earning a living to support their family had always been a struggle.

Viv wanted a better life for her daughter.

JULIAN

*J*ulian was about to concede defeat and slink away with his tail tucked between his legs, when Vivian surprised the hell out of him. "Would you like to grab a cup of coffee?"

Introducing himself with his medical title was a fail-proof come-on line, but it was low. At least it was true, though. The one about the article in the medical journal wasn't. But when Julian caught sight of the Kim Basinger doppelgänger looking over the pamphlet, he just couldn't help it.

As a kid, he'd had a huge crush on the actress. Impossibly, Vivian was even more beautiful than Kim. Except, she lacked the actress's sexy curves.

Picky, picky.

He was, but not so much as to miss an opportunity like this. The woman had the face of an angel.

"I would love to. Starbucks?"

"Coffee Bean." She pointed. "I like their Frappuccino better."

After getting their drinks, they carried them outside and found a bench.

"Are you enjoying the convention?" Julian asked to start a conversation.

She shrugged. "I guess. Most of it is useless. Between work and taking care of my kids, I don't have time for meditation. But maybe the next time I repaint the house, I'll choose colors to promote love and peace." She rolled her eyes.

"How old are your kids?" Julian didn't have a problem hooking up with a mother. But if her kids were little, he would suggest his hotel room instead of going to her place.

"Parker is twelve, and Ella is eighteen." She pulled out her phone.

Great, now she was going to show him pictures, and he would have to pretend he was interested.

"Ella wants to study nursing," Vivian said as she turned her phone to show him her daughter.

Not to be rude, he took a quick glance, and then sucked in a breath. It was like getting hit in the stomach. "Wow."

The girl was gorgeous, her big smart eyes staring at him from the picture as if seeing right through him. Needing a closer look, he took the phone from Vivian's hand and spent a good minute staring at the daughter before tearing his eyes away to look at the mother. "Nursing? She should pursue modeling or acting."

With a satisfied smirk on her full lips, Vivian took the phone away from him. "This picture is actually from the one photo shoot she's ever done. Ella is not tall enough to model clothes, but she scored one gig modeling running shoes. Her first and last. She said it had been brain-numbingly boring and not what she wanted to do with her life. Ella is a smart girl, and she knows that having a good profession is more important than being pretty. I'm so proud of her."

"What about acting?"

"That's not a good profession. It's more about luck than anything else."

"I can't argue with that. Is she starting college next year?"

Vivian shook her head. "Not yet. She took a year off so she could work and save up money first. We are going to take out student loans, but she'll need spending money."

"That's good," Julian said because he could think of nothing else to say.

His tuition had been covered by the clan, and his mother had taken care of all his other expenses. Most people didn't have the luxury of dedicating all of their time to study.

Vivian waved the hand holding the phone. "Turn your airdrop on. I'll send you the picture."

Once again, Julian didn't know how to respond. To refuse would offend Vivian, but to accept felt wrong on so many levels. The girl was eighteen, for Fates' sake.

A child.

He shouldn't look at the girl's photo and imagine how her lips would feel as he kissed her, which was precisely what he was going to do if he had it and kept looking at her beautiful face. "I don't think it's appropriate. I'm twenty-six. That's way too old for an eighteen-year-old girl."

Vivian's lush lips curled up. "And yet you had no problem hitting on a woman ten years older than you are. It seems to me that age differences don't matter to you."

She was direct, he had to give her that.

"You don't look it. But I would've done it even if you did. You're a gorgeous woman, Vivian."

"Thank you." She sighed. "I guess I understand. In the same way that you're too young for me, Ella is too young for you." She put a hand over her chest. "It's just that I have a feeling that the two of you should meet. A strong feeling."

Well, that was interesting. After all, Julian had come to

the convention to search for people with special abilities. Maybe Vivian was psychic.

"Do you get these kinds of feelings often?"

She eyed him suspiciously. "What do you mean?"

"Like you know that something is going to happen in a certain way."

"No, why do you ask?"

He waved a hand at the building the convention was being held in. "I assumed you came here to meet like-minded people. It is, after all, a psychic convention."

Her eyes narrowed into slits. "Is that why you're here, Julian? Are you a psychic?"

"Unfortunately, I'm not. But I'm very interested in the phenomenon. I hoped to meet people with special abilities."

Vivian's shoulders relaxed. "Yeah, I thought the same thing. There is that guy who teaches how to contact spirits. Did you attend his lecture?"

"I've been here the entire week. So, yeah. The last one on my list is the class on healing gemstones."

"A week is a long time. Are you from around here?"

"I'm from Los Angeles."

"Oh, yeah? Where do you practice?"

"I'm interning in my mother's clinic. She is a doctor too."

Vivian smiled. "That's awesome. Do you get along with your mom?"

"I do. My mother is my inspiration."

She put a hand over her chest. "That's so sweet. I wish Ella and I could work together, but she thinks that what I do is disgusting. I'm a dental hygienist." Vivian lifted her purse and took out her wallet. "Here." She handed him a business card. "If you need your teeth cleaned before going back to L.A., I can get you a rush appointment."

"Thank you." He took the card and put it in his pocket.

"Show me your teeth. I'll tell you if you need a cleaning."

As if he was going to let her take a peek at his fangs. A quick redirection was needed. "You know what? I changed my mind about the picture." He pulled his phone out and activated the airdrop feature. "Send it to me. I have an uncle with connections in Hollywood. Maybe he can get Ella a small part or two. Even the small ones pay well. It can help with her college fund."

"Thank you, that would be wonderful. I'm sure an acting job would be much more exciting than what Ella does now, which is waitressing at a diner."

"I bet." Feeling like an ass for lying to Vivian again, Julian smiled without showing his teeth.

Except, it wouldn't be a lie if he really talked with Brandon and got him to arrange a few auditions for the girl.

The clan's media specialist had a hand in several productions, including a couple of popular television series. He could get Ella a small role. It didn't even need to be a speaking one. If she had no acting talent, she could play the part of a cheerleader or a waitress or some other background character.

ELLA

"The guy in booth four keeps staring at you," Maddie whispered in Ella's ear as she brushed by her on the way to the kitchen. "He's cute. Do you want to take his order?"

As if a guy looking at her was something special. Everyone looked. Men, women, young, old. Ella was quite sick of it. Since she was a little girl, everyone had been commenting on how pretty she was, but it hadn't been so bad before she'd agreed to do that photo shoot.

She should've never done it. Not for the hundred bucks they'd paid her, and in retrospect, not even for a thousand.

The ad was supposed to showcase the shoes, not her face. It had appeared in an obscure teen magazine, and it hadn't even been a big one, but then someone had posted it on Pinterest, and that's when the circus had started.

The guy in booth four was probably trying to figure out where he'd seen her before. "He's all yours. You take his order."

Maddie shrugged. "Your loss. He is really cute."

Curiosity getting the better of her, Ella took a peek,

hoping she would catch him when he wasn't looking. But of course, that was too much to ask for.

The guy was looking right at her and grinning as if he'd overheard them talking about him.

Shit.

Still, Maddie was right. He was attractive, and he was also older, like maybe twenty-two or so. Ella had never gone on a date with an older guy before.

Perhaps she should give it a try?

Dating boys her age was a drag.

Like Jim, the quarterback all the girls were after. The guy had only two interests. Sports and his collection of girls' panties. When she'd refused to drop hers on their first date, he'd been graciously willing to accept them without having sex with her.

As if.

But at least Jim hadn't been a bad sport about that, and she still said hi to him whenever they bumped into each other. Unlike Tommy, who'd gotten offended by her refusal, calling her a frigid bitch to her face and then repeating it to everyone who cared to listen.

Maybe it could've been different with smarter guys, but, regrettably, none of the chess club geeks had had the guts to ask her out.

Ella would have taken brains and some basic manners over muscles any day. So yeah, the high school dating scene had been nasty. But maybe an older, more mature guy would be different?

It was worth a try.

She waved at Maddie and mouthed, "I'll take it."

Her friend gave her a discreet thumbs up.

Not to be too obvious, Ella stopped by her other customers, asking if they needed refills on their coffees or their sodas. Once she got to his booth, she lifted her tablet and peeked at him from the top of it. "What can I get for you?"

Up close, he was even cuter.

Dark brown messy hair, warm brown eyes framed by long lashes, and a clean-shaven face, which was a rarity among young guys. He had nice skin too, smooth and olive toned.

The guy opened the menu. "How are the pancakes, any good?"

"Excellent. Would you like eggs with them or a bowl of fruit?"

"Can I have both?"

"Sure. It will cost you extra, though."

"That's okay. And the coffee?"

"It's good too."

"Then I'll have a cup."

"Will that be all?"

"For now."

Up until the last sentence, Ella had thought he wasn't going to initiate anything, but then his voice dropped an octave on those last two words.

For some reason, she found his indirect approach sexy.

When she came back with his coffee, he glanced at her name tag. "Have you been working here long, Ella?"

"Only a couple of months. Right after I graduated from high school." Better let him know how old she was up front.

"That's cool. Any college plans?"

"Eventually, I want to study nursing, but I'm taking a year off to save up money first. How about you?"

He chuckled, the deep masculine sound sending shivers down her spine. "I don't need a college education for what I plan on doing with my life."

Ella put a hand on her hip. "Oh, yeah? And what's that?"

"To start with, I'm going to manage my uncle's pizzeria,

and then I'm going to open one myself. Then another one, and another one, until I have a whole chain of them." By his smug expression, the guy thought it was an awesome plan.

"Well, good luck with that."

Her tablet buzzed, announcing an order was waiting for pick-up at the kitchen. It could wait a couple more minutes. She wasn't done talking to the cute guy yet.

He poured sugar into his coffee mug and stirred it with a spoon. "Do you have anything against self-starters, Ella?"

"No, I find it admirable. That's why I said good luck. It wasn't meant as a put-down."

"My bad." He offered her his hand. "Romeo Giovani."

That was one hell of a sexy name.

"Ella Takala." She shook what he offered.

His handshake was firm but gentle, and lasted the appropriate two seconds.

"Takala, I've never heard that name before," he said as he leaned back.

"It's Finnish. It means remote dweller."

"Your father is from Finland? I've never heard anyone speak Finnish. I wonder how it sounds. Is it similar to Swedish?"

Embarrassed about how little she knew of her heritage, Ella blushed. "My dad's paternal grandparents were from Finland, but I don't think he knew the language."

Romeo frowned. "Knew?"

She nodded. "My dad was killed in Afghanistan when I was seven." Why the hell was she telling him that? A complete stranger?

He reached for her hand and squeezed it gently. "I lost my father in that fucking hellhole too."

MAGNUS

Two weeks ago.

𝓜agnus hated to admit it, but things were boring without Anandur around. His new roommates were decent, quiet lads, but they were both programmers who worked from home and hardly ever left their rooms. When they did, it was to get something to eat or talk about things he didn't understand.

They were literally conversing in a foreign language, but not one Magnus could absorb as easily as a human one. Computer languages, he'd discovered, had nothing in common with actual languages. It was more like math, a subject he'd never been good at.

Even their humor was different. He often joked that they were like real vampires, shunning the sun and sitting in dark rooms with the curtains tightly closed, but the fellows didn't find it funny. Apparently, it was a generational thing. He didn't get what was humorous about the silly YouTube clips they showed him, and they didn't get his jokes.

He should have roomed with other Guardians, but

everyone was already paired up, and there were no vacancies. His other option was to move into the new section that was finally ready and have a house all to himself.

Thank you, but no thanks.

"I'm heading out to the café. Do you want me to bring you something?"

Peter shook his head. "No thanks. I'm trying to cut down on sugar. I have a hard time falling asleep."

"That's because you drink twenty cups of coffee a day and stare at your monitor for hours. Get out of here and take a walk. That will help you sleep."

"I don't have time for walks." Peter lifted his coffee mug and went back to his room.

"It's all a matter of setting priorities," Magnus called after him.

Freddie refilled his mug. "Well, the break is over. Time to get back to work. See ya later." He followed Peter.

These guys lived in the virtual worlds of their games.

Perhaps it made them feel like gods to create whole new worlds and then get to experience them. Otherwise, they wouldn't be working on a Sunday, and a Saturday, and every other day of the week.

Well, good for them. While they were sitting in their dark rooms and playing gods, he was going to enjoy a nice walk through the village. Stuffing his phone and his wallet in his trouser pockets, Magnus headed for the café.

As he'd expected, since it was a Sunday, all the tables were taken, but there was a vacant chair next to the one Julian was sitting at. Magnus zeroed in on it before anyone else had a chance to grab it. The young doctor was well-liked and got along with everyone. If he didn't hurry, someone else would gladly join the guy.

"Hey, Julian. How was the psychic convention?" Magnus pulled the chair out and straddled it.

"Mostly a waste of time. They should have called it the mumbo-jumbo convention."

"A bunch of yahoos with crystal balls, eh?"

"I wish." Julian sighed. "That would have been at least entertaining. How about you? Did you hear anything from Anandur? He was your partner, right?"

"Yeah, he was. But then he got himself a mate who happened to be the Clan Mother's best friend when they were both girls. Annani wanted Wonder to be with her, so naturally Anandur had to follow."

"Yeah, I've heard. That's one hell of a story. Does he like it up there? I've never been to the sanctuary. My mother didn't go to stay at Annani's place when I was born. Doctor's duties and all that."

"Right. It's not like she could've left without arranging for a replacement. But there was no one. Now she has you."

"That was one of my main motivations for attending medical school. I thought that if I joined her, she'd have more time for her research. I never expected her to take on the heading up of a huge rescue operation."

"She's one of a kind, your mom."

Julian smiled. "I know. I'm very proud of what she's doing."

"Let me see if I have pictures of the sanctuary I can show you." Magnus got up, turned the chair around, and brought it closer to Julian before sitting back down. "Anandur and Wonder are having a blast over there. The Clan Mother is showing them some good times."

Magnus pulled his phone out and searched for Anandur's latest text message. "He keeps sending me pictures from all over the place. Look at this. Those are from New York and the previous ones are from Paris." He handed the phone to Julian. "I wouldn't mind an assignment like that."

Julian scrolled through the photos and then handed the phone back. "Nice. They look happy."

"Aye."

"Excuse me," Julian said as his phone pinged with an incoming message. "I've been waiting for this."

Magnus waved a hand. "Don't mind me. I'm going to get something to eat. Just don't let anyone take my chair."

"You've got it."

When Magnus returned with his sandwich, Julian was staring at his phone with a lovesick expression on his face.

"A lady friend?" he asked as he put his plate down.

Julian lifted his head. "What?"

"The message. Was it from a girl?"

"Oh, no." Julian waved a dismissive hand. "It was from Brandon. I asked him to arrange an audition for the daughter of a friend of mine."

If the kid had been staring lovingly at a message from Brandon, Magnus was going to eat the paper plate together with the napkins.

"Who's the friend?"

"A lady I met at the convention. Vivian. Her daughter Ella wants to study nursing, but she took a year off after high school to work and save up for it. Vivian showed me a picture of the girl, and I thought Brandon could find her a few gigs. She is very pretty."

So that was who Julian had been staring at. "Can I take a peek?" Magnus reached for the phone.

"Sure."

"Wow, pretty is an understatement. She looks a bit like the young Natalie Portman." He handed the phone back. The girl was indeed movie-star beautiful. No wonder Julian was infatuated. "Was she there with her mother?"

Julian shook his head. "No, and that's a funny story. I was

trying to hook up with Vivian, but she brushed me off and showed me her daughter's picture instead."

Magnus lifted a brow. "Hitting on a married woman? You've been a bad boy, Julian."

"She didn't wear a wedding ring. How was I supposed to know? Besides, Vivian is a widow."

"Is she as pretty as her daughter?"

"Vivian is a knockout. A Kim Basinger doppelgänger if I've ever seen one. Even more beautiful, but without the curves. And I mean none." He shook his head while smoothing his hand over his chest.

Some men were into breasts, but Magnus wasn't. Not that he would say no to a voluptuous beauty if one fell into his lap, but he preferred petite, delicate women.

"Is she tall?"

"Who, Vivian? Not at all. She is quite small, and so is Ella. That's why she can't model clothes even though she is so beautiful." Julian lifted his phone and gazed at the photo again. "Her being petite prompted me to think about hooking her up with Brandon. A lot of actresses are short."

Magnus laughed. "Are you sure hooking up is the term you want to use in the same sentence as Brandon? You seem to be fascinated by the girl."

Julian bared fangs that had suddenly grown an inch longer. "I meant for a job. She is eighteen. No one is hooking up with her. Not Brandon, and not me."

"Why not? Eighteen is kosher. Look at Anandur and Wonder. She is what, nineteen?"

"No, she is not. She is older than the Clan Mother."

"Stasis does not count. She has lived, like in actual living, for less than twenty years. And Anandur is over nine hundred years old."

"Vivian and Ella live in San Diego."

"Big deal. It's less than three hours' drive away. Give her a call, Julian."

The doctor crossed his arms over his chest. "She is a human."

Magnus chuckled. "Okay, then. Perhaps while you keep staring at her picture, she will age and magically turn into an immortal."

"I'm not going to pursue an eighteen-year-old."

5

VIVIAN

Two weeks ago

"May I be excused?" Parker asked.

Ella pinned him with a baleful stare. "Not so fast. It's your turn to wash the dishes."

He turned to Viv with a pleading puppy expression. "Ethan is waiting for me to play online. Can I do the dishes later?"

When he made that face, Viv could never say no, and the little scoundrel knew it. "Fine. But if you forget, and I have to remind you, you'll wash tomorrow's dishes too."

"I won't forget." Parker jumped up from his seat. "You're the best, Mom." He gave her a quick peck on the cheek before dashing to his bedroom.

Ella crossed her arms over her chest and pinned Vivian with a reproachful stare. "You should limit his screen time. All he does all day is play games on his computer."

In the absence of a father, Ella had taken upon herself the role of a second mother to Parker. Except, her contribution was mostly limited to giving Viv unsolicited parenting advice and the occasional babysitting.

"The future belongs to these computer-obsessed kids. I would've worried about him spending too much time gaming if he were doing poorly at school, but Parker is getting excellent grades. As long as he does his homework and completes his chores, he can play to his heart's content."

Ella shrugged and uncrossed her arms. "When he starts wearing glasses and develops a hunch, don't say I didn't warn you." She popped another piece of broccoli into her mouth.

"His posture is fine, and so is his vision."

Done chewing, Ella continued with her campaign. "I've seen guys like him in the chess club. Their IQs were useless for getting dates. He needs to do sports, and I'm not talking about attending PE class. That's not good enough."

There was something to it. The young doctor Vivian met at the convention had an athletic build despite the rigorous academic studies he'd done. Julian must've found time to visit the gym.

He and Ella would've been perfect for each other. But he hadn't called, and in the meantime, Ella had started dating someone named Romeo. Vivian hadn't expected it to last, but two weeks later they were still seeing each other almost every day.

She hadn't met the boy yet, but Ella had been waxing poetic about him.

"How are things going with Romeo?" Vivian asked.

For some reason, the name evoked images of someone sleazy.

Not that she should pass judgment based on something silly like that. There was nothing wrong with it. Romeo's family was from Italy. It might be a popular name over there.

"Great." Ella's eyes brightened and she smiled, the

concern for her brother's future dating success all forgotten. "His uncle in New York is opening a second restaurant."

"That's nice."

According to Ella, Romeo's dream was to own a chain of pizzerias. That was the excuse he'd given her for why he had no intention of getting a college education.

"He asked Romeo to come manage it for him once it's ready."

Vivian hoped that would be the end of their relationship. She wasn't a snob, but she'd always pictured Ella with someone well-educated.

She was a smart and beautiful girl, and she shouldn't settle for her first serious boyfriend, even if his name was freaking Romeo. "Is he going to accept the offer?"

"That's his dream. Of course, he is going to accept it."

"What about you? Is he just going to leave you?"

Ella would be heartbroken, but she'd get over it. And maybe Julian would call about those auditions he'd promised.

Looking down at her plate, Ella murmured, "His uncle is going to need waitresses."

Vivian snorted. "Forget it. You are not going to New York with a guy you met two weeks ago."

Crossing her arms over her chest, Ella glared at Viv with a pair of defiant eyes. "Romeo says that his uncle is going to pay me at least twenty percent more than what I'm getting now, and that the tips over there are much better. If I spend the rest of the summer working in New York, I could save up double compared to what I can save up working here at the crappy diner."

"Just as a reminder, you were ecstatic about getting the job in this *crappy diner*."

"That's because I thought it would be awesome to work in the same place as Maddie, and it was. But in New York, I'll get to work with my boyfriend, which is even more awesome."

Vivian mimicked Ella's pose, crossing her arms over her chest and pinning her daughter with a hard stare. "You're not going, so get it out of your head."

"Why?"

"Because you don't know anything about Romeo. For all we know, he could be a serial killer, or a druggie, or God knows what else. I'm not letting my eighteen-year-old daughter go to New York with a stranger!"

"What if I bring him over and you like him?"

Fat chance of that. "I would love to meet Romeo. You can invite him to dinner. In fact, I'm surprised he hasn't bothered to come and introduce himself like a serious boyfriend should. It just shows me that he is not really serious about you."

"Ugh, Mom. You're too young to have such outdated ideas about dating. No one brings their dates to meet their parents anymore—not until at least three months into the relationship."

Vivian waved a hand. "Here you go. If Romeo offered to take you to New York after you guys dated for at least six months, and after he'd come here and spent time with us at least once a week, and I'd gotten to know him better, I might have allowed you to go."

With a huff, Ella slumped in her chair. "Maybe I can ask Romeo to wait a little longer before he takes his uncle up on his offer."

6

MAGNUS

One week ago.

"What am I going to call you, my pretty girl?" Magnus picked up the Golden Retriever puppy from his back seat.

"Is it going to be Scarlet, or Nessie? Eh, girl? What's your preference?"

Since her coat was a nice deep golden shade of red, Magnus wanted to call her Bridget, but on second thought decided against it. The doctor might not find it amusing.

"I think Scarlet suits you best." He hugged the puppy close to his chest.

In response, she tucked her muzzle under his arm. He was lucky the dog hadn't pooped or thrown up as the breeder had warned him she would.

On the other hand, it might have been part of the sales pitch to get him to buy a trunk load of things the puppy supposedly had to have, or rather the owner of a puppy couldn't be without—like the special backseat cover to protect the upholstery.

Back in the day, all a dog needed were scraps from the dinner table and a kid to play with. Nowadays, there was specially formulated dog food, chew toys, a soft round pillow for a dog bed, two kinds of leashes, pee pads, dog shampoos and conditioners, dog toothbrush and toothpaste, anti-flea pills, and even a dog cologne.

And then there was the immunization record and the tagging. The number for an emergency vet was the only thing he'd gotten free of charge. All in all, Magnus had shelled out close to two grand for his Scarlet.

Perhaps he could ask Kian to reimburse him.

After all, his official reason for the adoption was to train her to sniff out immortals.

Except, Magnus hadn't been put in charge of the new dog training program, and he had bought the dog basically on a whim. He'd called Jeff—The Finder of Lost Things—and gotten the name of a local breeder the guy had recommended, then headed out to the boonies to get his puppy.

"What do you have there?" Carol abandoned her post at the café and rushed over as fast as her short legs allowed.

"This is Scarlet," Magnus told her.

"She is so pretty." Carol patted the dog's head. "What are you going to do with her when you're at work?"

"My roommates work from home, so she will never be left alone."

"Did you discuss it with them before getting her?"

"Of course I did. They liked the idea."

Carol sighed. "You know the problem with pets, right? They don't last."

"I know. The only reason I got her was because of Kian's idea to establish a training program for dogs to sniff out immortals. I want to test it and see if it works. What if dogs can sniff out Dormants? Wouldn't that be cool?"

Carol laughed. "What are you going to do, take your puppy out on a stroll and have her sniff up women's skirts?"

"Why not? It's the best pick-up method out there. The lasses are going to be all over the cute puppy, and I'm going to be all over the lasses."

"Pervert." She slapped his arm.

Baring her teeth, Scarlet growled.

"Just look at that." He bent his neck and kissed the dog's head. "She is already defending me. What a good dog you are, Scarlet."

Carol shook her head. "I'm surprised she isn't afraid of you. Dogs usually don't like immortals. And especially immortal males."

"That is why I'm sure they can smell the difference between us and humans, and why we can use them for detection. Personally, though, I've never had that problem. Dogs love me. Besides, if we get them as young puppies and treat them well, they will get used to our smell and not fear us. If dogs can grow up with lions and not be wary of them, they can do that with immortals."

"I wish you good luck."

"Thanks."

Now it remained to be seen what Kian would have to say about it. Magnus hoped he would reconsider and let him head up the dog training program. The boss wanted Arwel to find a civilian for the job, but for once Magnus didn't agree with the regent's reasoning. Just as police dogs were trained by police trainers, the training of dogs to sniff out immortals should be done by Guardians.

But before he took her to Kian's office, he had to let her do her business. Pooping on the regent's rug would not endear her to him.

The moment he put her down, Scarlet trotted behind a

bush, hiding from him like a shy lass. But as soon as she was done, she came back and looked up at him.

"You want me to pick you up?" Magnus bent down and scooped her in his arms. "Only because it's your first day. Tomorrow, you are walking." He sent a visual into her small brain.

She lifted her muzzle and wagged her tail in approval.

"Oh, sweet lass. You and I are going to have so much fun together."

Even though it was late in the evening, Magnus strode toward the office building and headed straight for Kian's office.

As he'd guessed, the boss was still there.

"Come in!" Kian called out when Magnus knocked.

"Good evening, Kian. I want to introduce you to the newest addition to the clan. This is Scarlet. Scarlet, this is Kian and he is the boss, so be a good girl and don't growl at him."

Crossing his arms over his chest, Kian leaned back in his chair. "I know that Onegus hasn't assigned you a new partner yet, and you are lonely, but he's going to find you one sooner rather than later. You shouldn't have rushed to get a dog. Did you take into consideration how much work a young one like that requires?"

The truth was that Kian wasn't too far off the mark with his comment, because Magnus had decided on adopting a puppy after Anandur had left.

Not that he was ever going to admit it.

As a Guardian, Magnus needed to protect his tough guy reputation. He was supposed to be okay with whatever life threw at him. The problem was that he hadn't been a Guardian for many years now, and living as a civilian among other civilians had apparently softened him.

Rather than descending all at once, the loneliness had crept up on him a little at a time.

The transition to living in the States and going back into the Guardian force had been made easy by partnering with Anandur. Even though the guy was at times annoying, there had never been a dull moment with him around. But then Magnus had lost Anandur as a roommate, and soon after that as a partner.

No wonder he was feeling lonelier than usual.

It was true that many of his Guardian buddies had moved to the States with him, but he missed his other friends back home—the civilians he'd lived among for the past several decades. He also missed his shop and the small clientele of discriminating gentlemen it had served. The demand for custom tailored clothing for men had dwindled in recent years, making the place barely profitable, but he would have kept it open just for the pleasure it had provided him with.

Except, just like most of the other retired Guardians, he couldn't refuse the call to serve. Because if not he and his buddies, then who?

Those girls needed saving, and he had what it took to do the job. It was as simple as that.

What he hadn't counted on, though, was how difficult that transition would be. Americans were different, especially the women. They were not as friendly as the Scottish lasses he was accustomed to, or maybe it was just a cultural thing, and he was still learning their ways.

Nevertheless, none of that was Kian's business, or anyone else's for that matter. The official reason for getting Scarlet was a valid one, and not merely an excuse to get a dog.

"I want to train Scarlet to sniff out immortals and hopefully also Dormants."

Kian lifted a brow. "I want a civilian in charge of that program."

"I know. But think of it as a pilot. First, let's see if it works. And if it does, I would very much like to be in charge of it. The dogs should work with Guardians, and therefore should be trained by us."

"You have a point. But one dog is not a program, and I can't release you from your duties just because you have a new pet."

"I'm going to perform my Guardian duties as usual. For now, training Scarlet is just a hobby. My roommates are both programmers who work from home. They are going to keep an eye on her while I'm on duty."

"Then, by all means. Let's see how it turns out." Kian smiled at the dog. "Welcome to my clan, Scarlet."

7

ELLA

One week ago.

*E*lla removed her apron, folded it, and put it inside her cubicle.

"Good luck with your mom," Maddie said.

"Thanks. I need it. But I'm not going home. I'm coming back here after my lunch break, so you will have to wish me luck again."

"No problem. Do you want me to come to your house for moral support?"

Maddie was the best, but she had a tendency to take over conversations. If she came, she would dominate the evening. "I would love to, but I think Romeo should have the stage. He needs to make my mom like him."

"As I said, good luck with that."

Ella frowned. "Why? What's wrong with him?"

"Nothing." Maddie lifted her hands in the universal sign for peace. "I like him, but your mom is not going to like any guy who tries to take you away from her."

"Yeah, you're right. That's why I'm meeting Romeo during my break to talk strategy."

Romeo would need to lay on the charm. And then there was Parker.

Hopefully the little dweeb was going to behave himself and not embarrass her in front of her boyfriend. She'd better warn him, maybe even threaten him with consequences.

This was too important for Parker to mess up.

Ella had decided she was going with Romeo to New York regardless of her mother's approval, but she would rather do it with her blessing.

They argued a lot, but mostly about little things. Until now, Ella had never gotten in trouble or done anything to really upset her mother.

Way to go all out on the first try.

The thing was, her mother was overreacting. After all, it wasn't as if Ella would be out of touch. Their psychic connection was not limited by distance, and they could talk whenever they wanted and wherever they were.

Unless Ella blocked Vivian, of course.

If she went without her mother's permission, she would be subjected to an endless tirade of scolding. Blocking that would be necessary to keep her sanity.

"I'll see you later." Ella pulled Maddie into a quick hug.

As she waited for Romeo in the parking lot, Ella heard the rumble of his ancient motorcycle's engine long before he pulled out in front of her.

"Hi, baby." He kissed her cheek and handed her a helmet. "Ready to go?"

"Yeah." She loved sitting pressed behind him, holding on tight with her arms wrapped around his slim waist. "Where are we going?"

"To the beach."

"Awesome." She put the helmet on and climbed behind him.

Regrettably, the beach was nearby and the ride ended way too soon. Ella would've loved to keep on riding with Romeo into the sunset.

Watching her remove the helmet and shake out her hair, Romeo put a hand over his heart. "I love it when you do that, baby." He took the helmet from her and leaned to kiss her lips. "I love you," he murmured.

"I love you too."

As usual, her heart had somersaulted at the words. No matter how many times he told her that, it always had the same startling effect as the first time. It was as if she couldn't believe that he really loved her.

Which was a bit odd. Ella was not aware of having insecurities of any kind. She shouldn't feel surprised that a hot guy had fallen for her. She had a lot to offer, and it wasn't all about her looks. She was smart, hard-working, and an all around nice person. Why shouldn't he love her?

When they found a bench, Romeo pulled a folded envelope out of his pocket. "I need you to fill this in."

"What is it?" Ella pulled out the contents.

"It's for the payroll department. My uncle emailed it to me and asked that you fill it in. That way everything is going to be ready once we get there." He produced a pen and handed it to her. "Make sure that your handwriting is legible."

One sheet of paper was a standard job application form, and the other one was for tax purposes. Ella remembered filling in similar forms when she'd applied for the job at the diner. The only difference was that this one asked for her driver's license number in addition to her social security number.

Well, this was probably how it worked in New York. The requirements were different than those in California.

She pulled her license and her social security card out of her wallet, wrote the numbers in the appropriate boxes, and then put them back.

The section on prior work experience had four subsections. "Does babysitting count as job experience? Because other than that, I only worked in the diner."

"You can skip that. Just write the diner's name. My uncle knows that you only had this one job and that you didn't have it for long. This is just a standard form." Romeo leaned and nuzzled her neck.

She pushed him away. "Stop it! I can't concentrate when you do that."

With a smirk, he leaned away and let her finish writing the rest of the information. Once she was done, he took the forms from her, put them back in the envelope, tucked it in his pocket, and wrapped his arm around her shoulder.

"Tomorrow, I'm going to scan and email both to my uncle. Consider yourself hired."

Ella leaned her head against his shoulder. "It's going to be fun working together."

She could imagine Romeo working in the kitchen or the back office while she served the customers. They would steal kisses when no one was looking, or maybe hide in the supply closet and do a little more than kissing.

Romeo was unlike any of the guys she'd dated before. He was a true gentleman and hadn't pressured her for more than she was ready for, or rather what he thought she was ready for.

It was true that they had only been dating for three weeks, but they were both adults and she was ready for more. Except, Romeo hadn't initiated anything, and she wasn't brave enough to do that.

On the one hand, it was sweet and old-fashioned. On the other hand, it bothered her. Didn't he want her?

The few other dates she had gone on, the guys had been desperate to get in her panties. Or in Jim's case, just get her panties.

Not that she thought it was okay, but according to her friends, most guys were like that, and it was up to the girls to set the boundaries. Romeo was the exception. The question was whether she should be glad or worried.

Back in the diner, she pulled Maddie aside. "Do you think it's weird that Romeo didn't try to get me in bed yet?"

"I think it's very weird," Maddie said. "He says he loves you, and he wants you to come live with him in New York, but he doesn't sleep with you? Maybe he is gay?"

Ella chuckled. "Not likely. He gets hard every time we kiss. He is not sexually indifferent to me."

"Maybe he's waiting for you to initiate?"

"You think?"

Maddie shrugged. "He knows you're a virgin, right?"

"Yeah? So what?"

"Perhaps that's why he is waiting for you to make the first move. He's probably never been with a virgin." Maddie snorted. "You're a unicorn, Ella. Who's heard of an eighteen-year-old girl who looks like an angel and never had sex before? You might scare the guy."

8

VIVIAN

"*Tell* me about your parents, Romeo," Vivian said.

Ella had told her that he'd also lost his father in Afghanistan, but she had never mentioned Romeo's mother.

"I was ten when my father was killed, and I don't remember much of him. My mother was too depressed to deal with anything, so we moved in with my uncle, her brother. It was supposed to be a temporary arrangement, just until she got back on her feet, but we ended up staying with him for many years. She does the bookkeeping for his pizzeria."

His uncle sounded like a nice guy. "Does your uncle have a family of his own?"

"He has a daughter. His wife died in childbirth, leaving him to raise my cousin on his own, and he never remarried. I don't think he's ever gotten over it. But since he practically raised me too, he thinks of me as his son."

"How old is your cousin?"

"Fifteen."

No wonder the uncle wanted Romeo to come back and

help him run his growing restaurant business. He had no one else.

"How come you are here in San Diego, then?"

He chuckled. "The weather, what else? I got sick of the miserable winters in New York and decided to give Southern California a try. I love the weather and the surf is great, but I miss New York."

"You surf?" Parker asked.

Romeo chuckled again. "Not very well, I'm afraid."

"I can surf," Parker said. "I bet I'm better than you."

"I'm sure you are. I would love to see you in action. Maybe you can teach me some moves? When is the next time you are going surfing?"

Parker grimaced. "I only surf during summer camp, but I have this awesome VR surfing game."

Romeo's eyes widened. "You have a VR headset?"

As Romeo and Parker ventured into a heated debate about virtual reality games and which were better than others, Vivian observed her daughter's boyfriend.

He was very well spoken for a Brooklyn kid who had never gone to college, and he sounded much older than his twenty-two years. That was until he'd gotten excited about computer games. Then he sounded like Parker, only with a deeper voice.

Perhaps he was well read. Vivian didn't have a college education either, but since she read a lot she had a rich vocabulary. That was why she insisted Ella and Parker read for at least an hour a day. Since the local public schools weren't the best, and she couldn't afford private ones, the enrichment had to happen at home. Which in a way was better because it instilled a habit of lifelong learning.

Or at least she hoped it did. As a parent, all she could do was show her kids the way. When they were all grown up, it would be up to them to choose their own paths.

Romeo seemed like a nice guy from a close-knit family. If he and Ella had been dating for a while longer, and if Ella were older, she might have considered letting her go with him to New York.

Vivian had never gotten to do anything exciting like that.

Upon graduating from high school, Viv and Josh had already been married and expecting a child. Josh had enlisted so he could support his family, and they had moved from Tulsa to San Diego where he had been stationed.

That was the extent of Viv's travels. Other than that, she had taken the kids to Disneyland, which was about two and a half hours away by car, and to Universal Studios, which was a little farther than that.

Perhaps she should let Ella go?

With their telepathic communication, distance was irrelevant. When Ella had gone on school trips, they had communicated just as easily whether she was in Washington DC or in Washington State.

Vivian could always check up on Ella. The moment she sensed her daughter was unhappy, she could buy her a plane ticket home, or even go get her.

"So how about it, Mom? Can I go to New York with Romeo?" Ella asked.

Vivian hated to quash the hopeful look in her daughter's eyes, but there was no way she could let her go. Not yet, anyway.

"I have an idea. How about Romeo goes first, gets the restaurant going, and in a few months, if you guys still feel as strongly about each other as you do now, you'll go and give it a try for a few weeks."

Romeo's lips pinched into a thin line.

"But, Mom! We love each other. I can't be separated from Romeo for so long!"

Viv hardened her heart. "Other than school trips, you've

never been away from home. You're too young and too inex-perienced to make life-changing decisions."

The tears misting Ella's eyes were like little arrows of guilt piercing Viv's heart. *Please, Mom*, she sent telepathically.

Reaching for her daughter's hand, she clasped it even though Ella tried to pull it away. "Before you dive into the deep, you need to dip your toes in the water first. I didn't say never. I only said later. If your love for each other is strong, it will survive a few months of separation." She glanced at Romeo. "Am I right?"

Schooling his expression to hide his irritation, he nodded. "I love Ella, and it's going to be hard to be apart. But we will do it your way. I'll go first, and once the restaurant is up and running, which I expect to happen in less than a month, Ella could come for a couple of weeks and see if she likes it. Then she can either stay or go home and come back again. Does that sound like something you can live with?"

Romeo had elegantly shortened the waiting period to one month, which was an attempt at compromise that Vivian appreciated and wished to reciprocate. But if she was to agree to his shortened timeframe, she had some conditions of her own.

"I'll tell you what. When the restaurant is ready, I'll come to New York together with Ella, have a talk with your uncle and with your mom, get to know them a bit, check out the place, and then stay for a week or two to see how she is managing and whether she likes it there or not."

It was a perfectly reasonable proposition, and Romeo was doing his best to appear agreeable, but she could tell he wasn't happy about the solution she'd suggested.

"I understand. You don't trust me, and that's okay. You're a mother and it's your job to worry about Ella. I'm sure my mom would love to meet you, and so will my uncle." He smiled suggestively.

Was he implying that his uncle might be interested in her? Or vice versa?

It was most inappropriate, even though she could understand where he was coming from. Both she and Romeo's uncle had lost their spouses and were single.

It wasn't the first time someone had tried to get her together with a friend or a relative. But she was not interested in a relationship, and especially not with a pizzeria owner in New York.

Vivian had a life in San Diego, and so did Parker.

It was best to ignore his comment though, pretending she didn't understand his meaning. "I'm sure we will all have a wonderful time. I've never been to New York. And I'm sure Parker is excited about seeing it for the first time too." She turned to her son, who had been suspiciously silent throughout the whole discussion. "Right, Parker?"

All she got in response was a glare.

Well, apparently he wasn't excited about going on a trip with his mom. Or maybe he didn't like the idea of his sister leaving.

After they had coffee and dessert, Romeo helped clear the table and even washed the dishes, which Vivian liked a lot.

When he was done, he asked Parker, "Can you show me your VR headset?"

"Sure." Her son didn't sound enthusiastic, but he took Romeo to his room anyway.

"What are your plans for the rest of the evening?" she asked Ella.

"We are going to see a movie?"

"Which one?"

Ella shrugged. "I don't know. We haven't decided yet."

When they were done cleaning up the kitchen, Romeo returned. "That was fun. I need to buy that headset for myself." He turned to Ella. "Are you ready to go?"

"Yeah." She kissed Vivian's cheek. "We are off to the movies, Mom."

Ever since Vivian had offered to accompany her to New York, Ella had been telepathically silent, which was fine. Once she gave it some thought, she would realize that this was the best solution and that her mother was not being mean to her just to make her life miserable.

"It was nice to meet you, Mrs. Takala." Romeo shook her hand.

"Same here. Have fun at the movies."

Parker still didn't say anything.

"What's wrong?" Viv asked once Ella and Romeo had left.

"I don't like him. He's a creep."

"You seemed to like him just fine when you guys were talking about computer games."

Parker crossed his arms over his chest. "No, I didn't. He was trying too hard. He sounded exactly like one of your boyfriends."

That was a low blow. "What do you mean, my boyfriends? I only had two and they were both very nice men."

"I didn't say they weren't nice. At least they weren't creeps like *Romeo*." He rolled his eyes as he said the name. "All I'm saying is that he sounded like an old guy trying to sound cool to impress a kid."

"Old guys don't play VR games."

"Yes, they do. My teacher, Mr. Biandi, does."

"And how old is Mr. Biandi?"

"Too old to play video games. He is twenty-eight."

Vivian ruffled his hair. "Let's have this talk when you are that age. I'm sure you will still be playing them, and I'm also sure that you won't think of yourself as old. Twenty-eight is still young."

9

EVA

Present day.

"Let me bring you a chair," Bhathian offered.

Eva waved a dismissive hand. "Anandur and Wonder will be here in a few minutes. If I sit, I'll get trampled by everyone rushing to congratulate them."

"At least lean on me. I'll hold up your belly." He took a step to stand behind her and wrapped his arms under her huge pregnant belly, hoisting it up. "Better?"

"You have no idea." Eva sighed and leaned back against him.

Him holding it up like that was the only respite she was getting from hauling it around lately. Even sleeping in bed was impossible, and she was spending her nights on the couch.

Not to mention sex, which hadn't been happening for a while now. Some women got hornier by the end of their pregnancy, but not Eva. She was as big as an elephant and felt just about as sexy.

Her little boy, who was obviously not so little, had been

trying to kick his way out of her belly for the past three months. Less so for the past week, though. There was simply no more room for him to move.

She hadn't been half as big with Nathalie. Although it was possible that after thirty-two years, she'd forgotten how it had felt toward the end of the pregnancy. What she remembered clearly, though, was that her belly had dropped a few days before the delivery, the same way as it had done now.

It was time.

Eva was more than ready to meet her little guy, and he was certainly ready to finally stretch his arms and legs.

Hopefully, it was not going to happen in the next hour or so. Everyone was outside in the village's central plaza, waiting for Anandur and Wonder's return. Eva didn't want to miss the party.

After being a loner for most of her life, she was finally starting to enjoy a sense of community, of family.

Even though she and Bhathian had moved into the village just a little over a week ago, the clan was already growing on her. Bhathian and Robert were still packing up the old house, including the boxes of files and the rest of her office.

Before moving, she'd thought it would be stifling to live in a place where everyone knew her. After all, she was an undercover detective, a corporate spy, and spies didn't like people to know who they were.

Eva liked the anonymity of the big city.

Except, her spying days were over, at least for now. For the next year or two, she was going to enjoy her baby and only supervise in the agency. It was Sharon's time to shine. Her assistant for the past seven years was going to take her place.

Hopefully, Sharon was up to the challenge. She might never be as good as Eva, but she was good enough to do the job, and that was all that mattered.

At the sound of excited murmurs, Eva looked up. At first, she could only see the top of Anandur's red hair, but then he and Wonder got closer, and the crowd erupted in hollers and whistles and clapping.

Holding her arms up and away from her belly, Eva joined the clapping. Out of all of Bhathian's Guardian buddies, she liked Anandur the most. Just like everyone else, she was glad that the Clan Mother had allowed Wonder and him to leave her sanctuary and come back to the village.

For good.

A trickle of wetness making its way down her inner thighs caused her to pause. Did she just pee herself?

It was possible.

With the constant pressure on her bladder, Eva sometimes didn't make it to the bathroom. There had been a couple of embarrassing accidents when someone had made her laugh.

This time it was going to be even worse. How the hell was she supposed to push her way through all these people?

The trickle intensified into a gush.

"Oh, shit!" She looked down. "I just peed myself."

Bhathian glanced at the puddle between her feet. "Are you sure it's pee? It doesn't smell like it."

He was right. It didn't. "Oh my God. My water just broke!"

"Quick! Get Bridget!" Bhathian hollered over the noisy crowd, and then started waving people out of the way. "Move it! Make room for the doctor!"

Her arms under her heaving stomach, holding it up, Eva stayed rooted to the spot, staring at the growing puddle at her feet.

Like the biblical parting of the sea, people moved aside, clearing a path for Bridget. The petite doctor came running, then skidded to a stop in front of Eva.

"I thought someone got injured." She looked at the puddle and smiled. "I see that we are going to welcome another member to our clan today." She looked up at Bhathian. "Don't just stand there like a doofus. Pick your mate up and carry her to the clinic."

"Yes, ma'am."

10

ELLA

*K*issing under the stars, with the ocean waves lapping at the shore only a few feet away, was so romantic.

Ella had never been so turned on in her life. Romeo's kiss was so intense, and he seemed so desperate for her, his hands roaming her body and touching her everywhere—except where she wanted him to touch her.

What was wrong with him?

The most he had done was to cup her butt and grind himself against her. He hadn't even touched her breasts, and she really wanted him to.

Sucking on the soft skin of her neck, he whispered, "Come to New York with me. I can't go without you."

He'd been saying that a lot. Except, as much as she wanted to go, Ella had to agree with her mother. What Vivian had suggested made sense, even to a lovesick, hormonal teenager like her.

Why couldn't Romeo accept it? He was supposed to be the more mature one.

Taking his hand, she led him to their favorite bench and

pulled him down to sit next to her. "It's only going to be for a little while. You said that you can have the restaurant up and running in less than a month. I will come with my mom and stay."

He sighed and shook his head. "I won't be able to concentrate on doing what needs to be done. I will be thinking about you every second of the day and dreaming about you at night. You have to come with me."

Before her mom had offered the very reasonable compromise, Ella had planned on running away with Romeo. But there was really no need to do it now.

They could survive one month without each other. It wasn't so bad.

And then there was Parker, who kept calling Romeo a creep. At first, she'd yelled at him to stop, but then she'd started to think that maybe the little dweeb was seeing something she wasn't. Perhaps he also had some psychic ability, and it was only starting to manifest now.

"My mom's request was very reasonable. It's not like she is forbidding me to go. I don't want to fight with her over one month. That wouldn't be fair. Don't you think?" Ella looked up at Romeo with hopeful eyes.

She didn't want to fight with him either, but it seemed it was either him or her mom. She couldn't make both happy.

"I was afraid you were going to say that." He reached into his back pocket and pulled out an envelope. "Here, take it."

"What is it?" She'd already filled in employment forms. Were there more?

He gestured with his chin. "Open it."

Inside the envelope was an innocent looking folded piece of paper. Except, when she unfolded it, Ella discovered that it wasn't innocent at all. "You bought me a plane ticket?"

"Just for the weekend." He pointed at the dates. "We leave Friday afternoon, you help me settle in, meet my mom and

my uncle, and then I stay and you go home Sunday evening.
You can tell your mom that you're staying at Maddie's."

It was tempting. Very tempting.

But could she do it?

It wouldn't be the first time she'd lied to her mother.
What teenage girl didn't? And a weekend in New York would
be so exciting.

She checked the dates again to make sure that her return
flight was Sunday night. It was a redeye, so she would arrive
at San Diego early Monday morning and would have to go to
work without sleep, but she could pull it off.

Ella smiled. "Okay. I'll do it."

A big grin split his face. "Really? You'll do it for me?"

She nodded.

Lifting her by the waist, he spun her and then crushed her
to him and kissed her hard, not letting go until they both ran
out of air. "You have no idea how happy you've just
made me."

ELLA

"*I*'m so excited to meet your family," Ella said as the plane lifted up into the air.

Romeo smiled a tight-lipped smile. "You should get some sleep. It will be late when we get there."

"I'm not tired."

"Then watch a movie." He pulled a set of bulky earphones out of his backpack and plunked them on his head.

He was acting kind of weird, especially for someone who was supposed to be ecstatic about his girlfriend joining him on the trip. Maybe he was afraid of flying?

Reaching over the armrest, Ella took his hand and gave it a squeeze. "It's okay to admit that you're scared. A lot of people are."

He moved the headphones, exposing one of his ears. "What did you say? These are noise canceling."

"I said that it's okay if you're scared of flying. It's nothing to be embarrassed about."

Incomprehension furrowing his brows, Romeo stared at her for a long moment. "I'm not scared of flying. I just don't like it." He leaned and kissed her cheek. "That's one of the reasons I wanted you to come with me. It makes it much more fun."

She wondered how exactly she was making it more fun for him when he was watching a movie and ignoring her. But maybe her presence alone was soothing to him.

"I'm glad."

He smiled and went back to watching his movie.

With nothing better to do, Ella pulled her earbuds out and chose a movie too. By the time she finished watching it, Romeo had fallen asleep with his headphones still on.

She might have not been in a relationship with a guy before, but Romeo's walk didn't match his talk. Ella had imagined spending the flight with his arm wrapped around her, and her head resting on his shoulder. There should've been kisses and whispers of love, not snores.

Was that what she'd lied to her mother for?

Perhaps her expectations were too high. With a sigh, Ella chose another movie to watch.

Her sleeping Romeo hadn't opened his eyes until the plane touched down the runway. "That was a good nap." He stretched his arms over his head.

"Do you think your mom is going to still be awake when we get there?"

"I'm sure she is." He lifted her hand and kissed the back of it. "She wants to meet my beautiful Californian girlfriend."

And just like that Ella's doubts evaporated.

Romeo had been tired, that's all. He still loved her, and he was looking forward to introducing her to his mother and his uncle.

After collecting Romeo's suitcase from the conveyor, they headed out into the street.

"Are we taking a taxi or the train?" Ella asked.

"Neither. My cousin Franco is picking us up." Romeo

pulled out his phone and checked his messages. "He should be here any minute."

That was odd. He hadn't mentioned a cousin named Franco. In fact, Romeo hadn't mentioned anyone picking them up from the airport.

"I thought your uncle only had a daughter."

Romeo waved a dismissive hand. "Franco is a second cousin from my father's side."

"Oh."

Still, why hadn't he mentioned him? Second cousins and all, they must've been close for the guy to come all the way from Brooklyn to pick them up.

"Here he is." Romeo waved at a silver old model Camry.

The car stopped next to the curb, and a moment later the trunk popped open.

Romeo hefted his suitcase inside and then reached for Ella's backpack.

"No, that's okay. I'll keep it with me. My wallet and my phone are in there."

Everything she'd brought with her was stuffed into her backpack. After all, her excuse had been a weekend at Maddie's, so it wasn't as if she could have taken a suitcase or even a carry-on.

"As you wish." He opened the back passenger door. "Scoot over." He got in with her.

The driver turned and grinned. "Pretty Ella. Lucky Romeo." He gave her a once-over.

That was an odd greeting. But whatever. "Nice to meet you, Franco."

"Very nice. Very, very nice," he murmured as he turned around.

"Is he okay?" she whispered. The guy seemed stoned.

Romeo wrapped his arm around her shoulder and

brought her against his side. "He's just acting dumb because he's never seen a girl as pretty as you."

Up front, Franco nodded. "Jackpot."

Did he mean that she was Romeo's jackpot? It was flattering in a weird way. Maybe Brooklyn had its own slang and everyone talked like that?

Fatigue catching up to her, Ella closed her eyes and leaned her head on Romeo's bicep. "Wake me up when we get there."

"Sure, baby. Get some sleep."

An hour or so later, Ella woke up as Franco parked the car in front of a two-story brick building.

"Come on. My uncle is waiting."

"Oh, okay. Aren't we meeting your mom first?"

"She's asleep. Let's go." He pulled on her elbow.

"What about your suitcase?" It was still in the trunk of Franco's car.

"I'll get it later. I don't want to keep my uncle waiting."

At the front door, Romeo pressed the buzzer for an intercom. "It's me," he said into the box.

As the door clicked open, they entered a dimly illuminated hallway. Half of it was taken by stairs going up, and the other half led to the back of the house. There was a living room on the left side, but it was too dark to see anything more than the general shape of a couch and a couple of armchairs.

"My uncle's office is in the back," Romeo said as he led her down the hallway.

That was odd. Wasn't it too late at night for the guy to be in his office? She'd expected a warmer welcome, like a cup of coffee in the kitchen with some leftover lasagna or some other Italian dish. Other than a bag of pretzels, Ella hadn't eaten anything on the plane and was quite hungry.

Romeo knocked on the door.

"It's open," an older sounding guy called out.

Opening the way, Romeo waved a hand. "Ladies first."

The uncle smiled, pushed to his feet, and walked up to Ella. "You're even prettier in person." He took her hands and kissed each in turn. "I'm Stefano, but you can call me uncle."

He looked and sounded exactly like what Ella had imagined a middle-aged pizzeria owner would—short, pudgy, with a friendly smile and the slight Italian accent of someone who had spent many years in the States.

"I'm going to get my suitcase," Romeo said.

Stefano didn't even spare him a glance. "Yes, you do that, and in the meantime, I will interview the lovely Ella."

Despite the uncle's friendly smile, when the door closed behind Romeo, a shiver of unease ran up Ella's spine. She'd just arrived at his house, it was almost midnight, and he wanted to interview her right there and then?

"Take a seat, dear." He pulled out a chair for her, then walked around and sat behind his desk.

"I hope Romeo told you that I don't have much experience."

"He did." Stefano smiled. "Which makes you so much more valuable than I originally expected. You and I are going to make a fortune."

Ella frowned. Even the most extravagant tips in the priciest restaurant would not amount to a fortune. Was he delusional?

Leaning back in his chair, Stefano pushed his big belly out and took a deep breath. "Let me explain."

JULIAN

"Thank you for dinner, Sharon. Or should I thank you, Robert?" Julian glanced at his ex-roommate.

"It was a joint effort," Sharon said. "I peeled and cut, and Robert cooked."

"You make a good team."

"Yeah, we do. But I'm afraid that for the foreseeable future, I won't be much help in the kitchen. I am now officially the sole field detective and head corporate spy of Eva's agency. I'll be going on missions all over the globe."

Robert frowned. "You said that Eva will try to stick to the States. You've already done a stint in Rio."

"She said she will, but I know her. If she gets a good enough offer she is not going to refuse it."

Robert's lips tightened into a thin line, but he was smart enough not to say anything. If Eva decided to take a mission abroad, Sharon couldn't refuse it only because her boyfriend didn't like it. Instead, the guy pushed to his feet and started clearing the table.

Sharon sighed. "Now he is going to give me the silent treatment."

Julian was saved from answering by his phone vibrating in his pocket. "Excuse me." He pulled it out. "Brandon, what's up?"

"I have an audition for your girl. Can she make it to Los Angeles by next Tuesday? Not the coming one, but the one after that."

Julian had emailed the clan's media guy Ella's picture the same day he'd gotten it. But up until now, Brandon hadn't found anything interesting enough to justify Ella coming all the way from San Diego.

"I can check. Is it worth the trip for her?"

"Definitely. I wouldn't have called you if it wasn't. It's a small nonspeaking role, but it's guaranteed. And because it's a Netflix series, it is also recurring. I just finished dinner with the director. When I showed her the picture, she said that Ella's looks precisely matched the character she had in mind."

"What's the series about?"

"A coming of age story of a group of high-school friends. She is the hot neighbor one of them is obsessing about, but he only sees her through her bedroom window and never talks to her."

Julian frowned. He'd watched movies like that, and it usually involved the girl taking off her clothes. "I hope there are no pervy peeping scenes."

"It's a PG-13 series. Someone is always going to interrupt, or the shutters will close a second before the shirt comes off. Our guy will never catch a glimpse and neither will the audience."

"You sure about that?"

"Stop fretting, Julian. I can promise you that your girl's virtue is secure, at least as far as the production goes. What she decides to do while she is here and with whom is not my or your business. She is over eighteen, right?"

"That's what her mother told me."

Julian still wasn't sure about the part. He trusted Brandon, but the media specialist was a mover and shaker, and he wasn't personally involved in the productions he helped put together. "Can you send me the script? I'm curious."

"I'll see what I can do. But just let me tell you, this is not how things work in this world. Your girl is not a star who needs to be wooed into accepting a role. I'll have to tell the director that the script is for me."

"Thank you. I really appreciate your help. I just don't feel right telling the girl's mother that everything is perfectly legit without making sure it really is."

"I get it. I'll email you the script as soon as I get it."

"Thanks. You're the best, Brandon."

"I know."

ELLA

*E*lla was starting to have a really bad feeling. Nothing was a big red flag, but there were many small peripheral things that were bothering her.

It was like the buzz of several annoying mosquitos. It wasn't enough to trigger panic, but it couldn't be ignored either.

Right now, though, those barely-there buzzes were starting to coalesce into one belonging to a big-ass scary hornet about to sting.

"You're a very beautiful girl, Ella," the hornet buzzed. "And sometimes, if they are very lucky, girls like you might catch the attention of very rich and powerful men who are willing to pay a fortune for the right one. And especially if she is a virgin."

Suddenly, the 'fortune' remark made sense.

Reaching for her backpack, Ella lifted it off the floor and pushed up to her feet. "I'm out of here."

"Sit down!" Stefano barked.

"I don't think so." She turned on her heel and rushed to the door.

"It's locked. Come back here and sit down."

With a sinking feeling, Ella tried the handle anyway. It was locked. "Help!" She banged on it. "Let me out of here!"

"Stop yelling. No one is going to hear you, and even if they did, no one is going to help you. I own this entire block."

"What do you want from me?"

She knew exactly what he wanted. But why her? There were so many pretty girls out there.

"Sit down, and I'll explain. It's not as bad as it seems. Every cloud has a silver lining."

He sounded so reasonable, so fatherly, but Ella was no longer buying his act.

Two things she now was sure of. Romeo had played her, and he was not coming back. On some level, she wasn't even surprised. Her subconscious had been aware of all the little things that didn't add up about him, she'd just refused to listen to it.

He'd never done more than kiss her, had never even invited her to his apartment. Now she knew why.

A virgin fetched a higher price.

"Are these men you're talking about into rape?" She turned around and glared at him. "Because if you think I'm going to do anything willingly, you're delusional."

Stefano chuckled. "If you sit down, I'm going to tell you what's in it for you. That's the carrot. But in case you're not into carrots, I'm also going to show you the stick."

She didn't have much choice but to do as he said.

Clutching the backpack to her chest, she sat on the edge of the chair. Her throat was dry and she would've killed for a glass of water, but she didn't dare ask. Instead, she tried to swallow some saliva, but her mouth was dry as well.

Stefano opened a drawer, pulled out a plastic water bottle, and tossed it to her. "You see? When you do as you're told you get rewarded."

Uncapping the bottle, she lifted it up and gulped its contents as quickly as she could before he changed his mind, or decided to show her the stick by taking the water away.

"Let's start with the carrot. A beauty like you could go for as much as a quarter of a million. A virgin beauty like you could bring double that. Thirty percent of that goes to you. Think of it as a college fund."

"You want to sell me?"

"Normally, I would auction you to the highest bidder. But I have a special client in mind, who might want you enough to pay double what I could expect you to fetch in an auction."

"You think someone is going to pay a million for me?"

"I said, he might. But I'm probably being overly optimistic. Three-quarters of a million is a more reasonable price. I'm going to start with a million, though, and let him haggle over the price."

"Why?" Not that Ella was going to agree to it, not even in exchange for three hundred thousand toward her college fund. But she was curious. Why would anyone be willing to pay so much?

"Let me put it this way. Why do you think Jennifer Lawrence gets paid twenty-five million for one movie?"

That was a dumb question. "Because she is a great actress and she brings in the audience."

"Yes, but there are plenty of good actresses out there. The reason she's getting paid so much is that there is just one of her. She is a commodity of one. Which means that whoever wants her, has to pay the price she demands."

"I'm not Jennifer Lawrence."

"You are to my client. There is only one of you."

"How do you know that?"

"Ah, I have my ways."

"It doesn't matter. I'm not for sale."

Shaking his head, Stefano sighed dramatically. "I was

hoping we could avoid discussing the stick. I'm a business-man, and what I like to do most is negotiate a good deal where everyone is happy. Think what you could do with two or three hundred thousand dollars. It could set you up for life. That much money would cover your tuition and a down payment on a house. All for a year or two of playing the role of a dutiful girlfriend to a rich man. Some buyers tire of their new toys even sooner than that. Most women would jump on the opportunity even without an upfront payment."

Evidently, Stefano didn't think highly of the female gender. To him, they were all greedy gold-diggers who were willing to trade their bodies for money and status.

"I'm not most women."

"No, you are not. Most women are not worth a million to some guy with way too much money on his hands. But you are. Now that I explained the carrot, here is the stick, dear Ella."

Fear clawing at her heart, she hugged the backpack tighter to her chest.

"If you don't cooperate, if you try to escape or give me or my client any trouble, we are going to hurt your mother and your brother. Your mother will be first. Nothing fatal, mind you. A car accident, or maybe a home invasion with a side of rape. If that won't bring you to heel, we will do the same to your little brother, Parker."

Tears running down her cheeks, Ella whispered, "You can't do that."

"Yes, I can, and I will. Are you so selfish that you are willing to sacrifice your loved ones?" He arched a brow.

Ella shook her head. Of course, she wasn't. But she could contact her mother telepathically and tell her to grab Parker and run. Once they were safe, she would run too.

As if reading her mind, Stefano continued. "And don't think that you can contact your family and ask for help or warn them. Romeo planted listening devices all over your house. We will know the moment your mother or brother make the slightest move that is out of the ordinary. You'll be getting them in a crapload of trouble because they are going to be punished for your actions."

Ella felt faint. She would have to block her mother out.

"You see, Ella. I've been in this business for a long time, and I know what works. A girl might be willing to take stupid risks to preserve her virtue, but not at the expense of her family, or her friends. This is the strongest deterrent, and it works like a charm. This is to ensure that you play nice and that you don't talk, not to your family, and not to anyone else." He smirked. "Yes, we also have a bug in your friend's house. Madeleine, I believe?"

JULIAN

*a*s Julian read the script Brandon had emailed him, he could vividly imagine Ella in the role of a teenage boy's obsession. The unreachable beauty in the tower, or in the second-floor window of a suburban house as was the case.

In some scenes, she was looking at the sky with her elbows braced against the windowsill, her chin propped on her hands. In others, she was practicing ballet moves in her room. To the boy, she always appeared angelic and serene.

In short, Ella was a perfect fit for that role. And Brandon was right about the PG-13 flavor. It was innocent enough to be aired on the Disney channel.

Now that Julian was sure the thing was legit, he could make the call.

Vivian would no doubt be surprised to hear from him. More than a month passed since they'd met at the psychic convention. She probably thought he was never going to call.

Pulling her business card out of his wallet, he remembered tossing it into the trash and then changing his mind and picking it up again.

After all, he'd promised Vivian to talk to Brandon about Ella. That was the only reason he needed to keep her phone number. It was not because he found himself clicking the photo app on his phone and staring at the girl's picture five or six times a day.

No, that wasn't the reason at all.

He was a man of his word. That's all.

The phone rang for quite a while before the receptionist picked it up.

"Bright Smiles dental office, how can I help you?"

"May I speak to Vivian Takala?"

"She is with a client, but I can make an appointment for you."

"It's not about an appointment. I'm a friend of hers. Can I leave my number for her to call me?"

"Sure. Oh, wait a moment. I see her coming out. Vivian, there is someone on the line for you."

"Who is it?"

"He says he is a friend of yours."

"Hello?"

"Hi, Vivian. It's Julian. Remember me? We met at the convention."

"I remember. How can I help you?"

She didn't sound happy to hear from him at all. In fact, she sounded troubled.

"Is something wrong?"

She sniffled. "You can say so. Ella is gone."

His heart sank like a two-ton anchor into his gut. "What do you mean by gone?"

"She went to New York with her boyfriend, and she is not answering her phone. I'm afraid something horrible has happened to her and the police are refusing to do anything because she's supposedly an adult."

Julian exhaled a relieved breath. "She might have forgotten to charge it. That's not a reason to panic."

"You don't understand. Ella told me that she was spending the weekend with Maddie, her best friend. When Ella didn't show up to work on Monday, Maddie called me and asked if Ella was home. Apparently, Ella had told Maddie that she was going away for the weekend and was coming back Sunday night or rather early Monday morning. She knew I would never let her go, so she asked Maddie to cover for her. It's Wednesday, Julian. Something's happened to her and I don't know what to do."

"Do you have the boyfriend's number?"

"If I had, I would have called him. I tried to find him online. There were several guys named Romeo Giovani, but none of them was him. I couldn't find him on any of the social sites either."

That didn't sound good.

"How long were they dating?"

"Not long. She met him the week after the convention." Vivian sighed. "I'm sorry to dump all of this on you like that. I'm sure you didn't call to hear all about my problems. What can I do for you?"

The original reason for his call was no longer relevant.

All he could think of were Ella's piercing eyes looking at him from that picture, calling to him to help her. He'd thought he was doing that by arranging an audition for her, but, apparently, Fate had a different role for him in mind.

His role was to save Ella.

But how? And from what?

"Julian? Are you there?"

"Yes, I'm sorry. I was just thinking about what you've told me. I called because my uncle arranged an audition for her.

But it seems we have a bigger problem than finding Ella a job. First we need to find Ella."

Vivian snorted. "Funny that you would say that. Romeo kept talking about his uncle in New York, and the waitressing job he was offering to Ella in his new pizza place. She wanted to move there with him."

"Maybe that's what she did?"

"I don't think so. When she asked me if she could go, I offered to come with her and check the place out first. I wasn't about to let my eighteen-year-old daughter move to New York without talking to that uncle face to face and making sure that it was all legitimate. Ella agreed that it was a good plan. Romeo must have tricked her into going with him."

The more details Vivian was supplying, the more suspicious Julian was becoming. He'd heard his mother and Turner talk about the different methods of luring unsuspecting girls into a trap. Ella's story sounded disturbingly familiar.

"I think you are right to worry. This whole thing sounds very fishy. My mother's boyfriend is an expert on stuff like this. Let me talk to him and get back to you later."

"I'll give you my cellphone number."

"No. I'll call you at work again. If what I suspect is true, your cell and your home phone might be tapped. Did this Romeo come to your house?"

"Yes."

"Then he might have planted a bug somewhere. Don't talk about any of it at home."

"Why would he do that?"

Crap, how was he going to tell a mother that her daughter might have been lured into a trafficker's trap?

"I might be jumping to conclusions, but if Ella is detained

65

against her wishes, they could be ensuring her cooperation by threatening to harm her family."

"But why would they do that? I'm not rich. They can't expect a big ransom from me."

"I don't think that is what they are after." Julian had a feeling Vivian still didn't understand what she was dealing with, and he didn't want to spell it out for her over the phone while she was at work. This was going to be difficult enough face to face.

"I called the police from home," Vivian said.

"That's fine. They know the police are not going to do anything. Ella went willingly, and she is legally an adult. But it's better they don't know you have anyone helping you."

"When are you going to call back?"

"Later today or tomorrow morning."

"Thank you, Julian."

"Don't thank me yet."

BRIDGET

"What's wrong?" Bridget asked as Julian entered her office. He looked troubled and smelled anxious. It wasn't like him.

Pulling out a chair, he sat on the very edge of the seat. "I need to talk to you. Remember the lady I told you about? The one I met at the psychic convention?"

Bridget smiled. "How could I forget. Is this the one you tried to hit on, but who gave you her daughter's picture instead?"

"Yes, her name is Vivian, and I just talked to her. She told me that her daughter is missing. Apparently, Ella hooked up with this character named Romeo, and he convinced her to accompany him to New York for the weekend. Ella went with him, lying to her mother and telling her that she was spending the weekend at a friend's house. According to that friend, Ella was supposed to be back early Monday morning, but she wasn't, and no one's heard from her since she left. Ella is not answering her phone. Naturally, Vivian is going out of her mind with worry."

Poor woman. Bridget could empathize with the mother.

The traffickers were destroying more than the girls' lives. Entire families were victimized. Mothers, fathers, siblings—none of their lives were ever the same after that. She wished the clan could offer counseling to the rescued girls' families as well, and she hated that Julian had found himself involved in a case. If she could, she would've protected him from the ugliness.

Except, he was a grown man, and not her baby anymore. She couldn't and shouldn't shield him from reality.

"Vivian is right to be concerned. If you visit our sanctuary in Ojai and talk to the girls we've rescued, you'll hear many stories like that. A charming guy pretends to be a loving boyfriend and lures the girl away with a tempting promise. Sometimes it's a too-good-to-be-true job opportunity, like modeling or acting, and sometimes it's just a promise of an all-expenses-paid vacation. Once the girl is delivered, he gets paid and moves on to his next victim."

As his fangs elongated, Bridget could practically see Julian's venom glands swell in his throat. She'd never seen him in such a state. Did he have feelings for Vivian? Or perhaps for Ella?

Except, he'd never met the girl. Could he have developed feelings for a picture?

It was possible. Stranger things had happened.

"If I ever catch that scumbag, I'm going to tear his throat out with my fangs," he hissed.

"Take a deep breath, Julian." She put her hand over his. "I know it's infuriating, but if you want to help rescue the girl, you need to find a certain level of detachment."

He glared at her, and then let out a long breath. "You're not telling me anything I don't know." Doing as she'd suggested, he took several more deep breaths, exhaling each one through his fangs with a loud hissing sound. "I never felt this kind of rage before. I don't think taking deep breaths is going to cut it."

Julian was a doctor, not a Guardian. He hadn't developed the tools needed to harness anger and aggression and channel them into positive action.

"As a doctor, you must've learned to deal with disturbing news. Try to use that."

He shook his head. "How can I help her? Where do I even start?"

Bridget patted his hand. "You've made the first step. You came to me."

"Now what?"

"Now we need to take it to Kian and try to convince him to approve an investigation, and then if needed, a rescue operation. There is still a good chance that Ella just wants to be with her boyfriend and is afraid to call home and get yelled at."

"I don't think so. Vivian is not that scary. But why do you need Kian's approval? Didn't he put you in charge of the entire operation?"

"He did. But this is personal, and I shouldn't approve a costly investigation and a resource-heavy rescue just because I'm the boss and my son asked me to. There is also a matter of scheduling. All of the Guardians are assigned their tasks and operations for the next six weeks. If I want to give your friend priority, I will need to rework the schedule, and I can't do that on a whim either. I need to discuss it with Kian first."

"Do you think he will object?"

Bridget shrugged. "He's going to say that we can't allocate resources to rescue a single girl, and then I'm going to point out that there are probably more girls wherever she's been taken to, and he is going to approve it. This is just a formality, but it needs to be done."

KIAN

*O*ne look at Julian, and Kian knew the kid was about to lose it. His fangs weren't fully elongated, but they were not their normal size either. His eyes, which he apparently had less control over than his fangs, were glowing so brightly that Kian was tempted to pull out his shades.

Syssi often remarked that the young doctor looked a lot like him, but that they had polar opposite personalities. Julian was supposedly easy-going and friendly, while Kian was intense and intimidating.

Seeing the doctor as he was now would've changed Syssi's mind.

Not one to beat around the bush, Bridget went straight to why she and her son were there. "Julian's friend is missing, and from what he told me, I think she's fallen victim to traffickers."

When she was done recounting the events as she knew them, Kian turned to Julian. "Did you check social media for the boyfriend's name?"

"Vivian, Ella's mother, did. She found several guys named

Romeo Giovani, but none of them was the one who'd taken Ella."

Kian snorted. "The name alone should've been a red flag. Romeo? Who calls their kid Romeo?"

"An Italian?" Bridget offered.

Julian didn't appreciate Kian's attempt to lighten things up. "Are you going to approve a rescue mission?"

"Of course. A friend of yours is a friend of the clan. And although you've never even met the girl, she obviously means something to you. Let me teleconference with Turner and see what he suggests."

"Thank you." Slumping in his chair, Julian released a relieved breath.

Luckily, Turner wasn't in one of his meetings and the call didn't go to voicemail. "How can I help you, Kian?"

"I have Bridget and Julian here. I think it's best Julian tells you the story. If it's okay with you, I'm putting you on the big screen."

"Go ahead."

"You're on. Give me a sec to aim the camera so all three of us are in the picture."

Turner waited until Kian was done turning his laptop around and then joined Bridget and Julian on the other side of his desk. "Hi, Bridget, Julian."

Bridget smiled and did a little hand wave. "Hello, Victor."

"Go ahead, Julian. I'm listening."

As Julian retold the story, Kian listened intently for any discrepancies between his version and Bridget's. Not that he didn't trust her account, but it was natural to omit some things, and give a personal spin to others.

"I see," Turner said once Julian was done.

Running his hand over his jaw, he stared into the distance, thinking.

Kian knew that look well. When Turner's pale blue eyes

looked unfocused, it was because his brain was working on formulating a plan of action. Evidently, Bridget and Julian were familiar with it as well. Neither of them moved a muscle as they waited for the mastermind to come up with a solution.

"Here is what I propose to do," Turner said after a long moment. "Since we must assume that Vivian's home is bugged, we cannot meet her there." He looked at Julian. "You said you called her at work."

"It's a dental office. She is a dental hygienist."

"Perfect. Make an appointment for teeth cleaning tomorrow at eleven. Most likely, she has another client scheduled for that time slot, but you need to impress upon her that it's imperative she clears enough time for you and moves the others to a different time or day. I'll come with you, and we will talk with her in the dental office."

"That's a good idea." Bridget said.

"I'm curious to see how the operation works from the family's perspective."

Kian had been wondering about Turner's wish to accompany Julian instead of sending a Guardian or two with him. "Just in case, I want you to take a couple of Guardians with you."

"In case of what?" Bridget asked.

"In case the dental office is being watched as well, and there is trouble. Julian is a civilian with no combat training. Besides, while you guys are busy talking with the mother, it's a good idea to have a Guardian watch your backs."

"I took the self-defense course," Julian said.

Kian ignored the comment. One self-defense class for beginners wasn't going to do him any good against trained opponents. Even humans. And there was always the possibility of Doomers being involved in human trafficking.

They used to limit their activity to acquisitions, but lately they had been changing a lot of things. Like the drug dealing, which they used to delegate to gangs and were now doing in-house. They might have done the same with acquiring girls for the island. Cutting the middlemen out would save them a lot of money.

Apparently, their backing had dried out, and they were desperate for other sources of income. Either that, or they had some major expenditures that needed funding. Hopefully, they hadn't ventured into nuclear weapons. Fates knew there was plenty of enriched uranium and nuclear warheads circulating the black markets.

"I don't expect anyone to physically watch the house," Turner said. "Or the dental office. That's a waste of resources. But they might have planted bugs in both. Although, that's not always the case either. The girls have no way of knowing whether the threats are real or not. There might be no bugs at all."

Kian put his arm around Julian's shoulders. "I'd rather not take a chance with this boy. I happen to like him."

Bridget, who should have seconded the notion, shook her head. "One Guardian should be enough. We don't want to scare poor Vivian even more than she already is."

"We need to write a new standard operating protocol for dealing with the family," Turner said. "I agree with Kian. We need to bring two Guardians with us because I might decide to leave them there to keep an eye on the girl's mother and brother. They will need to take turns."

Given Bridget's tight-lipped expression, Kian had a feeling she was not about to let him or Turner win the argument.

"You're in charge of field operations, Vic, so I'm not going to argue with you about safety, but I still think one Guardian should suffice. One man hanging around will not raise as much suspicion as two. He can even pretend to be a relative and stay at their house. Besides, a woman with a young son might be uneasy with two burly guys hovering over her and her child. I suggest you choose just one and make sure he's polite and kid-friendly."

The image that popped into Kian's head was of Magnus holding the Golden Retriever puppy in his arms. "How about Magnus?"

"Perfect." Bridget crossed her arms over her chest, making it crystal clear that this was how she wanted it done, and smiled at her mate.

Without batting an eyelid, Turner nodded in agreement. "Magnus is a good choice."

Smart man. Turner knew to choose his battles.

"Now that this is settled, should I book a flight back for you and Julian?" Bridget asked.

"Between the security checks and boarding and all that other nonsense, it's going to be faster by car. If Magnus stays to watch over Vivian, Julian and I will rent one for the trip back home."

Kian rubbed his jaw to hide his smirk.

That should be interesting. How would the son and the boyfriend feel about being stuck together in the car for two and a half hours?

Except, a sidelong glance at Julian revealed no negative reaction. Perhaps the guy was too agitated to think of anything other than the girl, or perhaps he and Turner got along just fine.

MAGNUS

*M*agnus dropped his duffle bag in the trunk of Turner's car and got in the back seat. "Good morning, gentlemen."

"I hope so," Julian muttered under his breath.

Glancing at Magnus through the rearview mirror, Turner said, "I heard that you got yourself a dog."

"A puppy. I'm going to train her to sniff out immortals and, hopefully, Dormants too."

"Who did you leave her with?"

"My roommates."

"Can we go already?" Julian asked.

"What's your hurry?" Turner pressed the ignition button. "The appointment is for eleven and it's only six in the morning. We have plenty of time even with rush hour traffic. By the way, did you talk to Vivian?"

"I made the appointment with the receptionist. By the time I called, Vivian had already left."

"Was her schedule open?" Magnus asked.

"It wasn't. I said it was an emergency, and that I was willing to pay double or even triple to see Vivian at eleven."

"And she agreed? That's unprofessional."

"Money talks. Besides, she thought I was one of Vivian's admirers. She said I wasn't the first one to offer to pay double to see her. Apparently, Vivian's schedule is full of guys who clean their teeth way too often."

Magnus crossed his arms over his chest. "Aha, that makes sense. She knew you'd become a repeat customer, and that's why she agreed to bump some other poor schmuck to a different time slot for you. Vivian must really be a knockout."

"She is. But the receptionist hinted that I would be just as disappointed as Vivian's other clients because she doesn't date."

"Not at all, or just her clients?"

"I have a feeling she doesn't date at all. When I flirted with her, she did everything to dissuade me, including pretending to be married. Only later, she admitted to being a widow."

That was strange. Why would a young, beautiful woman, who evidently could pick and choose from many contenders, refuse to date?

Was there a story there?

"Perhaps she still mourns her husband? When did he pass away?"

"He was killed in Afghanistan eleven years ago."

"That's a long time."

"Perhaps she is socially awkward?" Turner suggested. "Not everyone is comfortable with dating. It's a hassle. Personally, I detested it."

"You're lucky that you have Bridget. Miserable bachelors like us have no choice but to labor in the trenches, eh, Julian?"

"Yeah. It's a drag."

"Really? You're too young to feel this way. At your age, I was very happy chasing lasses. And mind you, back then it wasn't as easy as it is now. It took either a lot of work charming a lass into taking off her knickers, or a lot of coin. And since I was short on the latter, I had to perfect my skills in the former."

Julian snorted. "I bet you also had to walk seven miles to school, rain or shine, but mostly snow."

The kid needed to brush up on his history. "I was home-schooled. Back then there were no schools in the Highlands."

Julian turned around. "You're that old?"

"Not at all. I'm quite young for an immortal."

"So why are you complaining about having to date?"

Magnus sighed. "American girls are not as friendly as the Scottish lasses. Or maybe it's me. Don't get me wrong, I can still get as many hookups as I want, I just don't enjoy them as much."

Julian shrugged. "Sex is sex."

"Nay, it isn't so. I like to spend time with a woman before I take her to bed. But I find that I have nothing to talk about with American girls."

"Maybe you're just homesick," Turner said. "You should ask for time off and go home for a visit."

"Yeah. I might do that."

18

VIVIAN

*V*ivian glanced at the clock on the wall, willing it to be eleven already.

She'd been worried sick even before Julian's phone call, but after talking with him, the worry had turned into a full-blown panic.

The things he'd alluded to were even worse than what she'd allowed herself to imagine. The scenarios that she'd conceived of went along the lines of a controlling boyfriend who wasn't letting Ella go back home and brainwashing her against her mother.

The worst she could think of was that Romeo had Ella heavily drugged, and that that was the reason she wasn't responding to Vivian's frantic communication attempts.

The other two frightening possibilities were an unexpected illness or an accident.

But what Julian had hinted at was something much more nefarious.

Except, things like that didn't happen to smart girls living in middle-class neighborhoods in affluent American cities. Or did they?

Not likely.

Julian had probably overreacted.

He'd said that his mother's boyfriend was an expert in situations like that, but what had he meant by that?

Was the boyfriend a private detective?

At this point, Vivian was willing to take out a second mortgage on the house to pay for his services, but how would she know if he was any good? It was easy to take advantage of parents in her situation. People would give anything to get their child back.

A chilling thought had her pause with the scaler in hand. What if she had brought Ella's abduction about by giving Julian her picture?

What if he was behind the whole thing?

Ella had met Romeo a day or two after the convention. Julian might have sent him to entrap her. They could be in cahoots, keeping Ella drugged and locked up somewhere until they sucked Vivian clean of every penny she owned or could borrow.

Her patient opened her eyes and mumbled, "Is there summing wrong?"

"I'm sorry." Viv went back to scraping off tartar. "Everything is all right. In fact, you're doing very well. You must be flossing regularly."

The woman nodded.

Viv forced a smile. "I thought so."

Julian had seemed so nice, though. She couldn't be such a bad judge of character. But then she hadn't been overly suspicious of Romeo either.

Well, that wasn't true. Something had been off, but she couldn't put her finger on it. The only thing she remembered thinking was that he'd acted older than his age, and that he had a good vocabulary.

Parker, on the other hand, hadn't liked Romeo from the

start and thought he was a creep. She should've listened.

Except, looking back, Viv couldn't think of anything she'd done wrong. Other than keeping Ella locked up in her room, there wasn't much more that she could've done. Perhaps she should've investigated Romeo the moment he'd started dating Ella?

But who did things like that?

She wasn't the President or the head of the Secret Service. Those guys probably investigated the hell out of whoever dated their kids.

Besides, Vivian had thought it was just a fling, and that it wouldn't last more than a few weeks.

If Josh were still around, maybe this wouldn't have happened.

While Vivian used to believe that people were fundamentally good, not bad, Josh had always looked for ulterior motives. He would have picked up on Romeo's right away.

She had been too naive and trusting. But not anymore.

When Julian arrived for his appointment, she was going to be extra careful and look out for any signs of deception. She would ask a lot of questions and try not to appear as desperate as she felt.

"All done, Mrs. Shriver." Viv handed her patient a cup of diluted mouthwash.

"Thank you," her patient said once she was done gargling.

As Vivian escorted her to the reception area, the first thing she did was to peek through it at the waiting room.

Catching a glimpse of Julian's profile, her heart skipped a beat. He was just as handsome as she'd remembered, but that wasn't what had startled her. It was the pained expression on his face.

It eased some of her fears. Perhaps he was legit and was really here to help her?

"Your eleven o'clock is here." Dolores winked. "And he is

one hell of a looker," she mouthed. "Lucky girl, you." She handed Vivian the patient chart. "No insurance. He's paying cash." Another wink. "And a lot of it," she whispered.

Vivian had been wondering how Julian had managed to make a next day appointment without her arranging it. Apparently, Dolores had been bribed.

Opening the door to the waiting room, she called out, "Julian Ward?"

He hadn't written his doctor title on the chart. Had that been a lie? Perhaps he didn't want to call attention to himself. But if that had been his motive for omitting the title, he shouldn't have bothered. A guy looking like him couldn't escape notice no matter how hard he tried.

"Hello." He pushed to his feet and offered his hand.

"Good morning." Vivian wasn't sure whether she should pretend not to know him, but decided to play it safe and save it for the privacy of her treatment room. "Please, follow me."

In her room, she motioned for him to take a seat, and then closed the door.

"Thank you." He handed her a folded note before sitting down in the patient chair.

With an arched brow, Vivian unfolded the note and read it. *Your cell phone might be bugged. If you have it on you, take it to the front office and leave it there. Don't say a thing about Ella until you do.*

Talk about cloak and dagger. Was it all part of the setup to scare her into hiring him to find Ella?

The guy must be a superb actor to pull off that concerned expression so convincingly. Just in case, though, she decided to follow his instructions.

Maybe someone was really using her cellphone to spy on her conversations.

"I will be right back," she said. "I want to take a peek at your X-rays."

She knew he hadn't done any, because Dolores would have told her if he had. But it sounded like a legit excuse to leave a patient alone for a moment. If anyone was indeed listening in, they wouldn't suspect a thing.

When she returned a couple of minutes later, Julian wasn't alone in her room.

Two men were there with him.

He must've snuck them in through the back door. One was a short blond guy who seemed to be made from pure muscle, but it was the other one that had her suck in a breath.

Gorgeous and well-dressed, he looked like someone who belonged on the cover of one of her silly billionaire romance novels.

"I'm sorry to scare you like this," Julian said. "But I thought it would look odd if three guys followed you into your treatment room. I let my associates in through the back door."

"Yeah, I figured that was what you did." Her eyes were still glued to the tall, gorgeous guy with the goatee.

"This is Turner," Julian introduced the short blond guy. "He is the expert I told you about."

This was his mother's boyfriend? No wonder Julian saw nothing wrong about flirting with an older woman. Turner looked to be in his late twenties or early thirties, which meant that he must have been at least ten years younger than Julian's mother, even if she had him at eighteen like Vivian had Ella.

Or, what was more likely, Turner was Julian's accomplice and not his mother's boyfriend. It was probably just a cover story for how Julian knew the *expert*.

"I wish we'd met under more pleasant circumstances, Vivian." Turner offered his hand for a handshake.

She nodded.

"And this is Magnus," Julian continued. "He is here to keep you and your son safe."

Magnus flashed her a disarming smile. "At your service, my lady." He took her hand, but instead of shaking it, he dipped his head and kissed the back of it, sending an electric current from her hand straight to her center.

So his job was to charm and confuse her, and to her great embarrassment, it was working. That sexy accent was probably fake.

"Where are you from, Magnus?"

"Scotland, of course."

"I thought so, but I wasn't sure." She glanced at Turner and then at Julian. "Thank you all for coming. I'm touched."

It was on the tip of her tongue to ask why the three of them drove all the way from Los Angeles to see her, but Vivian suspected she already knew the answer to that.

Turner pulled a phone out of his pocket. "This is for you. I already programmed it with Julian's and Magnus's numbers, and all three of us have yours. If you need to contact us, use only this phone, and make sure not to do it from your house."

"Thank you." She took the phone from his hand. They were really laying it on thick.

"Take a seat, Vivian. This will take a while." He pointed at the only chair other than the dental one which Julian was leaning against.

"Yes, sir," she said with a thinly veiled sarcasm.

If the three of them thought to intimidate the little widow and scare her into paying them, they were in for a big surprise. Throughout Josh's enlistment, she'd met plenty of military types who thought they were all that.

She knew how to deal with them. Basically, it was about holding her chin up and not giving them an inch.

19

MAGNUS

*F*rom the moment Vivian had entered the room, Magnus couldn't take his eyes off her. She was a stunning woman. Without a trace of makeup, her thick blond hair gathered in a ponytail, she was more beautiful than all the actresses he'd been admiring combined. And he wasn't even into blonds.

Natalie Portman and Rachel Weisz had nothing on her. She bore some resemblance to Kim Basinger, but she was not her doppelgänger as Julian had claimed. She was much more beautiful.

The one thing Julian had been spot on about though, was the complete lack of curves. Vivian was petite, slim, and flat-chested. But then she might be hiding a few curves under the unflattering blue scrubs she had on.

Not that he cared one way or the other.

He liked petite, delicately built females. Bra size didn't matter. He also liked brunettes, but he was more than willing to make an exception in Vivian's case.

Once they found her daughter, of course.

He wasn't going to hit on a woman at a time like this. But

if she needed a shoulder to cry on, he would gladly offer his, and do nothing more than pat her slim back. Or maybe caress her hair. A kiss to the forehead should be all right too...

Yeah, he needed to stop before he got any more bright ideas.

While he'd been daydreaming, Turner had been asking questions and writing Vivian's answers on his yellow pad.

"You don't happen to know which airline Ella flew on?"

"No."

"Would her friend know, the one who told you about the trip?"

"Maddie said Ella didn't tell her. The only information she had was a late Friday evening departure and a late night Sunday or early morning Monday return. Will that help?"

"It's not really important. We can find out which flight Ella was on, and then hack into the airport's security cameras at the departure gate."

"What are you hoping to find?"

"Romeo's face. When we find the footage with Ella in it, he'll be there too. The name is obviously fake. But we can run his picture through facial recognition software and find out his real one. From there, it should be easy to find his address."

Vivian let out a breath. "And when you find him, you'll find Ella."

Turner shook his head. "Probably not. But he will tell us who he sold her to."

"Sold her? What are you talking about?"

Turner and Julian exchanged quick glances. Apparently, Julian hadn't told Vivian what she was up against.

Turner put the yellow pad away and leaned toward her. "What do you think happened to Ella?"

"I don't know. That's why I'm freaking out. I assume that

Romeo is not letting her go home. He probably has her drugged. Otherwise she would've found a way to contact me."

"That's possible, but I'm afraid there might be another, more sinister explanation. Romeo might be part of a trafficking ring. A young, handsome guy lures a pretty girl like Ella to go with him. He then transfers her to a handler who explains the situation. If she refuses to cooperate, they are going to hurt her family. That's why they plant listening devices. They collect details to prove that they have her loved ones under surveillance. That is how they blackmail her into cooperating. If she does what she is told, they promise her a cut of the profits, and that they will let her go in a year or two."

Vivian stared at Turner as if he was the devil himself. "You mean to tell me that they kidnapped my daughter and sold her into prostitution?"

Turner nodded.

Vivian threw her hands in the air. "You want to tell me that things like that happen in the United States of America, in middle-class neighborhoods?"

"More often than you know."

"But why Ella?"

"Julian tells me she is exceptionally beautiful."

Vivian nodded, then narrowed her eyes at Turner. "If what you're saying is true, why are the police ignoring me? Aren't they aware of what's going on?

"They are, but their hands are tied. Unless a crime is reported, there is nothing they can do."

"You are supposedly an expert on this. What can you do?"

"First of all, we get you and your son to safety. At the same time, we find Romeo and get him to tell us Ella's location. Then we raid the place and rescue her, along with any other girls who might be held there against their will."

Vivian's eyes were still narrowed. "Who are *we?*"

"We are a private organization dedicated to stopping human trafficking."

"How much do you charge for your services?"

"We don't. Our funding comes from contributions."

For some reason, Turner's last sentence brought tears to Vivian's eyes.

"Oh dear God. Up until now I was hoping this was all a scam, and that you guys had Ella and were trying to get money out of me."

Julian sucked in a breath. "Why would you think that?"

Turner patted Vivian's hand, his normally expressionless face showing compassion. "Because the alternative was much scarier."

She nodded. "What now?"

"How old is your son?" Turner asked.

"Parker is twelve."

"Do you think you can trust him not to talk about what's going on?"

"He's a smart kid. In fact, he was on to Romeo and called him a creep. I should've listened." She sighed. "Not that I would've done anything differently. I couldn't get him arrested based on a bad vibe."

"No, you couldn't," Turner agreed. "Here is what you do. Tell Parker what's going on when you pick him up from school today, but not with your phone around and not inside your car. You can also talk to him at home inside a bathroom with the water running. Out loud, start talking about cleaning up the closets and donating old stuff to charity. Pack all you and your son would need for a few days inside trash bags, and then ask him to help you carry the bags out to your car."

"How long are we talking about?"

"Hopefully, only a couple of days, but I believe in planning for contingencies. I suggest that you pack for at least a week."

"What am I supposed to tell the people at work? I can't just get up and go."

"Tomorrow is Friday. Do you work on the weekend?"

She shook her head.

"If everything goes smoothly, you'll be back home by Sunday. And if not, we can deliver a message for you. Something about a sickness or some unforeseen emergency."

Vivian nodded. "Okay."

"Tomorrow, drop your son off at school as usual and go to work. When it's time to pick him up, leave your cellphone here, but make sure it's connected to a charger. We don't want it running out of battery in case Ella calls. We will have your calls forwarded."

"Wow, you think of everything."

Turner's lips lifted in a sad smile. "That's what I do, Vivian, and I've been doing it for a very long time."

"Are you good at it?"

This time Turner smiled for real. "The best."

"I'll take your word for it. It's not like I can check references."

Magnus chuckled. "I can vouch for him, but then you'll have to take my word for it."

She didn't look amused, but then he couldn't blame her. Vivian was putting on a brave face, but he was sure she was screaming on the inside.

Turner continued. "After you pick up your son from school, head to the nearest mall." He pulled out his phone. "What's the name of the one closest to your home?"

"Westfield Plaza."

He brought up the map. "You will meet Magnus here." He pointed at one of the parking lots. "Tell Parker that you're taking him to the food court and then to watch a movie.

Don't say anything as you take the garbage bags out of your car."

"Do you think my car is bugged too?"

"It might be. From there, Magnus will take you to a safe house."

"We have a safe house?" Magnus asked. "Do you mean the sanctuary?"

"No, I mean a safe house. I'll have one ready by tomorrow."

20

TURNER

"*V*ivian is a strong woman," Magnus said as they got in the car.

She had put on a commanding performance of holding her shit together, which Turner found admirable, but that didn't mean she wasn't falling apart on the inside. "She has no choice." He pulled out of the dental office's parking lot.

Next to him, Julian stared ahead. "I can't believe she thought I orchestrated Ella's kidnapping so I could extort money out of her."

"That's because you look like a thug," Magnus said. "That good-boy pretty face of yours is a great cover for a criminal mastermind. Mwa-ha-ha."

Julian didn't find Magnus's attempt at humor funny. "Where to now?"

"The rental car office. You and I are going to head back to Los Angeles, and Magnus is going to keep the car and get a hotel room near Vivian's house."

"It's good that you have so many cars," Julian said. "You're not going to miss this one."

The kid liked to poke fun at Turner's car collection and

his continuous insistence on evasive maneuvers, even when it wasn't likely that he was being followed. The thing was, Julian couldn't understand that level of caution because he'd lived a sheltered life and had never been exposed to the darker side of the world like Turner had. This was his first personal brush with the ugly and rotten underbelly of humanity.

Naturally, he wasn't taking it too well.

"What about the safe house I'm supposed to take her to?" Magnus asked.

Turner merged into the fast-moving traffic of the freeway. "I have a place up in Big Bear that I use from time to time. You can take them there, or maybe Kian can spare one of the apartments in the clan's high rises, provided there are vacancies."

He pressed the personal assistant button on the steering wheel. "Call Bridget."

The phone rang a couple of times before she answered. "Hi, Vic. How did it go?"

"We are whisking Vivian and her son to a safe house tomorrow. Do you know if there are any vacancies in any of the clan's buildings downtown?"

"I have a better idea. You can use Amanda and Dalhu's cabin."

"I didn't know they had one."

She chuckled. "It belongs to the clan, but they are the only ones using it. I guess for sentimental reasons."

"Is that the one Dalhu broke into when he kidnapped Amanda?"

"Yep, that's the one. It was heavily damaged from the explosives the rescue team used, so Kian bought it and had it fixed."

"Is it big enough for three people?" Julian asked. "We need three bedrooms, or at least two."

"Originally it was just one big space with an open loft bedroom and one bathroom, but Kian had two bedrooms and a bath added downstairs. Magnus and Vivian can have those, and the boy can sleep in the loft. The place is the perfect safe house. It's in a remote location and it's off the grid."

"They must have nice memories from there if they keep going back," Turner said.

"I guess so. I remember that Amanda wasn't too happy about getting rescued. But that might have been Kian's fault. He was a real ass to her because she protected Dalhu from him."

"That sounds like one hell of a story," Magnus said. "I can't wait to hear the rest of it."

Bridget chuckled. "You have no idea. But I'm afraid that I've already said too much. It's their story to tell, not mine."

Turner had never heard the full story, just bits and pieces. Perhaps one day he would ask Amanda or Dalhu to tell him more. The important thing was that the cabin seemed like a perfect place for a safe house.

"So that's settled," he said. "Tomorrow, Magnus is going to take Vivian and her son to the cabin. Now, to the more important stuff. I need you to organize a group of Guardians. Arwel and four others. I'll also need the large plane ready, and flight arrangements for a New York airport. I don't care which one."

"What's the plan?"

"I'll tell you the details when I get home."

"Drive safely."

"I always do." He disconnected the call and turned to Julian. "Text Ella's full name and photo to William. I want him and Roni to find out which flight she was on and start working on the security cameras to find our *Romeo*."

"I'm on it."

21

KIAN

$\mathcal{O}$nce Bridget was done with her update, Kian asked, "What's the ETA on Turner and Julian?"

"They should be here any minute."

"Why is he asking for five Guardians and the large jet?"

Everyone's schedules had been set for the next six weeks. Freeing five Guardians to accompany Turner meant canceling one of the scheduled rescue missions.

"He said he was going to give us the details when he gets here. But I assume it's because he expects there will be more girls where Ella was taken, and he plans to bring them all back here to the sanctuary."

"That makes more sense. I would hate to think that we are dedicating so many resources to the rescue of one girl. Especially if we are pulling them away from other operations."

Bridget pinned him with a hard stare. "Every life is important. Besides, I asked for volunteers who were willing to give up a couple of their vacation days. The rest I managed to reshuffle so I didn't have to cancel any missions."

"Which means that you're sending out smaller teams. I'm

not sure I'm okay with that. Our first duty is to ensure our people's safety."

"Don't worry. I checked with each unit's commander and only took those who said they'd be fine with one less warrior."

"Spreading our teams thin is not the answer, Bridget. You have to accept that our resources are not limitless and we can't help everyone."

Bridget sighed. "Yeah, you're right. I won't do that again. I just wish we could rescue all of them."

"So do I. But there is no way around prioritizing. We can't save the whole world."

"I think I hear them coming." Bridget stood up and walked over to open the door. "Hi, guys. Come in."

"Did our hacker team come up with something?" Turner asked as he strode in.

Kian motioned him to a chair. "I haven't heard from them yet, so I assume they are still working on it."

Julian hugged his mother, and then the two of them joined Kian and Turner at the conference table.

Flipping to a new page on his yellow pad, Kian clicked his pen. "Do you really need the large jet?"

"If I want to bring the rescued girls to the sanctuary, I'll need the large one. I'm taking five Guardians with me. That leaves only two seats on the small one. But if that's a problem, we can put some of them on commercial flights."

Kian leaned back and crossed his arms over his chest. "What if this is not a kidnapping case, and the girl is just hanging out with her boyfriend and not giving a damn that her mother is worried about her?"

Julian pulled out his phone, scrolled until he found what he was looking for, and handed it to Kian. "Look at her."

The girl was beautiful, but Kian had seen many beautiful women, and beauty alone didn't impress him as much as it would another man. But he could see Julian's point. If whoever was holding Ella auctioned her, the girl would go for a lot of money.

The eyes staring at him from the picture were wise. How had a girl like this fallen victim to a con artist? Had she fallen in love with the scum?

Probably. Love blinded even the smartest people, and eighteen-year-olds had a right to their naïveté.

"Can I have my phone back?"

"I'm sorry." He handed it to Julian. "I was just thinking that Ella looks like a smart girl. She must've fallen in love to do something as stupid as to go to New York with a boyfriend she knew next to nothing about."

"They have the game perfected," Turner said. "That's why educating people about what to look out for is so important. Although in this case, Vivian was very careful, even though she wasn't suspicious. And Ella probably thought she was just going on a weekend adventure and would be back without her mother ever finding out."

"What about the cabin?" Julian asked. "Can we use it?"

Kian nodded. "It needs some cleaning up, though. The last time Amanda and Dalhu were there was more than two months ago. It needs airing and dusting and new bedding and such like."

"You don't have a cleaning service up there?" Bridget asked.

He chuckled. "It wouldn't be much of a safe house if I did. No. Whoever uses it, cleans it."

Turner nodded. "It's better this way. Julian can go and tidy up. I want to leave for New York as soon as possible. Hopefully by the time we get there, William and Roni will have the guy's information for us."

Kian lifted a brow. "I'm surprised that you're going at all. Don't you have a business to run?"

Other than the first test mission, Turner hadn't gone on any. He planned and advised and worked closely with Bridget, helping her organize and prioritize, but he had been adamantly determined about maintaining his independent status and running his private operation as he had done before his transition.

"I do. But family comes first." Turner glanced at Julian. "For some reason, this girl is important to Julian. And whoever is important to my mate's son, is important to me."

ELLA

*A*s the key rattled in the lock, announcing yet another of Stefano's visits, Ella put the book down and assumed a bored expression.

At first, she'd tensed every time she'd heard his heavy footsteps coming down the corridor, but after a week of his visits, she knew he wasn't going to touch her.

He would come in, tell her what her mother and Parker were doing so she would know he hadn't been bluffing about having them under surveillance, and then leave, locking her in the room.

If one could call it that. The bed was an old mattress on the floor, but at least there was an attached bathroom with a toilet, a sink, and a shower with a curtain.

Her phone and tablet had been taken away from her, there was no television or radio, and the only thing keeping her from going insane was a stack of tattered old romance novels that were mostly about sex. It hadn't been an act of kindness on Stefano's part. The wolf disguised as a friendly middle-aged man probably thought of them as education.

It was obvious that he was waiting for something or

someone—perhaps the rich buyer he'd told her about the day Romeo had delivered her.

Other than Stefano, it seemed like Ella was the only other occupant of the house. On occasion, she would hear other people downstairs, but then they would leave, and at night it was just her and him in the house. Sometimes, she wasn't sure he was there either.

Three times a day, Stefano brought her microwaved frozen entrees and a chilled soft drink. The rest of the time, she drank tap water from the bathroom.

The room didn't have a window, and neither did the bathroom. She could see the outline of a square where there had been one in the past, but it was now cemented over. Not that she would've tried anything even if there was an opening large enough for her to squeeze through and jump from the second floor down to the street.

With her family's safety at stake, Ella had no choice but to do what she was told.

"Get your things," Stefano said as he opened the door.

"Where are you taking me?"

His smile creeped her out. "It's time to recoup my investment. You should be happy. Your solitary confinement days are over. There will be other girls where I'm taking you." He waved his hand. "Now hurry up. I don't have all day."

While he watched, Ella stuffed her few belongings into her backpack, including the panties she'd washed last night which were still damp.

He took her out back into a courtyard where a car was parked, and pushed her into the back seat. "Here, take this." He handed her a couple of pills and a water bottle. "Those are sleeping pills. I don't want you to give Franco any trouble."

As if she would dare do anything and endanger her family.

Franco turned back and leered. "We meet again, pretty girl."

Pills in hand, Ella hesitated. What if the creep decided to take advantage of her while she was out?

Stefano leaned into the car through the driver side window. "You touch her, and you're dead. Am I clear?"

Franco lifted his hands in the air. "I swear to God that I wasn't thinking anything."

That earned him a loud slap. "Don't take the Lord's name in vain, you piece of shit. And no touching! Not even a hair on her head! Swear on your mother's life."

"I swear on my mother's life that I will not touch the girl."

Stefano stared him down for a long moment. "Get out. I'm going to deliver her myself."

Ella exhaled a relieved breath. At some point she was going to be violated, but at least it wasn't going to happen while she was out.

Franco didn't hesitate for a moment to vacate the driver seat. "I swear I wasn't going to touch her."

Stefano ignored him and turned the engine on. "Take the pills, Ella."

23

MAGNUS

While waiting in the mall's parking lot, Magnus scrolled through the information William's geek squad had assembled on Vivian, her late husband Joshua, her daughter Ella, and her son Parker.

With the number of details they'd been able to dig out, Magnus was surprised they hadn't listed the family's shoe sizes and the number of dental fillings each had.

Although with a dental hygienist as the matriarch, all of them probably had excellent teeth and had never needed to go under a dentist's drill.

Supposedly, it was a scary experience. Or maybe just for children.

Magnus chuckled. The reason Kian had chosen him for the babysitting job was probably Scarlet. The boss mistakenly assumed that if Magnus had gotten himself a puppy to raise, he must be kid-friendly.

As if dealing with a kid was in any way similar to dealing with a dog.

Other than all the expensive specialty stuff he'd had to

buy for Scarlet, taking care of a dog hadn't changed much since Magnus was a boy, and he knew what he was doing.

A twelve-year-old human was a different story.

At that age, Magnus had learned how to hunt, and how to fish, and how to build a fire, and how to put up a spit to roast his catch on. He'd also learned how to fight with his fists and with swords and how to make bows and arrows and shoot them. It had been fun, and he remembered enjoying his childhood. Well, except for when his mother had forced him to sit on his ass and study when he would've rather done anything but that.

Today's kids were different.

They stayed home and played computer games. As if that could replace the exhilaration of climbing a tree or besting a worthy opponent in a practice sword fight. They had no idea what they were missing.

Perhaps he could interest Vivian's boy in learning some of the outdoorsy things Magnus had loved when he was that age.

Or maybe it was time Magnus learned how to play computer games.

But if everything else failed, he had backup. No kid could resist a puppy. That was why he'd had Julian pick Scarlet up and bring her to the cabin. Hopefully, the trip to the mountains had been uneventful, and she hadn't pooped or peed in Julian's car. He'd told the guy to stop a couple of times on the way and let her do her business. But what if she'd run out on him?

Suddenly worried, Magnus pulled out his phone and dialed Julian's number. "Do you have my girl?"

"What do you mean? Vivian is not with you?"

That was hilarious. Why would he call Vivian his girl?

He would've liked to, that's for sure, but wanting and having were not the same thing.

"Do you have Scarlet?"

"Oh, yeah. She is already suffering from cabin fever and wants to get out. But I don't want to leave her alone in the yard. Even though the property is fenced, a predator can jump it and get her. She's still small."

"Make sure to keep an eye on her at all times. Did you pack her stuff?"

"Everything is here. Including her food, her toys, her toothbrush, toothpaste, and even the shampoo and conditioner. I felt like I was packing for a girl."

"Scarlet is a girl."

"Yeah, well. Not that kind of a girl, but whatever. It's cool. You're entitled to pamper your pet."

"What's the status with the hacking?" Magnus asked to change the subject.

He didn't need Julian to give him updates. As soon as Turner got something, he was going to let Magnus know.

But he didn't appreciate the civilian mocking him. It was bad enough that the other Guardians thought Magnus was soft because he happened to prefer well-made elegant clothing and didn't like jeans.

It was astounding what people could get prejudiced against. Apparently, freedom of expression was an ideal not yet internalized by humans and immortals alike. Being well-dressed didn't mean he wasn't one hell of a Guardian.

"They are still working on it," Julian said. "The guy is not as easy to find as we thought he'd be. Turner and the Guardians are already in New York, waiting for the info. I hope they'll have Ella in a few hours, and we can put this whole thing behind us."

"Aye, me too. See you later. And thanks for taking care of Scarlet for me."

"You're welcome." Julian disconnected the call on his end.

Things never worked that smoothly, but Magnus had

seen no reason to quash the young doctor's hope. And even if they did, it would be a long time before Ella could put the ordeal behind her.

The best they could do was avenge her.

Magnus would have loved nothing more than to turn every scumbag involved in the trafficking operation into hamburger meat, preferably using only his fangs and fists.

Damn it. This was not the time or place for getting all riled up.

As his venom glands filled up, and his fangs punched out over his lip, Magnus slapped a hand over his mouth. He was standing outside Turner's fancy SUV in the parking lot of a busy mall, with humans coming and going all around him. He should have known better than to allow his mind to wander in a direction that was sure to enrage him.

Kid-friendly my ass.

If he didn't get himself under control and fast, he was going to scare the crap out of both mother and son.

Glancing at his watch again, Magnus was glad that Vivian was running late. He needed a few minutes to calm down and retract his fangs.

Except, her tardiness worried him. If she'd picked up her son from school at three o'clock like she'd been supposed to, Vivian should have arrived already.

Several moments later, her car pulled up next to him.

Without saying a thing, Magnus pointed at a vacant spot two cars over and started walking.

When Vivian was done parking, a scrawny kid jumped out and hurried toward him with an enthusiastic expression on his face.

Magnus put a finger to his lips, signaling the boy to keep quiet as he waited for Vivian to pop the trunk open.

Pulling three full trash bags out, he started walking back toward the SUV with the kid following behind.

"Can I talk now?" Parker whispered when Magnus put the bags inside Turner's vehicle.

"Yes. Quietly." He offered his hand. "I'm Magnus."

"I know, Mom told me. And I'm Parker." The kid shook his hand. "Are you with the Secret Service?"

Another trash bag in hand, Vivian joined them. "I told you that they belong to a private organization." She handed Magnus the bag. "There was no room for it in the trunk."

Forcing a tight-lipped smile, Magnus took it and opened the passenger door for her. "My lady?" He waited for Vivian to get in and then closed the door behind her.

His damn fangs were acting up, and this time anger and aggression had nothing to do with it.

The scrubs Vivian had on yesterday had hidden her shapely figure. She was just as slim as he'd imagined, but she had perfectly shaped feminine curves. They were delicate, but not absent. Her hips flared slightly from her slim waist and she had a hint of cleavage.

Basically, she was his dream girl. The only variation was her being a blond and not a brunette. But since he found her perfect the way she was, Magnus was going to change the dream to fit the reality of her.

From now on, Vivian was his new ideal.

"Where are we going?" Parker asked as soon as he'd buckled up in the back seat.

"A cabin in the mountains."

"Does it have an internet connection?"

Shite, he'd forgotten to ask. "I don't know."

"Mom! You told me there would be internet! What am I going to do now?"

"You can use my phone as a hotspot," Magnus offered.

"Is there cellular reception?"

"My phone is connected to a satellite. I always have a connection."

"Cool." Parker's tone changed immediately.

"It must be expensive to use," Vivian said. "Parker plays for hours at a time."

"Don't worry about costs. Everything is covered."

In the back seat, Parker huffed. "I told you they are from the Secret Service. Only government employees don't care how much things cost."

"Parker! That's rude."

Magnus chuckled. "No, the kid is right. But no, we are not the Secret Service. We just have backers with deep pockets."

"Like who? Apple? Microsoft?"

The kid was smart.

Or maybe it wasn't just Parker, but this entire generation of kids who were connected to the net with an umbilical cord and fed off its endless supply of information.

"I'm not at liberty to disclose their names."

"Bummer."

24

VIVIAN

*D*isappointed with Magnus's answer, Parker pulled out his headphones and portable game console.

Vivian sighed. Unless he got hungry, Parker would keep playing for the entire duration of the drive, which meant that she would have to carry on a conversation with Magnus all on her own. A tough thing to do while she was torn between battling tears and fighting her most inappropriate attraction to the handsome Scot.

What was wrong with her?

How could she even notice how attractive he was at a time like this?

Besides, he wasn't even her type. She liked rugged all-American macho men like Josh, not sophisticated European fancy dressers.

It was those silly billionaire romances' fault.

Only, the heroes in her books were rough around the edges despite being rich, while Magnus oozed charm and good manners like some British lord, and he probably wasn't rich.

Otherwise, he wouldn't be a bodyguard. Under that suit

and tie were hard muscles, and behind the smiles and the sexy accent was steel.

Maybe that was the attraction. The sense of security that Magnus provided. He seemed like someone she could lean on, a strong man who could not only defend her and Parker, but also listen to her and offer comfort.

Right.

She should know better.

Josh had been the same. Even as an eighteen-year-old kid, he'd been strong and dependable. It had been so easy to lean on him and let him take care of all the things she'd felt overwhelmed by. They'd been so young, and everything had seemed so difficult, but Josh had found a way to get a job that provided housing and health insurance and allowed her to stay home with their baby until Ella was old enough to enter kindergarten.

But then tragedy had struck, Josh had been killed, and Vivian had been left to raise and support their two kids alone.

She'd managed, but it had taught her an important lesson.

Leaning on a good man was fine, it was part of being a team, and a man should be able to lean on his partner as well. But shit happened, and a woman should never rely on that support to the exclusion of being able to fend for herself and her family.

Except, that was true for everyday circumstances. Vivian worked to support her family and took care of her kids, but she wasn't equipped to deal with situations like this. Josh hadn't been either.

A helicopter mechanic was not a commando. He would've needed these people's help to rescue his daughter just as much as Vivian did.

Her chance meeting with Julian had been so fortunate, and she was grateful beyond words to him for mobilizing his mother's boyfriend and their entire organization to save Ella.

Even though Magnus's job was to safeguard her and Parker, she needed to remember that it was all part of the rescue mission. He wasn't there to provide emotional support to a distraught mother.

"How long to that cabin?"

"It's about three hours' drive away, but we should probably stop for dinner somewhere. Julian is supposed to restock the cabin, but I don't know what his idea of food supplies is. There might be nothing to prepare a meal from."

"We should stop at a supermarket then. The least I can do to repay you for your kindness is cook you dinner." Vivian wasn't a great cook, but she could throw a decent meal together.

"Please, I don't want you to feel obligated to me in any way." He cast her a piercing look that had her go weak at the knees.

Crap, had she made it sound as if she was offering more than a meal?

"Well, Parker and I need to eat too."

"I can cook for us."

"You can cook?"

He shrugged. "I can grill as well as the next guy. My roommates can survive on sandwiches, but I like to eat better."

Interesting. She hadn't thought of it before, but Magnus could've been married. He didn't wear a ring, but that didn't mean much. Many people didn't wear them for various reasons, and not all of them were meant to deceive. Because of her job, she couldn't wear rings even if she were still married.

Except, if Magnus was living with roommates, he probably was single. Unless one of his roommates was a woman. Or both.

"What do your roommates do? Are they also in security?"

"They are both programmers, and they work from home. Which means that they work until they drop and hardly ever breathe fresh air. I don't know how they do it. If I was cooped up in a room with a computer all day, I would go crazy. "

She looked him over. "You don't look like the outdoorsy type."

Magnus laughed. "I like to dress well." He turned to her and winked. "Even for outdoor activities. As a bachelor, I need to be ready to impress the ladies whatever the situation. Otherwise, how am I going to find my one and only?"

The handsome devil knew that he was attractive. She needed to stay away from talking about his looks. Asking Magnus about his work seemed like a safer topic for conversation.

"What exactly is your job? Are you a bodyguard? A detective? How does it work in your organization?"

Smoothing his hand over his meticulously trimmed goatee, Magnus took a long moment to answer. "I'm a cross between a policeman and a soldier. Sometimes I'm a detective, and sometimes I go on missions that require fighting skills, and sometimes I'm a bodyguard."

"Like military police?"

"Not really."

Maybe Parker was right, and Magnus was a secret agent. He certainly pulled off the 007 look well. "Like a Secret Service agent?"

"It's not like that either. I usually work with a partner or a group of people. Our organization provides in-house training, so it's tailored for its needs."

"How did you get recruited for the job?"

"I volunteered."

That wasn't telling her much either. It seemed that Magnus was an expert on dodging questions without refusing to answer them. But Vivian's curiosity had just gotten whetted, and she wasn't going to quit until she learned more about the people helping her.

"How did you know where to volunteer?"

He cast her an amused glance. "It's a family thing."

"Oh, I get it. So your father or uncles or brothers were, or still are, with the organization?"

"Uncles and cousins. I'm an only child and I don't know who my father was."

"Oh."

It wasn't unusual. Single motherhood was quite common. The only thing that troubled her about his answer was that he'd said *was* instead of *is*. Magnus was a young man in his early thirties or late twenties. If he didn't know who his father was, why would he presume that the man was dead?

Perhaps it was only a figure of speech, though, and he'd meant nothing by it.

MAGNUS

"That's a very nice cabin," Vivian said as Magnus parked the car. "It looks brand new."

"It was renovated recently."

He had to hand it to Kian. The guy didn't do anything half-assed. Magnus hadn't seen the property before, but cabins usually didn't come with a stone wall and an electric gate. There was even a portico over the parking area to keep the car shaded.

"Cool," was Parker's assessment.

"You can go inside," Magnus said as he opened the car door for Vivian. "There is a surprise waiting for you in there."

Parker eyed him suspiciously. "What kind of a surprise?"

"If I tell you it wouldn't be a surprise, right?"

The boy shrugged, hefted the trash bag containing his game console and all the wiring that went with it, and headed for the front door.

Hopefully, the cabin came with television. Magnus had managed to build some rapport with the kid over dinner, especially after letting him order the priciest steak on the menu. But all of that would be quickly forgotten if there was no screen to connect the game console to.

Vivian followed him to the back of the SUV and waited for him to open the trunk. "Let me carry some of it." She reached for the nearest trash bag.

Gently, he caught her hand and then lifted it to his lips for a quick kiss. "I got it. Go on inside. Julian is there with Scarlet."

She narrowed her eyes at him. "Who is Scarlet?"

"The surprise."

"Huh?"

He motioned with his chin at the front door. "Wait for it."

As soon as Julian opened the way, Scarlet bolted outside and attacked Parker with all the exuberant enthusiasm one would expect from a dog greeting its beloved owner and not a stranger she'd never sniffed before—paws on Parker's pants, tail wagging at the speed of a jet engine, a doggie smile, and a lolling tongue.

"You've got a puppy!" Parker squealed.

Lowering the trash bag to the ground, he lifted Scarlet who immediately started licking his face.

Leaning away, Parker laughed. "Stop it. Your breath stinks, boy."

"Her name is Scarlet," Magnus introduced his girl as he and Vivian stepped inside the cabin, leaving boy and dog outside. "Just don't let her get away. There are coyotes out there just waiting for her to sneak out." He pointed with his chin at the greenery outside the wall. "If you look closely, you can see them waiting with their bibs around their necks and their forks and knives ready."

"That's gross," Vivian said. "How can you joke like that about such a sweet puppy."

"I'll keep her safe." Parker sat on the front porch and scooped Scarlet onto his lap.

"Hi." Julian looked at the trash bags in Magnus's hands. "Let me show you to the bedrooms. You can choose which one you want. Parker can sleep in the loft."

"Thank you for preparing the cabin for us," Vivian said as she followed him to the first bedroom.

"My pleasure. They are identical in size. The only difference is the decor."

Magnus peeked into one, and then went to take a look at the other. Ingrid's touch was evident in both. The furniture was more rustic than what she'd used in the keep and in the village, but the way everything matched and the colors complemented each other was clearly the designer's work.

"They are both beautiful. Which one do you want, Magnus?"

He really had no preference. "I don't care. You choose."

"Then I'll take this one. If I leave the door open, I can see part of the loft from the bed."

"Good choice." He walked in and put the bags on the floor. "Did you take Scarlet on a walk?" he asked Julian. "With all the excitement, she might pee all over Parker."

"I did. But she didn't poo. I think she is shy around me. She kept giving me those looks as if hoping I'll get the hint and leave her alone to do her thing." Julian shook his head. "I've never had a dog, but this one seems like such a girl to me. Am I imagining it?"

Magnus clapped him on the back. "I don't know if it's her or us. But I treat her like a girl too. It just comes naturally. She has such a pretty feminine face."

"She does," Vivian said. "I can always tell if a dog is a male or a female. Girl dogs have more delicate features. Right, Magnus?" She looked up at him.

"I think so too."

For a long moment, he got stuck looking at Vivian's beautiful face. Porcelain skin, big blue eyes, and the most kissable lips he'd ever seen. They were like hypnotic magnets, pulling him closer to them...

As he caught himself starting to bend down, Magnus took a step back. "I should take Scarlet out for a walk, and if Parker wants, he can come along. If that's okay with you, that is. Julian will keep you safe until I'm back."

He needed to get out of there and go on a run to release some of the churning electrical currents running through him and messing with his head.

Vivian was not there for him to seduce. Only to protect.

Unfortunately, Scarlet wouldn't be able to keep up, and neither would Parker. Besides, Magnus was still wearing a suit. Not the most comfortable attire for outdoor activity.

"That's a great idea. He needs to stretch his legs after the long ride. While you guys are walking Scarlet, I'll put away our things, and then I'll prepare us an evening snack."

Magnus glanced at Julian. "I hope you'll find what to make it from."

Dinner had taken longer than he'd expected, and since Julian had been waiting for them in the cabin, they hadn't stopped for groceries on the way.

"I got bread and peanut butter and cold cuts and mayo and some vegetables..."

Vivian stopped him with a wave of her hand. "That's perfect. I'll make us sandwiches."

Magnus collected Scarlet's leash from the coat rack where Julian had left it and headed outside.

"Do you want to help me walk Scarlet?" he asked Parker.

"Sure. I'll just put this inside the house." The kid lifted the trash bag with his prized possessions and opened the door.

Thankfully, Magnus had seen a large screen in the living room and a smaller one in each of the bedrooms. The loft probably had one too. Parker was not going to be disappointed.

Thank you, Kian. Or was it Ingrid? Probably Ingrid. Kian just approved budgets. He didn't bother with small details like that.

When the kid came out, Magnus clipped the leash to Scarlet's collar. "Come on, girl. Let's scope the area."

"Are we doing a perimeter security check?" Parker asked.

Magnus arched a brow. "Where did you learn that? Games or movies?"

"Both."

"I guess they are not a total waste of time. Do you want to hold the leash?"

Parker grinned and reached for it. "Am I right? Is that what you're doing? Or are we really just walking the dog?"

"We are doing both. Wherever you are, always have your eyes open and check all the points of entry." Magnus opened the side walkway gate and then closed it behind them. "You see. This isn't locked, which is a security breach. Remind me to get a padlock for it when we come back."

"Is it safe to leave Mom and Julian like that? Should we tell them to lock the gate?"

The kid had good instincts, and he was right. Julian wasn't a Guardian, and Magnus shouldn't count on him to defend Vivian. Except, there were security cameras mounted every few feet on the cabin's exterior, as well as on the road leading to it. If any undesirable headed that way, Julian would know and lock the cabin up.

"Look over there." He pointed at one of them. "Those are security cameras. No one can get up here without Julian knowing about it. He will lock the place up."

"Is Julian also a secret agent?"

"I'm not a secret agent, kid, and neither is Julian. He is a doctor, and he isn't even part of our organization. His mom is. In fact, she and her mate are heading the rescue operations. I mean her boyfriend."

Parker hadn't noticed the slip of the tongue. "Is she like M in the James Bond movies?"

Magnus chuckled. "No, but I think I'll start calling her B. Her name is Bridget, and she's also a doctor like Julian. But she decided that rescuing girls is more important."

Parker hung his head. "I knew that guy was a creep. And I told Ella, but she didn't listen."

"How did you know? Did he say something that gave him away?"

Parker shrugged. "No, but he was trying too hard to make me like him. It reminded me of my mom's boyfriends. They tried to sound cool, and it was so fake. But they were old, so it was kind of okay. He was young, which was why it was so creepy."

"How many boyfriends were there?" Magnus blurted out before thinking.

It was wrong to ask the kid something like that. Besides, it was none of his business.

"Only two. My mom doesn't date anymore. She says she is too busy with work and with us. But I think she is just sad."

"Even before what happened to Ella?"

"Yeah. But it's much worse now. Ella and my mom are really close. Sometimes I think they can read each other's thoughts."

"Oh, yeah? What makes you think so?"

"If Ella catches me doing something I'm not supposed to, my mom knows about it right away, even if she's in another room. And the same works the other way around."

That was odd. "Can you give me an example?"

"Like that time Mom picked me up from school, and I told her that I flunked a math test. I thought I didn't need to study because I'm good at math, but the test was hard. Ella made fun of me the moment I got home. And I know Mom didn't call her because I was with her the whole time." He waved a hand. "Stuff like that happens all of the time, but they say that's because they can read me so easily."

"It's a family thing. My mother used to know every mischief I planned the moment I thought of it. She would wag her finger at me and say something like, 'I know that look, Magnus.'"

"What about your dad? Did he know too?"

Parker must have had his earphones on when Magnus had told Vivian about not having a father.

"I grew up without a dad."

"Did he die?"

"A long time ago."

"Mine too. I don't even remember my dad. I was a baby when he was killed."

"I'm sorry to hear that, lad."

"Did your dad die in a war?" Parker asked.

Magnus had no idea, but he nodded. "Yeah."

"Bummer."

26

ELLA

*A*s Ella blinked her eyes open, a girl's face was hovering several inches above hers.

"Finally, you're awake."

"Where am I?"

The girl handed her a water bottle. "You're in the auction house. Hi, I'm Rose."

"Hi, I'm Ella." She opened the bottle and gulped down its contents. "How long was I asleep?"

"I don't know how long you were asleep before Stefano dumped you in here, but you slept for about two hours since then."

"Where is here?"

The girl rolled her eyes. "Are you stupid or something? I told you. This is the auction house."

"I heard you. But where is the auction house and what is it?"

"You really are dumb," Rose muttered under her breath. "We are somewhere in the state of New York. That's all I know, and an auction house is exactly what it sounds like. That's where you'll be auctioned to the highest bidder." She gave Ella a look over. "In your case it's going to be a lot. You're very pretty, and on top of that you're a virgin."

"How do you know that?" It's not like she had Virgin tattooed on her forehead.

"Stefano told me."

Ella pushed back to a sitting position. The room was much nicer than the one she'd come from. There were twin beds, each with a bunch of fluffy pillows and a thick comforter. Apparently, the condemned were treated nicely before their fate was sealed.

"Are you getting auctioned too?"

Rose stretched her arms over her head. "Not tonight."

That didn't sound good. "Am I getting auctioned tonight?"

Rose smiled. "Tomorrow night. And because you're so special, it's going to be a closed auction with just one item on the list. You."

Hugging the comforter to her chest, Ella shook her head. "Whoever is going to buy me will be very disappointed. I'm not going to go to him willingly, or let him touch me." She knew it was a lot of bravado that she couldn't back up, but it had felt good saying that.

Rose's horrified expression didn't bode well. "God, you are really stupid. Who do you think you're dealing with?"

Ella pinned Rose with a hard glare. "I'm really sick of you calling me stupid."

"So stop talking like a moron. You're lucky that you're a virgin, otherwise you would've already been drugged and raped, and not necessarily in that order. These people are not playing games. There is tons of money in this. I heard of a girl who refused to cooperate and they raped her mother to teach her a lesson, and told her that her little sister was next."

Ella shivered. That sounded a lot like what Stefano had threatened her with.

"What am I supposed to do? Just lie down and take it?"

"You have to do more than that. You have to pretend that you like it."

"Are you shitting me? How am I supposed to do that?"

"If you care about your family, you're going to do exactly that." Rose put a hand on Ella's trembling knee. "Look, it's not going to be as bad for you because you're a virgin. You will probably get bought by some rich dude who is not going to share you. You're lucky."

"Yeah, right, lucky. That's me."

"You are. If it makes you feel any better, you can think of it as an arranged marriage. In the old days, girls were delivered to men they never saw before and were supposed to accept as their husbands. It still works like that today in many countries."

"That doesn't make it right."

"No, it doesn't. But if so many girls survived this and still do, so can you."

Ella hung her head, bracing her forehead on her upturned knees. Maybe Rose was right. She'd been willing to have sex with Romeo because she'd thought she loved him and he loved her back. But it had been an illusion, a lie.

Except that lie had been perpetrated against her, while taking Rose's advice meant lying to herself.

Could she do it?

Did she have a choice?

Ella was so tempted to open the channel to her mom and ask for her help. She could explain that they were being watched and tell her mom to be careful. After all, no one would ever suspect Ella's means of communication with her mother.

But how was Vivian going to find her, when she herself didn't know where she was being held?

Besides, according to Rose, these people were monsters.

They might hurt her family even without proof of her contacting her mom.

They might hurt Parker.

She couldn't take the chance that her actions would lead to that.

Enduring pain and humiliation at the hands of some pervert was a thousand times preferable to losing her brother or her mother, or being responsible for them getting hurt.

27

VIVIAN

*V*ivian lifted the first trash bag and upended it over the bed. Before putting her clothes and toiletries in the bag, she'd packed them inside various sizes of ziplock bags, so everything was well-organized and ready to be placed on the shelves.

"Do you need help?" Julian asked.

"No, I got it. Thank you." She turned to him. "I want to thank you again for your help. I don't know what I would've done without you. I think fate arranged for us to meet at the convention."

She'd expected him to scoff at her statement, but he nodded instead. "I think so too."

For some reason, his sad expression broke the dam on the tears she'd managed to keep at bay so far. He was a stranger who had never met Ella, and yet was distraught enough over her kidnapping to mobilize every resource he could think of.

He was the proof that good people still existed out there. And to think she'd suspected him of having been involved in Ella's disappearance.

"I'm sorry." She sniffled and wiped her tears away with the back of her hand.

"That's okay. If you need to cry, just cry. Holding it in is not healthy."

Vivian shook her head. "That's not what I'm sorry for. I'm sorry for having had such bad thoughts about you. Just shows how little I know about people. I thought that scumbag Romeo was okay, and I suspected an angel like you of scheming to defraud me." The tears started flowing again, and this time there was no stopping them.

Julian pulled her into his arms. "I'm far from an angel, but I think that I'm a decent guy." He rubbed her back. "I was a bit offended at first, but once Turner spelled it out for me, I understood why. It was easier to believe that I was hiding Ella to get money out of you than to accept the alternative."

She nodded and pulled out of his arms. "Still, it was stupid of me."

Stuffing his hands in his pockets, Julian looked down at his feet, seemingly lost for words. "Would you like tea, or coffee? I could make some."

"Sure." It would give Julian something to do, and her a chance to pull herself together. "I would love some coffee."

"Cream and sugar?"

"Cream. No sugar." She managed a thin smile. "It's bad for your teeth."

"I'll get right on it."

"Thank you."

After a quick visit to the bathroom to wash her face and brush her hair, Vivian got busy putting the rest of her stuff in the closet. Parker's things were next.

"Does the loft have a closet?" she asked Julian.

"Yes, it does. The coffee is almost ready."

"It won't take long."

She lifted the trash bag with Parker's things and climbed the stairs to the loft.

He was going to love it. The bed was big, there was a screen mounted on the wall on one side, and a bathroom on the other. At home, Parker shared a bathroom with Ella, which was the source of endless complaints about how long each took in there.

Right now, Parker would probably give up his favorite game console for a chance to fight with his sister about bathroom time again.

Oh, God. The tears came back with gusto, and this time there was no stopping them or the sobs rising up from her aching chest. Rushing into the bathroom, Vivian closed the door, and let herself collapse on the floor sobbing.

She'd been holding up for as long as she could. First, it had been for Parker's sake, and then because she didn't want to appear weak in front of strangers. But eventually this was bound to happen.

Except, crying on the floor was not going to help Ella or anyone else. She needed to be strong and not further burden the people helping her with an emotional breakdown. They were doing enough by keeping her and Parker safe and rescuing Ella. Comforting a hysterical mother was not part of what they'd signed up for.

There was a stack of brand new towels next to the tub, the price tags still attached to them. As Vivian picked up one to dry her face with, she thought about Julian buying all of these things. Did he pay for everything out of his own pocket? Would the organization reimburse him for it?

She should offer to pay him back.

But first, she needed to finish putting Parker's clothes in the closet.

Taking several calming breaths, she glanced at the mirror.

Her eyes were red, but there wasn't much she could do about it.

Getting busy was the best remedy. Just as she'd done with her bag, Vivian upended his on the bed. Three ziplocks toppled out. One with Parker's clothes, another one with his toiletries, and a third one with Josh's framed picture wrapped in several T-shirts.

On an impulse, she'd grabbed it off the mantel at home, adding it to the things she'd taken with her to the cabin. In times of stress Vivian found comfort in it, often talking to him late at night after the kids were asleep.

She needed him now more than ever, even if it was just an old picture of him in uniform.

Taking it with her downstairs, she put it on the fireplace mantel.

"Is this Ella's father?" Julian asked.

"Yes."

"I can see the resemblance."

"Josh was very handsome."

Julian handed her a mug of coffee. "Cream, no sugar."

"Thank you." She took a sip. "It's good."

"Air Force?"

"Josh was a helicopter mechanic." She sighed and took her mug to the coffee table. The couch faced the fireplace and Josh's picture. "He enlisted because I was pregnant with Ella, and it was the fastest way to train for a well-paying job that included housing and health insurance."

Holding a mug of his own, Julian joined her on the couch. "You must've been very young when you had her."

She took another sip and nodded. "Eighteen. The same age Ella is now." She chuckled. "I thought I was so grown up and ready for motherhood. But when I look at Ella, I realize that I was still a child myself."

"What about Josh? How old was he?"

"The same age as I. We were both kids. We struggled, but we did fine. When Ella was born, she didn't lack anything. Life was good."

"When did he die?"

"A year after Parker was born. I was so sure that as a mechanic he was safe. But no one is safe in a war zone."

"Afghanistan?"

She nodded.

MAGNUS

"*L*et's head back. Scarlet is getting tired."

So was Parker, but Magnus didn't want to embarrass the kid. A twelve-year-old shouldn't be huffing and puffing after an hour-long brisk walk through the woods. Not even a human.

It had been a long time ago, but Magnus still remembered running around with a bunch of human boys before his transition. They had been much more resilient than Parker, spending long days outdoors and being active most of the time.

"Maybe you should pick her up?" Parker asked.

"Nah. She needs the exercise. But we can slow the pace."

"Finally," Parker muttered under his breath.

Her tail no longer wagging and her muzzle down, Scarlet trotted slowly for several more minutes, but then a few hundred feet from the cabin she just plopped on the ground and refused to move.

"Okay, girl. You win." Magnus scooped her into his arms and increased the pace.

Parker could use the exercise.

When they reached the front porch, the kid sat on the steps. "Give me a minute to catch my breath."

"No problem. Take your time." Magnus opened the door.

"I was starting to worry," Vivian said. "That was a long walk."

"Indeed." Magnus put Scarlet on her doggie bed. "Parker will sleep well tonight." And so would Scarlet.

The puppy plopped on her side and closed her eyes with a very human sounding sigh.

"Don't bet on it." Vivian waved a hand. "He is going to play video games no matter how tired he is." She walked out onto the porch. "Come inside, Parker. I made sandwiches."

Vivian was putting on a brave face and smiling, but Magnus could still smell the tears she had shed earlier. He wanted to pull her into his arms and comfort her. The instinct to reach for her was so strong that he had to fist his hands and keep his arms locked at his sides.

"Are you coming?" Vivian glanced at him. "I made enough for everybody. And there is also salad for the grownups." She ruffled Parker's hair. "My son thinks that eating veggies is not manly. I thought that watching a couple of very manly dudes eat a salad might change his mind."

Magnus grinned. Sneaky woman.

On the one hand, he was flattered that she thought him manly, but on the other hand, he was now obligated to eat the damn salad even if it wasn't good.

He shouldn't have worried, though. Everything was not only appetizing but also nicely presented. It seemed that Vivian appreciated esthetics. The sandwiches were crust-free and cut into small triangles, and the salad was made with beans and creamy dressing, so it was filling on top of looking good and being tasty.

"Thank you for the meal," Julian said. "But I really need to get going. I left a bunch of movies in the media cabinet. If you want to watch a subscription channel, use the satellite connected laptop." He pointed at the one he'd left on the coffee table. "Nothing else works here."

"Can I play online with my friends?"

Magnus shook his head. "Right now, it's best if you disappear from the grid. You can use my subscription to watch movies."

"Do you have a gaming subscription?"

"No, I don't play. I don't even know how."

The kid eyed him with a frown. "Dude, you're not that old. Didn't you play Atari or Nintendo as a kid?"

"Nope. I prefer outdoor activity."

"Figures. I guess I'll have to play solo games. May I be excused, Mom?"

"Yes, you may."

Parker grabbed the bag with his game console and took the stairs to the loft.

"Cool," they heard him say.

"Did you hear anything from your people in New York?" Vivian whispered.

"Not yet. They are still waiting for the hacker to find who Romeo is."

"Does it usually take so long?"

"No, it doesn't. But apparently he and his organization are more sophisticated than we've given them credit for. He is either a foreign national who isn't registered anywhere, or he's done something to camouflage his features and fool the facial recognition software."

"So how are they going to find him?"

"I'm not familiar with their methods, but our hacker team is the best in the world. One way or another they will find him."

She arched a brow. "Best in the world? I'm sure you're exaggerating."

"Well, I may be a tad. But I'm confident in their ability to locate anyone anywhere in the world."

Vivian paled. "Do you think they've taken her abroad?"

"No, I don't. It's much more complicated to cross international lines."

She slumped back. "Oh, thank God. That would've made finding Ella so much harder. Even impossible."

He reached over the table and clasped her hand. "We are going to find her. I promise."

Looking at him with her big blue eyes, Vivian didn't pull her hand away. Instead, she put her other hand on top of his.

"I know that you're just saying it to cheer me up, but I appreciate the effort."

Her hands were so small compared to his.

For a long moment, they stared into each other's eyes, and an entire subliminal communication passed between them.

Or perhaps it had happened only in his head.

In either case, this innocent touching of hands brought about not so innocent musings, and it needed to stop.

Magnus let go of Vivian's hand and pushed to his feet. "I'll clear the dishes."

Pink coloring her pale cheeks, Vivian shook her head. "No, that's okay, I'll deal with the table. It's the least I can do."

"Together, then. I'll clear the table and you'll wash the dishes."

"Okay."

When they were done, Vivian dried her hands with a dishtowel. "I'm going to take a shower and go to sleep."

It reminded him that there was just one bathroom downstairs, and that they were going to take turns. "I'll lock everything up for the night. When you're done, let me know, and I'll grab a quick shower too."

Vivian smoothed her hand over her long hair. "Yeah,

about that. Because the bathroom has two doors, one from each bedroom, we need to knock before entering."

"I'll try to remember that."

He wasn't going to forget. That part was easy. The tough part would be to hear the shower running and not to imagine Vivian in the nude.

29

VIVIAN

*A*wake, even though she'd retired to her bedroom hours ago, Vivian lay in bed and sent message after message to Ella.

Some of them were verbal, telling her daughter that she and Parker were safe and that help was on the way, and some of them were visual, showing her the cabin and Magnus and Julian. She'd even sent an image of Turner, since he was the one who would be doing the saving.

Her head ached from the strain, and she knew that as long as Ella was blocking her it was futile. But Vivian harbored a tiny hope that Ella might lower her guard for a split second and one of the messages would go through.

Except, if Ella had received anything, she would've responded by now.

Magnus wasn't sleeping either. She could hear him pacing around the living room and conversing with someone quietly on his phone. Was it a girlfriend?

Vivian strained to hear, but it was no use. He was keeping his voice low, probably thinking she was asleep and not wanting to wake her up. Besides, it was such a silly thing to be concerned with. What did she care if he had a girlfriend?

It wasn't as if she was interested in anything.

When Magnus was done talking, he turned on the television and started watching something that sounded like a political debate. Several different voices were arguing, but again, she couldn't make out the words. Not that it was important. She was just curious about what Magnus found interesting.

Was he restless? Or was he one of those people who didn't need much sleep?

Under normal circumstances, Vivian had no problem falling asleep and staying asleep until morning, but since Ella had been taken, she hadn't been sleeping for more than two hours at a time.

The lack of sleep had an adverse effect on her already depressed mood. Vivian was well aware of it, but who could sleep at a time like this?

Perhaps a cup of tea would help.

There was no need for her to get dressed. The sweats she had on were fine, and with her modest cleavage, she could get away with not wearing a bra.

Magnus wouldn't even notice.

Well, without the pushup bra, he might notice how really flat-chested she was. But whatever. Looking attractive was not a priority.

Liar.

Even if she wasn't interested in anything, Vivian still wanted Magnus to find her attractive. She just didn't feel like putting any effort into it.

Flat slippers to match her flat chest, she shuffled out into the living room.

"Can't sleep?" Magnus turned to look at her and then got up. "I can make us some tea."

Vivian swallowed.

Without the suit and tie, all those impressive muscles she'd suspected he'd been hiding under it were clearly visible through the plain white T-shirt he'd put on.

Suddenly, she felt very awkward about her lack of bra and the house slippers.

Not only was Magnus a foot taller than her, but his pectoral muscles were also more pronounced than her breasts.

She shook her head. It didn't matter. This wasn't the time or the place for it, and there were also other reasons why a relationship with him or anyone else was not on the cards.

Magnus misunderstood her head shaking. "If you don't want tea, I can make coffee. But that would be counterproductive given that you have a hard time falling asleep."

She forced a smile. "I would love a cup of tea."

Sitting on the couch, she stared at the talking heads on the screen without hearing a word they were saying. Perhaps their droning voices would make her sleepy.

"Here you go." Magnus handed her a steaming mug. "Do you like cream and sugar in your tea?"

"No, thank you."

"Good, because I didn't put any in." He sat next to her on the couch. "I can switch to something else if you like."

"That's okay. You can keep watching the debate."

He waved a hand. "It's the same crap over and over again. How about a movie?"

That might distract her from the storm raging inside her head. "I would love to."

A patter of light feet on the wooden stairs announced Parker. "Can I watch with you?"

"Sure." Magnus patted the spot between Vivian and himself. "What kind of movies do you like?"

"*Star Wars* and all the superhero movies. Batman, Superman, Avengers."

Vivian rolled her eyes. "He's seen them all a gazillion times."

"How about you?" Magnus turned to her. "What's your pleasure?"

"Please, Mom." Parker turned a pair of puppy eyes on her.

"Fine. I guess you're going to watch it for a gazillion and one times."

"Thanks."

Scarlet lifted her head, and a moment later her tail started wagging.

"Come here, girl." Magnus tapped his thigh.

The puppy didn't wait for another invitation, but instead of leaping into Magnus's lap, she jumped into Parker's.

"Tsk, tsk, you naughty girl. Betraying me for a younger man."

Parker patted her head. "She likes me."

"Yes, she does." Magnus searched for the movie on the laptop Julian had left behind. "*Rogue One*, okay?"

"Awesome," Parker said.

As the movie started playing, Vivian didn't pay as much attention to it as to the improbable homey scene of Parker stroking Scarlet's coat while leaning against Magnus.

If Ella were with them, it could have been a Hallmark moment. Well, except for the nonverbal communication that would've been going on between them.

Ella would have said that Magnus was hot and that Vivian should totally go for him. And Vivian would've teased her back with images of Julian in a tuxedo and Ella in a white dress dancing at their wedding.

With a sigh, she picked up a pillow and hugged it to her chest. It was such a nice fantasy. Except, with her rotten luck she had no business entertaining silly dreams like that.

Instead of providing solace, they only made her sadder.

30

TURNER

*A*s Turner's phone buzzed in his pocket, he put down the fork and whipped the device out. "It's about bloody time," he muttered before accepting the call. He and the Guardians had been waiting all night for the hackers to find Romeo's real name and his address. They hadn't even bothered with hotel rooms, passing the time either in the jet or in nearby restaurants and coffee shops.

"What do you have for me, William?"

"The guy's name is Morris R. Weber. Guess what the R stands for?"

"Romeo."

"You got it. Check your email. Roni just sent you all the information we gathered on him."

"How come it was so difficult to find the guy?"

"Plastic surgery and contact lenses. Romeo didn't use to be so pretty."

"I'm not going to ask how you managed to find him."

William chuckled. "You can stop by when you have some spare time, and I'll let Roni explain. It was his idea that helped us solve the puzzle."

"I will. Thanks, and thank Roni for me too."

"Good luck."

Turner signaled the waitress. "Check, please."

Pushing aside the plate with his half-eaten breakfast, he brought up the email Roni had sent him and started reading. Surprisingly, the address was in Brooklyn where the uncle's pizzeria was supposed to be.

By the time the girl returned with the bill, the Guardians had finished shoveling in the rest of the food and were ready to roll.

As their van slugged along with the rest of the rush hour traffic, Turner continued reading the email. Romeo, or Morris, was thirty-two years old, not twenty-two. He was the son of two immigrants, an Italian mother and a German father. The parents had divorced when he was two, and the father had returned to Germany.

The mother had raised him alone and was still living in Brooklyn. She had three brothers and one sister, all of them living on the East Coast. Roni had included the addresses of the mother and her siblings.

If Romeo had already moved on to his next victim, Turner was going to pay the mother a visit. One way or another, he was going to find where Ella was being held, and he wasn't above threatening the scumbag's mother.

"That's where he lives?" Neil asked as he parked the van in front of the building. "I would think thugs like him made more money and could afford someplace nicer."

"He's probably spending everything on drugs," Arwel said.

Turner glanced at the Guardian. "What makes you think that?"

"Call it a hunch. Usually when things don't add up, it's because a piece of the puzzle is missing."

"Good observation. Arwel, you come with me." Turner pointed at Neil and then at Edan. "You two circle to the back of the building and watch the fire escape staircase." He turned to the remaining two Guardians. "Neil and Gregor, you stay in the van and watch the front."

Given the four disappointed expressions, the Guardians weren't happy about missing out on the interrogation.

"He might not even be there," Arwel said.

The guy was excellent at reading emotions, and his range was quite impressive. Walls and other barriers didn't impede his telepathic ability either. It had its limitations though. It extended as far as receiving visuals but not verbal communication. Arwel could thrall humans and get into their heads, but then almost any other immortal could do that. Thralling, however, had to be done up close and didn't work on other immortals.

With one exception. Yamanu could blanket-thrall humans from a distance, provided it wasn't from too far away. On the other hand, Yamanu was useless on other immortals, while Arwel could feel their emotions as well.

Turner was still learning, but unlike other skills he'd acquired throughout his life, thralling had proved difficult to master.

Romeo's apartment was on the third floor, and his door was locked—not surprising given the shitty neighborhood he lived in.

"Someone is in there," Arwel said. "He's sleeping."

"Good." Hopefully it wasn't a roommate.

Pulling out his burglar tools, Turner opened the two locks and then pushed the door open, yanking out the security chain together with the screws fastening it to the wall.

He hadn't even exerted much force to do so, and managed it without making too much noise. Immortality came with many perks.

Evidence of Romeo's drug use was scattered all over the

messy coffee table and the floor of his bedroom, where they found him passed out on a filthy bed.

"Wake up, dirtbag." Turner slapped him.

When the guy cracked one bloodshot eye open, Turner yanked him up by his T-shirt and flung him into a chair. Arwel stood behind it, ready to restrain the scum if he tried to run, or hold him in place for the beating Turner was planning to deliver.

"What's going on?" Romeo mumbled. "Who are you people?"

"Where is Ella?" Turner asked.

When the guy tried to stand up, Arwel pushed on his head, forcing him back down.

"I'll ask again. Where is Ella?"

"I don't know who you're talking about."

Turner had hoped Romeo would resist at first. The punch to his surgically enhanced jaw was most satisfying. Arwel could've thralled the information out of the human's head, but it was way more fun to get it out of him the old-fashioned way.

"That was a light one. The next one will undo all the nice work your plastic surgeon put into making you pretty."

Romeo lifted a pair of startled eyes. Apparently, getting beat up was not a novelty for him, but someone knowing about his surgery was.

"Yes, Morris, we know everything about you, including where your mother and her brothers and sister live. If you love your mama, you'd better talk. Where is Ella?"

"I don't know where she is. I swear!"

Why were thugs so stupid?

The guy should know that another punch was coming, and then another one, and that eventually he would talk. Why prolong the torment?

Nevertheless, Turner was more than happy to hit that

fake jaw again, this time dislocating the implant along with the bone.

Romeo was no longer pretty.

As the guy groaned, Turner pushed it back into place, knowing it would hurt even more.

"Okay, okay. Just don't hit me again." Romeo rattled out an address.

Behind him, Arwel shook his head. "He's not lying. That's where he brought her. But she's no longer there, and he knows it."

Romeo's panic-stricken eyes confirmed Arwel's words.

"Where is she now?"

"I swear on my mother that I don't know. All I know is that it's an auction house. I don't know where it is or who runs it. I deliver the girls to my uncle, and he auctions them off. But it doesn't belong to him. It works like any other auction place. Many operators use it."

Romeo kept spilling out information, probably thinking that as long as he was talking he wasn't going to get punched.

"Who's your uncle and where can I find him?"

Romeo started crying. "He's gonna kill me."

Turner crouched in front of him. "If you don't tell me where he is, I'm going to kill you. But if you tell me, I'll keep you safe." For the time being.

First, he was going to lock the scum up in the keep's dungeon and interrogate him until he extracted every last bit of information out of him.

Only when there was nothing left of Romeo's brain, was Turner going to put him out of his misery and kill him.

MAGNUS

"*A*re you taking Scarlet out?" Vivian asked. "I'm about to make breakfast."

Magnus crouched in front of the puppy and clipped the leash to her collar. "I'm just taking her out to the front yard."

He would've preferred to take Vivian and Parker with him on a long walk through the woods, but just as she'd predicted, the kid had spent half of the night playing games and was still asleep.

With all the security cameras planted along the road leading up to the cabin and around the cabin itself, no one could sneak up on them. The place was safe. Nevertheless, he didn't want to be more than a few paces away while they were alone inside.

There was always the possibility of an aerial attack. A very remote possibility, but still, he wasn't going to take chances with Vivian and Parker's lives.

Last night had been one of the most surreal experiences of Magnus's life, and that was saying a lot. Battles were old news to him, disasters didn't faze him, but the illusion of having a family threw him an unexpected curveball.

Sitting on that couch with Parker leaning against him, Magnus had an out of body experience. Well, not really, but for a moment it had felt like it. In his imagination, he was standing in front of the screen and watching himself with Vivian and Parker on the couch, thinking that if they were in a movie, the three of them would've made a nice family. Or rather the four of them, once they got Ella back.

He'd even gone as far as imagining taking Julian aside and warning him against hurting Ella's feelings before allowing the handsome doctor to take the girl out on a date.

The thing was, Magnus was not prone to wishful thinking. He simply lacked the imagination required for conjuring fantasies. So where the hell had that come from?

Vivian was as close as it was ever going to get to his dream woman, but she was a human and so was the boy. Magnus could never be more than a passing stranger in their lives.

As Scarlet rushed into the bushes to do her business, the leash tightened on Magnus's hand, forcing him to follow. He would've let her roam the yard without a leash, but the gate's slats were too far apart. Scarlet was still small enough to squeeze through them, and he had no intention of chasing after her into the woods and leaving Vivian and Parker unprotected.

When his phone rang, he didn't pull it out right away.

If Turner's crew had found Ella, it would be wonderful news for her mother and brother, but it would also mean that his time with them was coming to an end.

Don't be a selfish bastard.

Shaking his head, Magnus pulled the phone out of his pocket. Just as he'd expected, Arwel's face was on the display. "I hope you're calling with good news."

"Regrettably, no. We found Romeo, but he delivered Ella to his uncle, who in turn took her to an auction house, and

Romeo doesn't know where that is. We are dropping him at the jet and then heading to the uncle's house."

"Are you sure he's telling the truth?"

Arwel chuckled. "I'm sure. As Turner had his fun beating the crap out of the guy, I monitored the scumbag to verify the information he gave us. He was telling the truth as he knew it. We'll know more when we have the uncle."

"Keep me updated."

"I will."

Damn, despite his momentary loss of reason, Magnus had hoped to have good news for Vivian. Perhaps he should wait until the team got the uncle?

Except, finding the next scumbag on the list was no news. When they found the auction house and got Ella out, then it would be news worth delivering to her mother.

But that was too much to hope for.

If Magnus were a parent, he would have wanted to be kept in the loop. Hell, he would've been out there with the men, meting out justice the old-fashioned style.

"Come on, girl." He pulled on the leash. "Time to go home."

"That was short," Vivian said as he opened the door.

"I've got updates."

Her smile vanished. "By the look on your face they are not good."

"They found Romeo, and he told them that he delivered Ella to his uncle. But she is not there either. She was taken to an auction house. They are on their way to the uncle's place to get that information out of him."

"An auction house?" Vivian's chin started quivering, and then her entire body followed. She was shaking all over. "They are going to auction my baby?"

Fuck, he should've phrased it differently.

Up until now, Vivian must've harbored a sliver of hope

that this was all one big misunderstanding, and that Ella was just hanging out with her boyfriend.

Refusing to believe that the most feared thing had actually happened was a natural tendency, and it wasn't limited to humans. In the same situation, an immortal mother would have also preferred to live in denial.

Not knowing what else to do, Magnus wrapped his arms around Vivian and started rocking her. "That's actually good news. It means that she wasn't violated yet. The crew might get to her before the auction takes place."

He didn't believe half the things he was saying, but right now his top priority was comforting a distraught mother. A little false hope was better than none.

Besides, it felt good to hold her in the shelter of his arms and offer her some solace. There was nothing sexual about it. He wasn't the type of guy who could get it up while a woman cried. Any other time, even when it was inappropriate, he had no such problems, but female tears were his kryptonite.

As Parker walked by them and out the door, Vivian pulled out of Magnus's arms and wiped her eyes. "He's upset."

"I'll go talk to him."

She hesitated for a moment, and then nodded. "It's difficult for him too."

Magnus had a feeling that Parker's hunched shoulders had more to do with seeing them in each other's arms than the lack of good news about Ella. But he knew what or rather who would cheer the boy up.

"Come, Scarlet."

As soon as he opened the door, the puppy bolted out, her nails skidding on the hardwood floor as she rushed to leap into Parker's lap.

Sitting on the porch's floor with his feet on the step below, the kid patted her while leaning away to escape her tongue. "Don't lick me. It's gross."

Magnus sat next to them. "Did it bother you that I hugged your mom?"

Parker glanced at him with a frown. "She was sad and you were trying to make her feel better. I get it. I'm upset because of what you told her before the hug. I hoped your friends would find Ella before I woke up. I even stayed in bed and forced myself to sleep longer to make sure of it. I know it's silly."

"Not at all." Magnus rose to his feet. "It's perfectly natural. Come on, your mom is waiting for us with breakfast."

ELLA

a knock on the door startled Ella. Heck, everything startled her. A sneeze somewhere down the corridor got her heart racing. She was like a little mouse trapped in a cage, waiting to get fed to the snake.

"Relax." Rose didn't even lift her head from her book. "It's only the esthetician coming to give us our beauty treatments."

"Beauty treatments? Are you serious? Like in facials?"

A moment later, the door opened and a chunky woman in a white coat rolled in a cart full of equipment. "Hello, girls, I'm Grace. I'm here to make you look fabulous."

Right, as if Ella wanted to look good for some old pervert. Except, what choice did she have?

None.

Any act of defiance would mean Parker and her mom getting hurt. She had to do what she was told.

"Hit the shower, girls. Wash your hair but don't shave. I'm going to wax you."

Ella had never done waxing before, but Maddie had, and supposedly it was painful as hell. Whatever, waxing should be the least of her concerns right now. She was so numb it was doubtful that she would even feel the pain.

"Do you want to go first?" she asked Rose.

"Sure." The girl padded to the bathroom.

"I can do your facial while Rose is in the shower." The woman picked up a magnifying glass from her cart. "Come closer." Taller than Ella by at least half a foot, Grace leaned down to look at her nose. "Blackheads. Let's start on those."

Would it get her in trouble if she rolled her eyes at the esthetician?

This was so stupid. As if the old pervert would check her nose with a magnifying glass.

Lifting the only chair in the room, Grace put it under the light fixture. "Sit here."

As the torture began, Ella tried to ignore the poking and the squeezing and consider her possibilities. What if she could contact her mother and tell her to act as if nothing happened, then go to the supermarket or a coffee shop and call the police from there?

But what would the police do?

There was nothing anyone could do for Ella.

Stefano had told her that her mother had already called the police. She'd been told that there was no reason for them to get involved, since Ella was an adult and had left of her own accord. After all, it wasn't as if she'd been seen being dragged by force through the airport. In her stupidity, she'd gone willingly with Romeo, may he rot in hell for eternity.

Could Vivian make a case for why she and Parker needed protection?

What if the police agreed to come to their house and search for listening devices?

Would that be proof enough that Parker and her mom were in danger?

Perhaps they could enter the witness protection program?

Except, they hadn't witnessed anything, so the police had no reason to protect them.

Maybe they could run, though.

First, her mom would have to find all the listening devices and get rid of those that were in her car or her purse. The ones in the house could stay. They could leave the television going so it would sound as if they were still there. It should buy them some time.

Ella could leave the channel open and get updates from them. If no one came after her family in more than a day, it would mean that they'd gotten away, and she could try to run. If she got caught, the slavers could only punish her, which was a risk Ella was willing to live with.

Or die for.

But that was a stupid plan, and she knew it.

First of all, Stefano had taken her wallet and her phone, so she didn't even have an ID or money to pay for a bus ticket.

Secondly, her mom wasn't some super-agent who could find every listening device Romeo had planted and get rid of it somehow without anyone noticing that she'd done it. The moment Vivian and Parker tried to get away, these monsters would go after them just to teach her and Ella a lesson. They would make an example out of her to scare the other girls into compliance.

Perhaps it would be better to wait for when she was bought by the pervert. It might be easier to run then. It didn't make sense for the monsters to keep tabs on the families of all the girls that were ever sold. At some point, they must stop monitoring their activities.

Yeah, and that point was probably when the buyer got tired of his new toy and let her go. Or sold her to someone else to recoup his investment. Ella didn't believe any of the things Stefano had told her. She was not getting a portion of the proceeds from her auction, and she was never getting released.

Those were all tactics designed to make her cooperate. The carrot and the stick.

"All done." Grace wiped her nose. "The blackheads are gone. Now let's put a mask on you." She got closer to inspect Ella's skin. "Not that you need it. But it's part of the package deal."

Ella could no longer hold her tongue. "How can you work for them when you know what they do here?"

The woman patted her shoulder. "It's a tough world, girlie, and the sooner you realize it the better. You don't know how lucky you are. A pretty thing like you is going to be bought by some rich guy who is going to pamper you. You're going to get designer clothes, go to fancy restaurants, and all you have to do for it is spread your legs and pretend you're enjoying it. That's not hard at all." She patted her shoulder again.

Apparently, people had an endless capacity for selling themselves lies to justify their actions. Or maybe Grace's view of what was good and what was evil was as totally messed up as Rose's.

There was another knock on the door, and a guy in a white coat entered, pushing another cart.

He wasn't an esthetician, though.

"I'm Doctor Smith." He introduced himself with what was for sure a fake name. "I'm here to verify the virginity of Ella Takala. I assume it's you?"

33

MAGNUS

*B*reakfast was a tense affair, and Magnus was at a loss as to how to lighten things up.

Vivian was holding back tears the entire time, and Parker used anger to stave off his own, frowning at his pancakes and cutting into them aggressively as if they were the enemy.

Things didn't improve once it was over. Vivian grabbed the dishes before he was even done and dropped the entire pile in the sink. It was a miracle none of them broke.

"How about the three of us take Scarlet on a walk and look for a nice branch to make a bow from?"

That got the kid's attention. "You can make a bow out of a branch?"

"What do you think they are made from?"

"I don't know. Some composite material?"

"Well, maybe that's how they make them today. But originally they were made from wood. I can teach you how to make your own, including the arrows, and then teach you how to shoot."

Parker's eyes shone with newfound enthusiasm. "That

would be awesome. But why do we need Mom to come with us?"

"Because I have to keep an eye on both of you at all times. Yesterday, when we went on our walk, Julian was here to keep your mom safe."

"But you said that Julian is a doctor. What could he have done to protect her?"

The kid had a good memory. "Julian has some training and knows how to fight. I'm sure your mom doesn't. Right, Vivian?"

She shook her head. "I'm afraid I don't. I never had the time to take a self-defense class."

"I can remedy that. When we come back, I'm going to teach you some basic moves." He glanced at her slippers. "Did you bring comfortable walking shoes?"

"I did. I'll go put them on."

"Ready?" he asked when she returned a couple of minutes later, looking adorable in a pair of black leggings, an oversized pink sweatshirt, and sneakers.

"Can I walk Scarlet?" Parker asked as Magnus closed the gate behind them.

"Sure. Just hold on tight. If she sniffs a squirrel, she'll start chasing it."

"What kind of branch should I look for?"

"You need a mostly straight one that's about one and a half to two inches in diameter and about five feet long. Which is about as tall as you are."

"Got it."

Tail wagging and muzzle close to the ground, sniffing for something interesting, Scarlet led Parker from one bush to another.

"Bringing the dog was a great idea," Vivian said.

"She is new. I didn't want to leave her behind if I didn't

have to. My roommates are fine watching her, but they leave cleaning up her mess to me."

"Does she still poo and pee in the house?"

"Sometimes she pees when she gets overly excited, and sometimes because my roommates forget to take her out."

"She didn't pee in the cabin yet."

"I hope not. I need to check she hasn't left me a present somewhere."

Vivian pointed at the duo in front of them. "I think they are going too fast."

It was still an acceptable distance, but Magnus could understand why she was feeling overprotective of her son.

"Don't get too far away from us," he called out.

Parker looked over his shoulder. "Yes, sir."

"He likes you," Vivian said. "You're good with kids."

"I came with a puppy. Of course, he likes me."

"It's more than that. You didn't have to take him out on walks, or promise to make him a bow. You did that to take his mind off his worries, and you found a wonderful way to do that. I really appreciate that."

Her gratitude made him uncomfortable. "I didn't promise that I would make it for him. I promised that I would teach him how to make it himself. It's going to keep him busy for hours, outdoors in the fresh air, and with the sun shining on his skin, instead of the glow from a screen. Being cooped up in that stuffy dark loft is not good for his mood."

With a sigh, Vivian lowered her head. "Ella said that he was spending too much time gaming. I guess she's right. I know that computer skills are valuable, but so is fresh air and physical activity. It's just that I'm not much of an outdoors woman myself, and all of Parker's friends are exactly like him. None of those boys go outside to play."

Without thinking, Magnus wrapped his arm around her. "Tell me about Ella and Parker's dad."

He'd seen the picture she'd brought with her and put on the mantel. A handsome young man in an Air Force uniform. Perhaps talking about an old pain would distract her from the new one.

She didn't make a move to remove his arm, but she didn't lean on him either. A pity, since he would've liked that very much.

"What do you want to know?"

"How did you meet?"

"We met as freshmen." There was a smile in her voice. "It was love at first sight. For both of us. We dated throughout high school, and even though we were careful, I got pregnant halfway through senior year. We knew we were going to get married. We just didn't plan on it to happen so soon."

She sighed. "Anyway, we got married and Josh enlisted. He got trained as a helicopter mechanic."

"Good decision."

"Not really. He didn't have any other choice. That was the fastest route to a good salary with medical benefits and housing. But it was also what got him killed. His helicopter crashed in Afghanistan. He wasn't even supposed to be on it. Josh repaired them, he didn't fly them."

She wiped a tear away. "Anyway, it's my fault that he's dead. If not for me getting pregnant, Josh wouldn't have had to enlist and he would have been alive today."

Damn, that was a lot of guilt to carry around on those slim shoulders, and totally misplaced. "You must know that's nonsense, right?"

She shrugged.

Magnus stopped and turned her toward him. "Look at me, Vivian." When she did, he continued. "It's natural to feel guilty for being alive while Josh is not. Soldiers who lose friends often feel the same. But it's irrational. Life is chaotic, and shit happens to good people for no good reason. We are not born with a crystal ball and the ability to predict the future."

"In my case it's more than a random tragedy. I'm a magnet for them."

"What do you mean?"

He could see why she would think that. A husband killed in a war, and a daughter kidnapped by sex traffickers was more bad luck than any woman should ever experience.

"Magnus! I found the perfect stick." Parker came running back with a long thin branch in his hand and Scarlet trotting behind him with her tongue lolling. "It's already curved."

"Let me see." He took the stick and pretended to examine it carefully. "You're right. It's perfect. Let's go back to the cabin, and I'll show you how to determine which side is the belly and which side is the back."

Parker eyed the staff. "It's kind of obvious. The inside of the curve is the belly, and the outside is the back."

"Smart boy. I'll mark the center for you and then you'll get to work removing the wood. You never touch the back, you only remove from the belly side. But not in the middle and not on the tips. Those should stay straight or have very little bend."

Vivian tapped his arm. "Are you talking about using a knife to cut out the wood?"

"Naturally."

"I'm not sure I'm comfortable with Parker handling a dangerous tool like that. He's only twelve."

"Mom!" Parker's cheeks got red, and not because of the brisk morning walk.

"I was nine when I made my first bow," Magnus said. "Compared to me back then, Parker is a man." He winked at the boy.

34

VIVIAN

*H*and on her chest, Vivian watched through the window as Parker handled the knife Magnus had given him.

The two of them had been sitting on the porch steps for over an hour. When Magnus had done the cutting to show Parker how it was done, it had looked easy, but the boy lacked the muscle power of the man, and she was afraid the knife would slip from his hand and cut him.

Her heart skipped a beat when Magnus squeezed Parker's shoulder in encouragement, got up, and opened the door to get back in.

"You can't leave him alone out there with that knife!"

"He is fine, Vivian. I showed him how to handle it." He took her elbow and turned her toward the window. "The staff is propped against the ground, and he's cutting away from his body. He can't hurt himself even if his hand slips."

She watched Parker for several minutes as he chipped away at the wood with an expression of deep concentration on his face, which was turning red from exertion. "He is not going to last long."

Magnus chuckled. "I know. But he is stubborn and determined."

"Tell me about it."

"Those are excellent qualities. He is not a quitter."

"I guess."

"Come on." He turned her away from the window. "Don't hover over him like a mother hen. How about some tea?"

"We can have it out on the porch."

"Not a chance." He pulled her into the kitchen. "Black tea or something herbal?"

"Black."

He pulled out a chair for her. "Take a seat."

For some reason, Vivian felt uncomfortable sitting and doing nothing while Magnus was preparing tea for her. Not that it required much effort, but she just wasn't used to people doing things for her. She was the caretaker, not the other way around. The only time the kids waited on her was on her birthday and on Mother's Day.

Putting a steaming mug in front of her, Magnus pulled out a chair for himself and sat down with his own mug. "I'm not much of a tea drinker, but since meeting you it seems I prefer it to coffee."

Holding the cup with both hands, Vivian grimaced. "I'm not much of a tea drinker either, but the coffee Julian bought tastes awful. I prefer the tea."

"Right, we should do a grocery run."

That didn't sound like something people hiding in a safe house did.

"Is it safe?"

Magnus puffed out his chest. "Have no fear. As long as you and Parker are with me, you're safe."

Vivian shook her head. "Men and their over-inflated egos. That was something Josh would have said." She smiled. "He would've probably given Parker the knife to work with too.

Poor kid is growing up with two mother hens smothering him and not letting him be a boy."

Magnus reached for her hand and gave it a little squeeze. "Don't worry about it. I grew up without a father and I turned out fine. But what I don't understand is how come a beautiful woman like you hasn't been snagged already by some guy. Not that I'm implying you need one to raise your son, because I'm definitely not, but it must get lonely sometimes."

"It does. But I can't have another death on my conscience. Every man who gets close to me dies. I'm a black widow."

She wasn't surprised by the look he was giving her. Magnus thought she was nuts. That would change once he heard the whole story.

"I know you don't believe me. Heck, I can't believe it myself, but I can't argue with three deaths."

"Tell me about them."

She didn't want to. Even the most rational of guys would get wary of her after hearing her story, and she liked having Magnus's easy-going company even though nothing could ever come of it.

He was attracted to her, it was quite obvious, and she was attracted to him. It was better to quash any ideas he might have about hooking up with her before the attraction turned into something more.

"So you already know about Josh. He was killed in Afghanistan. Whether it was my fault that he was even there or not is debatable. But let's put it aside. Four years after his death, the dentist I work for introduced me to a friend of his. Frank was a general contractor and was doing well for himself. He was divorced, had no kids, and had no problem with dating a widow who had two. A lovely man, really."

She paused to take a sip from her tea. "We dated for about

five months when he fell off the ladder on one of his jobs and broke his neck."

"It had nothing to do with you."

Vivian arched a brow. "He was on the phone with me when it happened. If I didn't call, he would still be alive."

Crossing his arms over his chest, Magnus frowned. "He should not have answered his phone while climbing a ladder. You could not have known that he was doing that when you called."

"That's true. I didn't say I killed him, but I played a part in his death."

"That's it? You decided that you're a black widow because of two random and unrelated deaths?"

"There was a third." She took another sip from her tea. "Al was an accountant. His firm managed the dental office's books."

"What happened to him?"

"A fatal car accident."

"Let me guess. He was on his way to pick you up for a date."

"How did you know?"

Oblivious to her sarcastic tone, Magnus waved a hand. "Otherwise you wouldn't be blaming yourself for his death."

"He wasn't picking me up for a date."

"Oh, yeah?"

"Al was going home after our date. He wanted to spend the night at my house, and I said no. If I'd said yes, he would still be alive."

"That's a lot of crappy coincidences."

"Maybe. But I've had enough grief to last me three life-times. I'd rather stay alone than go through that again."

35

MAGNUS

*T*hat was a lot of bad luck, so much so that for a moment Magnus allowed himself to get sucked into the story Vivian was telling herself.

Except, he didn't believe in superstition or that some people were magnets for bad luck. Vivian had just suffered an excruciating amount of it.

Poor woman, no wonder she didn't want to get emotionally involved with anyone.

If he could, he would've told her that she had nothing to fear with him because he was practically indestructible. With him, she could let go of her fears.

But to what end?

All he could offer her was a short-lived affair, and then he would have to disappear from her life. She would probably think it was her fault again.

"I understand that you're afraid of losing someone close again, but I can assure you that your fears are irrational, and that what happened to you was a series of unfortunate events."

"I'm not willing to take the risk of having another death

on my conscience." Vivian pushed to her feet. "But enough about me. I'd better check on Parker and then start working on lunch. After all that hard work he's going to be hungry."

She walked over to the living room window and peeked outside. "He's still at it."

Standing behind her, Magnus put his hand on her shoulder. "Parker is doing better than I expected. He made quite a bit of progress while we were having tea. Impressive, given those scrawny arms of his."

Vivian chuckled. "They are not as weak as they seem. He's quite strong. Typing away on a keyboard must give him some sort of a workout."

"Not really. I'm going to look for a couple of brooms."

As he turned around and headed back toward the kitchen, Vivian followed. "Look in the utility closet. I've seen one in there."

"Nice. Exactly what I was looking for." He pulled out a broom with a wooden pole. "That's one. I'll check the shed for another."

"What are you going to do? Have him clean the cabin?" Vivian snorted. "Good luck with that."

Magnus upended the broom and unscrewed the pole. "Nope, I'm going to teach him staff fighting."

"Perhaps you should wait for tomorrow. I think Parker's had enough physical activity for today."

The boy hadn't had nearly enough. "I'll let him rest a little."

Vivian started opening cabinets. "First, let's see if we have anything to make lunch from." She eyed the neatly organized row of cans on the top shelf. "Can you get those cans of kidney beans down for me?" She pointed.

"No problem." Leaning over her, Magnus reached for the first can, keenly aware that he was caging Vivian between his body and the counter as he pulled one and put it down and then the other.

Apparently, so was she. Her pulse speeding up, Vivian's breathing became soft and shallow.

He was having an effect on her.

Except, he shouldn't start thumping his chest yet. Her reaction was probably not because of his irresistible male magnetism.

Viv hadn't been with a man in a long while. She might have responded like that to any guy standing so close behind her and invading her personal space.

At least she wasn't scared of him.

Even though he was caging her small frame between his outstretched arms, Magnus didn't detect even a whiff of fear, only of arousal.

Did he dare start anything?

Since the moment they'd met, they had been dancing a polite dance around each other, suppressing their mutual attraction. On his part, Magnus had thought the timing was wrong, and that making advances was inappropriate given the situation. But his issues were tame and mundane compared to Vivian's.

If he initiated anything, he would be taking advantage of a woman in a vulnerable situation.

But what if she felt the same gnawing need to get closer?

Neither could make long-term promises to the other, for completely different reasons, but they could give each other something. A momentary escape, a stolen moment of passion, an affirmation of life.

"I want to kiss you so badly," he murmured into her hair. "I know it's a bad idea on so many levels, but right now it feels like the best one I've had in my entire life."

She turned around inside his outstretched arms and lifted her eyes to him. "You are a danger seeker, aren't you?"

"I see nothing dangerous here. All I see is a beautiful woman whose lush lips I've wanted to kiss from the first moment I saw her."

Barely breathing, Vivian gave him the tiniest of nods. He wasn't even sure that she'd done it consciously.

Slowly, as if he was dealing with a skittish little mare, he lifted his hand to her neck and cupped it gently. When she didn't tense, he dipped his head, stopping with his lips a fraction of an inch away from hers.

He was giving her the option to either close the distance or pull away.

Closing her eyes, Vivian lifted her chin and their lips touched.

Was it his imagination, or had the bells of destiny just rung? It felt as if the world had righted itself, or some other monumental shift had occurred. Logically, he knew it was all in his head, and that nothing had changed in the outside world.

Only in his.

His fingers on her neck gently massaging, he licked at the seam of her lips, coaxing her to open for him.

With a barely audible moan, Vivian lifted her arms, wrapped them around his neck, and pressed herself to him.

As her willing participation broke the dam on his restraint, he gripped her hips and lifted her up on the counter. Pressing himself between her spread thighs, he pushed his tongue inside her mouth and plundered her sweetness.

Through the haze of lust, he heard the front door opening. It took him a second longer to process the information and quickly step away from Vivian.

"Mom, what are you doing sitting on the counter?"

Realizing that his fangs must be showing, Magnus dove

into the utility closet and pretended to look for something until he got them under control.

"I was trying to climb up and get these cans from the top shelf, but Magnus took them down for me." She slid to the floor. "It's nice to be tall. I could use him around the house when I can't reach places."

Grabbing the two cans, she turned around so she was facing away from Parker and started opening drawers. "Where is the can opener? I thought I saw it here somewhere."

"It's on the counter, Mom. Right there." He pointed.

"Oh, silly me. I forgot that I already pulled it out. Can you check if there are any bell peppers left in the fridge? And onions?"

"Sure. What are you making?"

"A stir-fry."

"That's what you always make when we don't have ingredients for something better."

"Exactly. We need to go to the supermarket and get some groceries."

Magnus exhaled a relieved breath. Parker seemed to suspect nothing, which was good since he and the boy were just starting to build a relationship, and it would've been a shame to ruin it by being caught kissing his mom.

But why did it matter?

Tomorrow or the following day, he was going to drive mother and son back home and never see either of them again.

Right. As if he could do that after what had just happened.

Like a boy after his first kiss, Magnus touched a finger to his lips. They still tingled as if they had been touched by fire.

Damn. Maybe the woman was indeed a witch.

A bewitching temptress he felt powerless to resist.

ELLA

*R*ose lit up a joint and took a fat hit. "Want some?" She offered it to Ella.

"I don't smoke pot." She didn't smoke at all.

Taking another long drag, Rose puffed out a stream of smoke. "You should. It will help you relax. You look like you're going to lose your shit. It ain't good." She waved the hand with the joint, spreading the noxious smell all over the room.

"I don't know how you can be so calm."

It was beyond Ella how the girl could act so indifferent to her situation. Wasn't she worried about what was going to happen to her?

Except, maybe Rose wasn't stressing because she wasn't getting auctioned tonight. Still, Ella would've been freaking out even if hers wasn't imminent. Were they going to have her strip naked? Would there be a room full of perverts ogling her? And what if the one who bought her was some old smelly guy with twisted sexual tastes?

It was worse than waiting for an execution.

Rose shrugged. "To tell you the truth, I'm kind of excited.

I'm not a virgin like you." She snorted. "I gave it up when I was fourteen." She gave Ella a once-over. "With that face and that body, I don't know how you managed to keep your cherry for so long, or why you wanted to. Are you religious or something?"

"I'm not. I just haven't met the right guy." She'd thought she had, but wasn't that a big joke.

After taking another puff, Rose waved a hand over her own body. "Other than this, I don't have much else going for me. I'm not smart, I don't have rich parents, and no one gives a shit about me. The way I see it, I was going to sell this one way or another, and probably for much less than my cut of the auction money. Even with only thirty percent, it's going to be more than what I can make in a year of busting my butt waiting tables or doing some other crap like that."

Ella shook her head.

It almost sounded as if Rose was in cahoots with Stefano or the auction people, and she was trying to convince Ella that things were not as bad as they seemed, so she'd play nice.

Or maybe it was the pot talking, and everything seemed sunnier when people were high. Perhaps she should take Rose up on her offer and give it a try.

Surviving the morning alone had been exhausting, emotionally and physically. The intrusive probing had been the worst, but the waxing, especially of her intimate parts, had been a close second. The other stuff could've been fun under different circumstances. Except, the pedicure, manicure, makeup, and hair had all been done in preparation for the auction.

A reminder that the worst was still to come.

"Let me try." She reached for the joint.

Rose's smile looked victorious. "Don't suck in too much. Take a small drag and hold it in your mouth."

Ella coughed and gave it back. "It's disgusting. It tastes

like mildew." She should have known that since it smelled like it too.

"Do you feel anything?"

"Other than the need to throw up? No." She grabbed a water bottle and gulped half of it down to clear the foul taste.

Rose pointed at the garments Grace had left on the chair. "You'd better get dressed. It's almost time."

"How do you know?" They didn't have a watch.

Besides, no one had bothered to tell her when she should be ready.

The suspicion that Rose was working with the auction people resurfaced. She was like an old pro who could anticipate their every move. Maybe she'd been auctioned several times?

But that didn't make sense.

She must've been planted to either spy on Ella or just make her more relaxed for the upcoming event. Yeah. That made more sense. If Stefano's expectations were realistic, then a lot of money was riding on Ella's performance at the auction. Naturally, they would want to make her less nervous and more cooperative.

The girl shrugged. "Grace told you to get ready."

Ella eyed the short silk robe and thong. There was no bra. As she picked the two items up, her hands shook.

Don't cry! she commanded herself as she ducked into the bathroom. It had been easier to pretend to be brave in front of Rose. The girl was about the same age as Ella, but acted tough as if she was a thirty-year-old pro.

What if Rose wasn't a spy and was just holding up better?

If Ella allowed herself to go into full freak-out mode, feeling sorry for herself, she would undermine not only herself but her roommate as well.

Don't cry! Don't cry! she kept repeating as she stripped out of her clothes and put on the barely-there panties, then covered up as best she could with the too- short robe.

37

VIVIAN

*T*he trip to the grocery store went by with Parker and Magnus talking about the different kinds of bows and which one was good for killing what—a gruesome subject the two guys found fascinating.

She could understand Magnus talking about lethal weapons with the same emotional detachment as if he were talking about golf clubs. After all, he was a soldier of sorts. But it surprised her that Parker was regarding it in the same way.

Then again, the computer games her son was playing weren't about petting kittens or growing flowers. Most were extremely violent.

Was it a male thing?

Did they need an outlet to release excess testosterone? If so, she preferred Parker doing it in a pretend game.

Trying to tune them out, Vivian shifted in her seat and looked out the window at the greenery passing them by. This high in the mountains, it was cold enough for pockets of snow to survive the midday sun. It wasn't a lot, just little patches of it dotting the sides of the road. There was more snow on the mountain peaks.

The monotonous landscape wasn't much of a distraction, though, and it didn't take long for her mind to go back to the kiss Parker had interrupted.

She touched a trembling finger to her lips.

The hunger that kiss had awakened was terrifying in its intensity. Up until then, suppressing her attraction to Magnus had been easily manageable. Between her worry about Ella and her determination to never enter a relationship with a man again, her libido had remained mostly dormant.

Not that there hadn't been sparks. She would've been blind and half-dead not to notice how incredibly handsome Magnus was, or how wonderfully protective and supportive he was of her and Parker. In a different life, she would've fallen in love with him just for that. But until the kiss, Vivian had managed to extinguish those sparks before they ignited an inferno that could only be put out in one way.

Would it be so terrible to give in to the hunger, though?

After this was over, she would probably never see Magnus again. And if they weren't in a relationship, perhaps her curse wouldn't affect him. A one-night hookup didn't count as a relationship, right?

Except, she'd never tested that theory, nor did she dare to.

Besides, she wasn't the type who could do casual sex, and this wasn't only about sex. She had feelings for him that could easily morph into love, and if she loved him, her curse would kick in for sure.

On the other hand, Vivian wasn't sure she'd loved Frank or Al. She'd liked them, had enjoyed their company, and both had been suitable husband material, but the relationships hadn't had the depth of feeling like the one she'd had with Josh. At the time, she'd thought it was because nothing could ever compare to what they had, and no man could ever replace the father of her children.

It was still true, but she had a feeling that if she let it happen, Magnus could come pretty close.

"You have arrived at your destination," the navigation system announced in its eerily realistic feminine voice.

"She sounds sexy," Parker said.

"You think?" Magnus got out and opened Vivian's door. "Because I don't." He winked at her, sending a wave of heat to her cheeks. "Your voice is much sexier," he whispered into her ear as he helped her out.

Given the sexual innuendo, it seemed Magnus assumed there was something going on between them. She should set him straight before Parker caught on.

"Please don't do that," she whispered back.

"Do what?" He winked again and opened the back door to help Parker with Scarlet.

"I think she needs to pee," Parker said a little too late.

As soon as Magnus got her out of the car, she squatted next to the wheel and peed, some of it landing on Magnus's shoe.

"Shite, girl, could ye no wait a minute?" He shook his leg out.

It was funny how his accent reverted to his native Scottish whenever he was upset. Other times it was barely noticeable.

Reaching into her bag, Vivian pulled out a couple of tissues. "Here, you can wipe your shoe with these."

"Thank you."

As Magnus took the leash from Parker and led Scarlet to the store, she looked shamed even though he hadn't really scolded her. Her head and tail pointing down, she was stealing furtive glances at Magnus to see if he was still mad at her.

The guy at the register jumped as soon as they entered the store. "I'm sorry, but you can't bring the dog inside."

With a broad smile, Magnus stared the owner down for a moment. "Scarlet is well-behaved. Good dogs are allowed in stores."

"Yes, good dogs are allowed in the store," the guy parroted.

That was so weird. Magnus had been polite. He'd even smiled. And yet, he'd somehow scared the owner into agreeing to let Scarlet in.

Stealing a sidelong glance at him, Vivian tried to see Magnus as others did. He was tall but not huge, muscular but not overly so, and he had a kind face. There was nothing intimidating about him.

Was it the clothes?

With the slacks and the dress shoes and the button-down shirt, Magnus didn't fit in with the other customers in the grocery store.

He'd worn exercise pants and shirt around the cabin and to walk Scarlet, but she'd never seen him in jeans. Was it a European thing? Did they dress fancier for everyday activities?

"Do you dress like this all of the time?" she blurted out, realizing it sounded rude the moment the words left her mouth. "Don't get me wrong. I think you look great. But people usually don't wear slacks and dress shoes to go grocery shopping."

Magnus shrugged. "I'm not a jeans man." He leaned to whisper in her ear. "But I'll buy some if you fancy seeing me in a pair."

Luckily, Parker had wandered into the cereal section and wasn't there to see her get all flustered. "Please don't do this."

He shrugged. "Let me know if you change your mind. There is a clothing store next door."

Obviously, he was playing dumb. Although she'd learned that with men one never knew. They were very literal creatures.

Bundling all men in the same basket was a mistake, though. Up until now, Vivian had been fortunate to be exposed only to the good ones—decent, hard-working, moral men. Maybe that was why she hadn't been more suspicious of Romeo.

One could only judge people based on one's own experience, and hers had been positive. She'd encountered a few jerks in her life, who hadn't? But overall she'd had no reason to be wary of men.

Naively, Vivian had thought that she and her children were safe in their quiet suburban neighborhood, leading their average suburban lives.

She would never make that mistake again.

Apparently, she'd been blind and deaf to the fact that the world was full of predators who considered people like her easy prey.

When this was over and Ella was back home, they were both going to take self-defense classes and maybe even learn how to handle a gun. They'd get permits, and, if possible, a permit to carry.

"About the staff fighting you were going to teach Parker, can you teach me too?"

Magnus's brows furrowed. "What has prompted this? Do you want to beat me into wearing jeans? I already said I would."

It took talent to say something so silly with such a serious expression. He was a good actor. She should remember that.

"I want to learn self-defense. But since I'm short and skinny and have no muscles to speak of, I figured I'd do better with a staff."

Still affecting a serious expression, Magnus pretended to

measure her bicep, his large hand encircling it with room to spare. "I see what you mean." He shook his head. "I can tell you one thing, though. Training with a staff is not easy. Those tiny muscles of yours are going to grow. Are you okay with looking like Popeye?"

"Popeye?"

"The sailor." When she still looked at him with puzzlement in her eyes, Magnus waved his hand. "The one who loves spinach?"

"Oh, yeah, I remember now. My dad used to sing the theme song whenever my mom served spinach. What kind of cartoons are they showing kids in Scotland? That one is ancient. It was a thing when my parents were kids."

Magnus's smile turned into a frown. "I guess Scottish public television lags behind." He let go of her bicep. "I'll go look for a good broom we could use for the staff."

38

ELLA

As Stefano entered the room without knocking, Ella's heart sank all the way down to her toes. She felt dizzy and faint, but that might have been the pot's fault. Rose had smoked one joint after another, filling the small room with noxious fumes.

"It's time." He sounded out of breath, excited.

Was he going to watch? Or was he anxious to get his hands on the money from her sale?

Probably the money.

If he'd wanted to see her naked, he could've commanded her to strip for him during the week he'd kept her locked up in his house. Or he could've installed a camera in the bathroom. But there hadn't been one.

She'd checked.

Stefano's perversion was all about greed.

"What are you waiting for?" He waved a hand to hurry her along. "Get up!"

Doing her best to hold her shit together, Ella tried to stand up, but her knees buckled, and she fell back down on the bed.

Faster than she would've expected from the fat middle-aged man, Stefano leaped, catching her by the elbow and helping her up. "Now, now, Ella, don't go fainting on me," he said as he pulled her toward the door.

"Wait, what about my things?"

"Don't worry about it. Before you get shipped off to the buyer, you're coming back here to get dressed."

That was a relief.

"Good luck!" Rose called after her. "Whip them into a frenzy, girl. I'll hold my fingers crossed for the bidding to go wild."

As Stefano closed the door behind him, his grip on her elbow tightened. He turned her around to face him. "Listen to me, Ella, and listen good. The buyer I had in mind for you requested a private viewing before the auction. If he likes what he sees, he's going to pay top price for you."

"I don't care about the money."

Even if Stefano hadn't been lying about her share, Ella wouldn't touch a penny of it. All of the blood money would go to charity.

"Maybe so. But think of it this way," he smirked. "What's better, stripping naked for only one man, or for a roomful of ogling men?"

Someone kill me now.

If there was a God, she wished He'd strike her down with a thunderbolt and end her misery.

"What do you want me to do?" she managed to say through the lump in her throat.

"Just do whatever the proxy tells you. Nothing more and nothing less."

"Proxy?"

Stefano chuckled. "You think a man like him will come here in person? He sent a proxy. The auction house has a viewing room, where buyers can inspect the merchandise from wherever they are in the world."

Ella's knees buckled again, this time from relief.

She might get humiliated and degraded, but she wouldn't get raped.

Not today.

The viewing room Stefano brought her to reminded Ella of the one photoshoot she'd done for the running shoes commercial. It looked like a modeling studio, complete with a stage, a backdrop, and several modeling lamps. The difference was that one of its walls was made of glass, and that several video cameras and other equipment were mounted on the walls instead of perching on top of a tripod or in the hands of a photographer.

Without further preamble, Stefano pushed her onto the stage, and then left her alone in the viewing room.

Ella strained her eyes, trying to see the person on the other side of the glass wall, but that room was steeped in darkness. As far as she knew, Stefano could've lied to her and there was a bunch of leering perverts sitting on the other side and making lewd comments about her.

"State your name," a woman's voice came through the loudspeaker.

The proxy was a woman?

"Ella," she whispered.

"Louder. The buyer wants to hear your voice."

"Ella."

"That's better. How old are you, Ella?"

"I'm eighteen," she managed to croak.

"Tell us something about yourself."

Between the lump in her throat and the panic seizing her mind, Ella couldn't find a single thing to say.

"Would you rather remove the robe and show us your other assets?"

Was there an option for her not to disrobe?

Swallowing the little bit of moisture in her mouth, Ella cleared her throat. "I was a good student in high school and I got accepted to several colleges. I wanted to study nursing." She looked down at her bare feet. "Maybe one day I will."

"Why do you want to be a nurse?"

What was this, a job interview?

In a way it was, but the job description was not something anyone could put in an ad. Except, the alternative to answering was taking off her robe, which she still might be required to do. But on the off-chance that she wouldn't, Ella decided to answer.

"I like helping people. I wanted to become a doctor, but that takes too long and costs too much money, so I settled on nursing."

For several long moments, nothing came through the speakers, and Ella wondered if the buyer and his proxy were discussing the terms of her purchase.

This was nothing like the auction scenes in the billionaire romance novels she'd pilfered from her mother. Those had been arousing. This was terrifying, humiliating, and as far from sexy as it could get.

Perhaps the difference was that the women in those romances offered themselves willingly. But even then she couldn't imagine how anyone could do so without knowing who the buyer was.

In the romances, he was always a hot guy the woman was immediately attracted to. In reality, he would probably be some old, fat guy.

Besides, anyone who bought women in an auction was a disgusting pervert.

"The buyer is happy so far," the woman said through the speaker. "You have a pleasant voice and not a shrill one, which would have been a deal breaker, and you seem fairly intelligent. He also finds you very beautiful. The last thing he wants to verify before finalizing the purchase, is that you're not hiding some deformities under that robe. Please take it off, and then turn in a slow circle."

39

TURNER

"I can't sense anybody inside," Arwel said.

The address of the two-story brick building they were parked in front of was the one Romeo had provided but, apparently, no one was home.

Unacceptable. Turner had hoped someone would be there, and it didn't matter if it was the uncle or one of his minions.

He had a van full of Guardians and no one to shake down.

Pulling out his phone, he went over the information Roni and William had compiled about Romeo and his family.

One of his uncles on his mother's side was indeed named Stefano, but the address didn't match. It didn't mean that they were in the wrong place, though. It only meant that the trafficker didn't do business where he slept.

Unlike this old building, which was in one of Brooklyn's shittiest neighborhoods, his real home was in the much more affluent Cobble Hill.

They could split up, and Turner could send two Guardians to the other address, but he doubted the guy was there. In fact, he hadn't really expected to find Stefano anywhere other than the auction house.

Ella was a rare beauty who was going to bring in lots of money. The scumbag would want to be there and supervise the proceedings to ensure everything went smoothly.

"That's okay. Let's go inside and search the place. I'm pretty sure we can find the auction house's address in there."

"Can you hack into a computer?" Arwel asked. "Because that's the first place I would look."

"I can give it a try."

Roni had taught him a few basic tricks. It didn't make him a hacker, but then an older guy like Stefano was probably using an easy to figure out password that Turner might be able to deduce.

Disarming the alarm took him several minutes, and opening the two locks on the back door a couple more.

As was often the case when going on missions in person, Turner had learned a valuable lesson. Not even one of the Guardians he had with him knew how to disarm an alarm, and none of them carried burglar tools.

"When we get back, I'm going to have a talk with your chief and suggest training on breaking and entering. You rely too heavily on your superior strength and thralling abilities." He put the tools in his pocket and opened the door. "In some instances, both are of no use, and more mundane, human methods serve the purpose better."

Arwel followed him inside. "I know how to use those. I just didn't think to bring them with me."

"You should always come prepared. Just as you strap on a couple of knives before going out on a mission, you should bring along your burglar tools. You can never know when they'll come in handy."

The guy shrugged.

"You and I will start on the office." He turned to the other three. "You search the rest of the place."

Since Edan had been left to watch over the bound and gagged Romeo in the jet, Turner was short one Guardian.

After the dose of drugs they'd had the scum ingest, the bounding and gagging hadn't been necessary. But Turner derived sadistic pleasure from making the motherfucker as miserable as possible.

Another thing Turner had learned on this mission was that thralling was complicated and it had its limitations. Apparently, it was not the same as compulsion, and none of the clan members possessed the latter. Except maybe for the goddess, but that was beside the point. It wasn't like he could take her with him on missions.

Thralling Romeo into obedience was possible, but not guaranteed to hold. The other option was turning the guy into a zombie by erasing a big chunk of his memories. Except, since Turner still wanted to interrogate him, he needed the guy to have a functioning brain.

In Romeo's case, drugs had been a safer and more straightforward solution to getting him on the jet without dragging him through the airport bound and gagged.

To do that, they would've needed someone of Yamanu's caliber to shroud them. None of the Guardians were even close.

"That's interesting," Arwel said.

Turner looked up. "What do you have there?"

Arwel handed him a magazine, opened on a folded page. "Look at the picture."

"That's Ella." He flipped the magazine to the front. "*Teen Life* magazine." He went back to look at the picture. "It's a running shoe advertisement." He looked at the front again. "And it's five months old."

The implications were clear.

Ella hadn't been a random victim. Someone had seen that picture and had ordered either her specifically or a girl who looked like her.

But if that was indeed so, why take her to an auction house and not deliver her straight to the buyer?

Perhaps the guy wanted to inspect what he was paying for first and do so on neutral territory. Or maybe the uncle and the buyer were haggling over the price and needed an intermediary.

This was both good and bad news.

The good news was that in all likelihood Ella hadn't been violated yet. A buyer who'd gone to all the trouble of ordering a specific girl, wouldn't want anyone else touching her.

The bad news was that a man like that was probably extremely rich and powerful. Either a drug lord, a major arms dealer, or a Mafia boss.

Law-abiding citizens didn't buy sex slaves.

Which meant that it was crucial for them to get her out before the transaction was finalized. Once Ella was delivered to her buyer, the operation would become much more complicated.

Those kinds of men had armies of thugs at their disposal, and lived in heavily guarded fortresses. Even worse, the buyer didn't necessarily reside in the States.

If he took her out of the country, it would further complicate things.

They were wasting time.

"Call your men," Turner said. "While they keep searching, you and I are going to pay Romeo's mom a visit."

"Why?"

"I'll threaten her and have her call her brother and beg him to come to her rescue. I hate doing that to a woman, but we are running out of time."

"What makes you think he'll come?"

"He may or he may not. But while she has him on the phone, we will zero in on his location."

"Can William do that remotely?"

"I believe so. If my hacker can do it, so can he."

Caterina's place was not far from her brother's home; the real one, not the one he used for his shady business. From the information William and Roni had gathered, Stefano was her sole source of support, so chances were that the two were close, and that he would come running to her rescue.

"May I help you?" The woman opened the door but left the chain on.

The only one standing on her stoop was Arwel, who didn't look threatening, especially given that perpetually suffering expression of his. "I'm a friend of Stefano. He asked me to deliver a message. You need to invite my friend and me inside."

The thrall worked like a charm. Caterina released the chain and opened the door wide. "Please, come in."

As Arwel and Turner stepped inside, she closed the door behind them and put the chain back up, locking herself in with the wolves.

This time, Turner was going to let Arwel do the talking. Since the woman seemed responsive to thralling, hopefully Turner wouldn't need to slap her to make the point. He would hate it, but he'd do it if necessary.

"Please take a seat, Caterina." Arwel pointed at the couch.

When she was seated, he pulled out one of the dining room chairs, put it down right in front of her, and sat on it. "Yesterday, Stefano took a girl to the auction house."

Turner tensed. That wasn't what they had agreed on.

As Arwel lifted his arm, signaling for Turner to wait, Caterina nodded.

"I need you to tell me where the auction house is."

What was wrong with the guy? How the hell was she supposed to know that?

As the woman nodded again and proceeded to give Arwel the address, Turner was dumbfounded.

"Thank you." Arwel patted her hand. "You will now escort us to the door, close it, and lock it behind us. Then you'll forget that you ever saw us. You will go back to the couch and continue watching your soap opera."

"Yes. The soap opera. I was watching it."

Turner waited until they were in the car. "How the hell did you know she'd have the address?" he asked as Arwel eased into traffic.

"I wasn't sure she would, but her guilt was so thick that I was almost choking on it. I knew then that she was aware of her brother's activities, and I took a chance." He cast Turner a sideways glance. "What now?"

"Now we go and rent another van. We got an auction house to raid."

ELLA

"Thank you for your cooperation, Ella. You can put the robe back on," the disembodied female voice said. "The buyer is very pleased with you."

As if that was supposed to make her feel better.

Lifting the robe off the floor with shaking hands, Ella put her arms inside the kimono sleeves, brought the two halves together, and wrapped the sash around her waist so tightly that it pinched, then double knotted it for good measure.

Except, nothing was enough to make her feel covered.

All she wanted was to crawl into a bed, pull the covers over her head, and never get out. If only there were a magic trick that could've made her invisible.

Heck, if there were, she would've used it after the first time someone had commented on how pretty she was. What was supposed to be a gift, was in fact a curse.

But then she'd always suspected that.

That was why she wore her hair in a ponytail, didn't use makeup, and dressed in clothes that made her look younger than she really was and obscured her shape.

In the past, her main motive was not to stand out as much

and to be liked. She'd never been comfortable with the looks she'd been getting. Could it have been some sixth sense warning her that there were predators out there? Evildoers who were attracted to her like cats to catnip?

Stefano opened the door and pulled her into a bear hug. "You did good, girl, very good."

He wrapped his fat arm around her shoulders and led her out of the viewing room. "Seven hundred and fifty thousand dollars he paid for you. I threw the most obscene number I could think of and he didn't even haggle. That's two hundred thousand dollars going into your account, girl. Think of all the things you could do with that money."

She didn't care about the money. As far as she was concerned, Stefano together with the mystery buyer could stuff it up their butts, preferably one dollar bill at a time.

Besides, she didn't believe a single word coming out of his mouth, and she wanted him to stop touching her. Shrugging her shoulders, she shook his arm off. "The lights in there were hot." She forced the excuse instead of telling Stefano how disgusting she found him.

If he still had her mother and Parker under surveillance, she didn't want to antagonize him no matter how satisfying it would have been to call him a filthy pig.

His meaty hand closed on her shoulder, and he spun her around so she was facing him. "Listen here, girl, and listen good. The buyer paid a lot of money for you, and he expects to get his money's worth. You won't see a dime of that money until he releases you, and your mom and brother will stay under close watch to ensure your full cooperation. Am I clear?"

"I didn't expect anything else."

His hand on her shoulder loosened its grip. "Smart girl." He patted her back. "You have half an hour to get dressed and collect your things."

After unlocking the door to her room, he pushed her in and then locked it again.

"How did it go?" Rose asked.

"I was sold."

The girl smiled as if it was good news. "Congratulations. How much did you get?"

"I didn't get anything. Stefano got seven hundred and fifty thousand dollars. Or so he says."

Rose whistled. "The highest I heard of was three hundred. Good for you." She lifted her hand for a high-five.

"Really?" Ella grabbed her backpack and headed for the bathroom.

After stripping for the pervert who'd bought her, she didn't feel like changing clothes even in front of another girl.

Taking her things out of the backpack, she wished she was a smoker and had a lighter so she could set the thong and robe on fire.

Rose had one.

Maybe before leaving she could borrow it for a second and burn them in the bathtub?

It was an old iron one, so the fire would be contained. As much as she didn't like Rose and her blasé attitude toward the flesh market, Ella didn't want to cause the girl harm by setting the room on fire.

But first, she needed to use the tub to take a shower and wash the makeup off, together with the shame and the humiliation.

Regrettably, she didn't have enough time to scrub it all off. Not that there would ever be enough time to do that. It was a stain on her soul that was never going away, and it was only the first of many more to come.

When she was done, Ella gathered her wet hair in a ponytail and secured it with a hair tie, then put on her cotton panties, sports bra, jeans, and T-shirt. It was warm, and the sweatshirt was unnecessary, but it was another layer of insulation. The more layers she had on, the better she felt.

"Why did you wash off the makeup?" Rose asked as she came out. "You looked so good in it."

"I hate makeup. Can I borrow your lighter?"

Rose narrowed her eyes. "Why? Do you want a joint? I can roll one for you."

"No, I just want to burn what I wore before."

As Rose started to shake her head, the door opened and an elegant forty-something woman in spiky heels walked in. "Hello, Ella. Are you ready to go?"

She recognized the cultured voice. "No. But does it matter?"

"It doesn't." The woman opened the door wider and motioned for Ella to get out.

"Good luck, Rose." Ella waved at her roommate.

"Thanks. You too."

The woman closed the door and started walking, expecting Ella to follow.

What if she made a run for it? With those spiky heels, the woman wouldn't be able to catch her.

Even though she knew it would bring her nothing but more misery, the impulse was almost overwhelming. What was it called? The fight or flight instinct? Or was it the flight or fight?

"You might think it's the end of the world, Ella. But it really isn't. You are a very lucky girl. As long as you cooperate, you'll be treated like a princess. The buyer is a very rich and influential man. If you please him, he'll reward you beyond your wildest imagination. But don't ever dare to displease him. You wouldn't like the consequences."

The woman turned and pinned her with a hard stare. "Don't dawdle, Ella. Walk purposefully."

"Toward my own doom," she muttered under her breath.

The woman chuckled. "You're such a silly teenager. I don't know what a man like him expects to get from you." She gave her a once-over. "Except for that, of course. You are beautiful."

She said it as if she was appraising a piece of art, deeming it pleasing to the eye but worthless because it wasn't made by some well-known artist.

As they reached the end of a corridor, the woman pressed an intercom button and lifted her face to the camera. A door to the outside buzzed and clicked open.

A limousine was parked right by the door. The driver leaning against it with his bulky arms crossed over his chest was the tallest man Ella had ever seen.

He had the expression of a bulldog.

"Can you hand me a water bottle, Yuri?" the woman asked.

Without a word, the guy opened the limo's passenger door, leaned in, and pulled out a bottle.

"Thank you." She handed the bottle to Ella, and then pulled out a packet of pills from her bag and tore it open. "Sleeping pills. Take them."

Ella glanced suspiciously at Yuri. As big as he was, he didn't look like a pervert, but then neither did Romeo.

The woman laughed. "Don't worry about Yuri, dear. Now that you're Dimitri's property no one is going to lay a finger on you."

So that was the name of the perv who'd paid three-quarters of a million for her.

Dimitri.

41

TURNER

*I*t was late evening when Turner and the Guardians arrived at the auction house.

As was the case with most dark deeds, flesh auctions were usually held at night. There was a good chance Ella was still there.

The place was in a rural area, about an hour's drive away from Brooklyn. It was sparsely populated, which meant that two rental vans would have stood out even to an amateur. They had to park half a mile away and jog back.

The thing was, five men jogging on a deserted rural road would've stuck out too, but Turner had come prepared. A quick stop at a sports supply store had outfitted them with matching sports shirts and pants. With the five of them jogging in loose formation, they looked like a team practicing for a marathon.

Hopefully, it would do.

The only other thing he could've done was to wait for the cover of darkness, but he didn't want to take the risk of Ella being taken away while they were waiting.

When they got closer, he asked Arwel, "Can you sense how many people are inside?"

"I'm working on it. Let's pass it and then come back."

"No problem."

They jogged about a mile beyond the house, when Arwel stopped and pretended to stretch his calves. "I don't think there is an auction going on tonight. There aren't enough people in there. I could sense about four apprehensive females, two indifferent ones, and four bored men."

"How can you tell the difference between males and females?"

Arwel lifted a brow. "It's impossible not to. They project a completely different emotional landscape."

"I'll take your word for it. Let's just hope Ella is one of the four apprehensive females."

Liam shrugged. "This operation should go down easy with only four guards."

"The indifferent women might be guards as well," Turner said.

"Six is still easy."

"There are five of us, and I can't thrall."

Arwel rubbed his jaw. "I can thrall two at the same time, but I need them to be together in the same room."

"We'll figure it out." Turner looked at the other Guardians. "Who wants to be the runner with the sprained ankle?"

"I'll do it," Liam said.

Turner doubted the guy had ever sprained anything. "Do you know what to do?"

"Of course, I do. I've been a Guardian since long before you were born, when people still fought with swords and sticks. I know what a broken or twisted ankle feels like."

It was easy to forget that these men were much older than

they looked. "Okay. Let's jog back. When we are in sight of the house, the show begins."

Liam saluted. "Got it."

He had, but his acting skills were laughable. "Neil, Gregor, pick him up. And Liam, tone it down a bit. You're overacting."

Arwel knocked on the door, and several moments later a guy opened the small window at the top. "What do you want?"

"Please open the door. Our friend twisted his ankle and we need to use your phone to call for an ambulance."

Thankfully, Arwel's thrall was strong enough to overcome the goon's suspicious mind.

Once the door was opened, the rest was easy. Neil and Gregor carried Liam into the monitoring room, where the guards had been playing cards while watching their victims on the screens.

In minutes, the Guardians had them face down on the floor and hogtied.

"Let's get the others. Bring everyone here."

Five girls and one older woman were brought in, which accounted for everyone Arwel had sensed. Except, none of them was Ella.

"Where is Ella?" Turner asked.

"You're too late," one of the girls said. "She's been sold already."

Fuck. "Do you know who bought her?"

She shrugged. "How should I know? Some rich dude."

"Did you see him?"

The girl glanced at the men hogtied on the floor. "No. A woman came to take her, but I don't know where."

"A proxy," Turner said to no one in particular. "Arwel. See if any of these people know who the woman was and where we can find her."

It took the guy nearly an hour to interrogate the four guards, the five girls and the woman esthetician, who acted the most hysterical of the bunch.

The guards, as well as the girl who'd shared a room with Ella, could all describe the proxy in detail. One of the guards even had the name she'd identified herself by when she came in—Madame X.

That wasn't much help.

Turner's eyes went to the monitors. "Where do they keep the recordings?"

Arwel got the answer for him. "It's in that closet." He pointed.

"We need to go over them, find Madame X, and send her portrait to William. Hopefully, this one hasn't undergone extensive plastic surgery and will not give the facial recognition software as much trouble as Romeo did."

He turned to the girls huddled together in one corner of the room. "Who wants to go home?"

Four pairs of hopeful eyes lifted to his. The fifth girl, the one who'd shared Ella's room, shrugged. "I have no home. I was hoping for some rich dude to buy me and take care of me."

"We have a place for you where you can take your time and figure things out."

She eyed him suspiciously. "What kind of a place?"

"It's a sanctuary for girls who had been taken against their will and abused. You'll have access to job training, therapy, and even some pocket money. You can take your time and figure out what you want to do with the rest of your life."

"Who runs it?"

"It's run by volunteers and funded by donations."

"Can I come too?" one of the other girls asked.

"All of you are coming with us. We need to figure out who

193

took you, and if they are threatening your families. You'll go home only after we make sure it's safe."

"I just want to go home." One of the girls started crying.

Crap, that was the part Turner was not equipped to deal with. "Arwel? Can you help her?"

42

ELLA

*G*roggy, Ella opened her eyes, closed them again, blinked a couple of times to make sure she wasn't dreaming, and then opened them again.

The room she was in was like something out of a gaudy fairytale, or in her case, a nightmare. It looked like a replica of some Russian tsar's master bedroom, and was probably the size of her entire house.

The ceiling was at least two stories tall, the frames of the paintings on the walls were gilded, and the green velvet curtains flanking the windows were edged with gold tassels. The four-poster bed she was in was huge, and it had a velvet canopy, also edged with gold tassels.

Hopefully, it wasn't the perv's bedroom.

The good news was that it didn't look lived in. Other than the over-the-top everything, she could see no personal mementos. There were no framed family pictures on the massive fireplace mantel, and no aggrandized painted portraits of patriarchs or matriarchs that one would expect to find in a room like that.

Big windows overlooked grounds that went on forever,

and there was even a balcony with French doors leading to it, which were most likely locked.

After paying all that money for her, the perv wouldn't want her jumping off and running away.

Just for the heck of it, though, she got out of bed, padded to the doors, and tried the handle, not really expecting it to budge.

Surprise.

The doors weren't locked, and Ella stepped outside. From the looks of it, she was on the second floor, but it was much higher up than in any regular house. The first floor was probably three stories high. If she jumped, she would probably break something. Not that she would. Stefano had made it clear that her family was still being watched.

With a heavy heart, she walked back inside and searched for the bathroom. The first door she opened led to a huge walk-in closet that was thankfully empty. It confirmed that she wasn't in the owner's master bedroom.

The second door she tried was the bathroom. It looked like another Kremlin replica, but with modern amenities. The toilet was in a separate room that also housed a bidet. After using the former, she decided to give the latter a try.

It was a pleasant experience, she had to admit, and it even had a drying cycle so no towel was needed.

Cool.

Out in the main bathroom, she washed her hands and then took stock of the toiletries someone had left for her on the counter. Other than several hair brushes and combs, there was also a new toothbrush, toothpaste, a selection of soaps, perfumes, and lotions, and a stack of neatly folded small towels.

Ella used the toothbrush and redid her ponytail.

Except for the sneakers that someone had taken off her,

she was still dressed in what she'd had on when she'd left the auction house.

Did the driver bring her backpack up to the room?

All she had in there were a few items of clothing. Under different circumstances, it wouldn't have mattered to her if the thing got lost or misplaced, but right now what she had in her backpack was the only connection to her old life.

A piece of home.

And just like that the tears she'd been holding back came gushing out, and then the sobs, and finally Ella just let herself drop to the bathroom floor.

The door opened, and an older woman in a maid's uniform rushed in. "What happened you? Why you cry?" she asked in a heavy Russian accent.

With knees that protested the move with loud cracking, the woman crouched next to Ella and started patting her back. "Tell Larissa what you cry for."

Lifting her head, Ella's eyes landed on a huge cross. Dangling from a thick neck, it rested on the woman's hefty bosom. "Do you know who I am?"

"Yes. You are Ella. My best friend's name is Ella, but she is in Russia, and I don't see her in many years."

"Do you know why I'm here?"

The woman sighed. "I know. Master bought pretty girl. He told me take good care of you."

Ella eyed the cross. "How can you be a God-fearing woman and work for a man who buys people and holds them against their will?"

Larissa shook her head. "Master is a good man and treats loyal people good. You loyal and good, he good to you."

A disturbing thought crossed Ella's mind. What if Larissa had once been a beautiful girl, and the perv had bought her as well? Then, when she was no longer young and pretty, he demoted her to housekeeping duties.

"Did he buy you too?"

Larissa laughed, her heavy bosom heaving. "Who will pay money for this?" She grabbed her fat belly and gave it a squeeze. "No, master did not buy me, he pay me salary. He bring me from Russia to manage the house because I'm loyal and good."

With a grunt, Larissa pushed herself up and offered Ella a hand. "Come, I bring dinner. Good food make you feel better." She laughed again. "It always make me feel better." She patted her belly.

Ignoring the offered hand, Ella got up. "Where is your master?"

"He coming back Monday. Master fly airplane all over the world. Lots of business."

"He's a pilot?"

"He know how to fly, but he has many pilots. Master has many planes."

The perv was an airline mogul?

Drug lord would have been a more fitting occupation for a scumbag who bought girls for sex. But what did she know? Lack of morals did not necessarily mean criminal occupation. The guy could run a legitimate business and still be rotten to the core.

She had two more days before he showed up to find out more about him, and she could start by talking to his household manager.

Larissa was the enemy, but she was also a source of information. Not that Ella had any idea what she could possibly learn that would benefit her in any way.

Know thy enemy. Wasn't there a saying like that?

Following Larissa back to the bedroom, Ella glanced at the sitting area where previously she'd seen only a couch and two chairs. Now there was also a round table set for one. "Aren't you going to eat with me?"

The woman eyed the table setting. "I sit with you if you want."

"Thank you. I don't like eating alone."

The truth was that Ella didn't think she could eat at all. She was nauseous, either from the sleeping pills or the fear churning in her stomach. Maybe she could get away with pushing the food around her plate while she coaxed Larissa into talking about her boss.

"Your master's name is Dimitri, right?" she asked when the woman brought another chair to the table and sat down.

"Yes."

"Can you tell me a little bit about him?"

43

MAGNUS

*A*fter reading the message from Arwel, Magnus's first instinct was to punch something. Except, as solidly as the cabin was built, he was mad enough to do some damage. Besides, it would scare Vivian, who was already on edge and barely hanging on.

"Fuck," he muttered under his breath.

How the hell was he going to tell her that the crew had arrived too late to rescue her daughter?

Scarlet whimpered and trotted to the furthest part of the porch, cowering away from the waves of anger and frustration he was emitting.

"It's okay, girl. I'm not mad at you." He crouched. "Come here."

Head hanging low and tail tucked between her legs, she trotted back to him.

"That's a good girl." He scratched behind her ears.

When he'd gotten the update about the uncle not being home, Magnus hadn't even told Vivian about it. It had been a minor setback, and he'd known Turner would find the auction house's address one way or another.

Naturally, he'd told her what he'd thought was the good news about the team getting in position to raid the auction house. Vivian had been a nervous wreck ever since, cooking up a storm for dinner and then eating none of it.

Now he had the most unpleasant duty of delivering the worst news yet.

Ella had been bought and taken away to the buyer's place, and the team was tearing the auction house apart, searching for his identity. They were going to find her, he had no doubt about that, but probably not before the buyer took what he'd paid for, either by coercion or by force.

It was going to devastate Vivian.

"Come on, Scarlet, let's get it over with." He opened the door and let the dog go in first.

In the kitchen, Vivian took one look at his face and paused with the coffee carafe in hand. "What happened?"

He strode toward her, took the carafe, and put it down. "You may want to sit down."

"Oh my God." She paled. "Just spit it out before I get a heart attack."

"They were too late. Ella was already gone by the time they raided the auction house. Apparently, she was bought straight out without being auctioned."

As Vivian's hands started shaking, he quickly added, "At least she wasn't paraded in front of a crowd."

Parker stormed up the stairs to the loft with the dog trotting after him. Thank the Fates for the puppy. Both mother and son needed someone to comfort them, but there was only one of him, and Magnus needed to take care of Vivian first.

A moment later sounds of gunfire filled the space. The boy was taking his frustration out on imaginary bad guys, but the mother had no such outlet.

Frozen in place, she stared at Magnus without seeing

him, the tremors that had started in her hands spreading to the rest of her body. Magnus would've gladly volunteered to be Vivian's punching bag, but the small woman in front of him was in no shape to even make a fist.

In fact, she seemed to be on the verge of collapse.

Instinct taking over, Magnus scooped Vivian up in his arms and carried her to her bedroom. Holding her up with one arm, he lifted the comforter with the other, and laid her on the bed. When she kept shivering even after he'd tucked the blanket around her, he joined her on the bed and pulled her into his arms together with the comforter.

"They are going to find Ella. And I'm not just saying that to make you feel better. I know Turner, and I know the guys he took with him. They are the best there is. It's just taking a little longer. That's all."

Slowly, the shivering subsided. "I can't imagine what she's going through," Vivian whispered.

His thoughts exactly, but he had to give her something better than that. "She is young and she will survive. We will get her the best therapy there is to make her forget and move on with her life." To help the girl put the ordeal behind her, he would gladly thrall Ella himself, but for some reason, the clan therapist was against it.

Something about the memories remaining in the subconscious, and if not dealt with, poisoning the victim from the inside. He had to trust Vanessa's professional opinion.

With a sigh, Vivian freed her arms from the cocoon he'd wrapped her in and put them around him. "You're such a good man, Magnus. I don't know what I would have done without you." She put her forehead on his chest. "You have such a big, strong heart."

Damn.

As long as Vivian had been distressed, her proximity hadn't affected him. He was there because she needed comfort, and not for any other reason. Except, he wasn't a saint, and now that she'd calmed down, he was reminded of that, and in a moment, she'd realize it too.

He had to pull back.

"Don't go," she said when he lifted his arm off her. "I need you."

Okay... maybe he could shift his hips back a little and still have his arm around her.

Except, as soon as he'd done that, Vivian snuggled even closer. There was no way she didn't feel him, even through the comforter. He was still wearing the loose nylon pants he'd put on for the staff training with Parker, and those were no barrier at all.

He now understood the appeal of jeans. The thick fabric held things in place and prevented embarrassing moments like this.

"I'm sorry," he murmured into her fragrant hair. "I can't help the response."

"It's okay. I don't mind."

Right... apparently she didn't mind torturing him.

At least he hadn't turned on the lights and the room was dark, so she couldn't see the other signs of his arousal. As long as he kept his eyes closed, and his fangs away from her, he was good.

"Am I making you uncomfortable?" Vivian whispered.

"You could say so."

"I like it that you're such a gentleman."

He snorted. "I don't feel very gentlemanly."

"It feels different here in the dark with you. It's like the world doesn't exist outside the circle of your arms."

She was killing him. Didn't she realize that what she was saying sounded like an invitation to sex?

44

VIVIAN

What am I doing? Vivian thought as soon as the words left her mouth.

Magnus sucked in a breath and tried to pull away in an effort to hide his hard-on. Again.

It was the honest truth, and she'd meant every word, but she hadn't meant for it to sound like a seduction.

For some inexplicable reason, feeling him get hard for her was reassuring. Right now, his primal response felt like the only solid thing in her liquid world. She was drowning, and he was her life raft.

Apparently, desperation had an odd effect on her.

Everyone responded differently to trauma. For some it triggered the flight or fight response, while others froze in place, unable to make the decision to either run or hide.

Her response seemed to be to seek the protection of a strong man.

Admittedly, it wasn't very flattering to her ego, but right now she was beyond caring about stuff like that.

It didn't matter that she'd been on her own for years,

supporting her family and managing just fine without a man, and it didn't matter that she had Magnus's protection whether she had sex with him or not.

When her world was falling apart, and she felt like her life energy had been drained away, leaving her cold and empty, she could count on him to replenish it.

On a rational level, it didn't make any sense.

But Vivian wasn't thinking with her head. She was thinking with some primitive feminine part of her that was drawn to Magnus like a starving succubus who needed to feed on the man's sexual energy or shrivel away and die.

If she was honest about it, though, using Magnus like that was degrading to her and unfair to him.

It was difficult to admit, and she couldn't look into his eyes when she confessed her need. "I feel empty, Magnus. Depleted. There is nothing left inside of me to give. I can only take."

"Tell me what you need, and it's yours." He stroked her hair.

"Can you make love to me? Can you lend me your energy and your life force when I have nothing to give back?"

Hesitantly, she lifted her eyes to him.

There was a good chance he might refuse her request despite his obvious attraction to her. Magnus might think that she was in shock and talking nonsense. In which case he'd decline politely, telling her that her mind wasn't in the right place and that her decision-making ability was impaired.

That was what she would have thought if she'd heard a woman talk like that. Except, she knew the instinct wasn't wrong.

In the dark, Vivian hadn't expected to see Magnus's eyes. But when he opened them, she was taken aback, not only because the hunger in them seemed even greater than hers, but because they glowed. From the inside.

"There is nothing I would deny you, Vivian. Not my body, not my energy, and not my very soul. Everything I have is yours for the taking."

That was so much more than she'd expected. "Why?"

"I don't know. I've never felt so strongly about anyone before. It just feels right. Maybe we are both a little looney right now." He cupped her cheek and pressed a soft kiss to her lips. "But I'm fine with a few moments of insanity. Are you?"

"Yes."

"Don't move from this spot." He got off the bed. "I'm going to check on Parker and then lock the door."

At least one of them was still thinking straight, and it wasn't her. Not that Parker ever wandered into her bedroom at night, not since he was a toddler. But locking the door was a good idea.

It was too dark to see anything, but as the door opened, the sounds of gunfire and explosions drifted down from the loft and then were cut off when the door closed again.

Vivian heard the lock click into place, and then Magnus's nearly silent footsteps on the hardwood floor.

The bed dipped as he got in.

"Close your eyes, Vivian, and keep them closed until I tell you to open them."

"Okay." She couldn't see anything anyway.

Which meant that he couldn't see her either, and that was good.

With her pretty face and lush hair and the right push-up bra, Vivian could look good when dressed. But not so much in the nude. Flat-chested and bony, with no muscle definition, her body was far from sexy.

"I'm going to take care of you, love." His words came out a

little slurred. Perhaps he was drunk on the moment because she knew he hadn't touched alcohol. "You don't need to move a muscle. Just lie back and feel."

Vivian couldn't do anything more than that even if she tried, and she was grateful to Magnus for understanding that.

It should have felt awkward to go straight from their first and only kiss, one which had been abruptly interrupted, to being undressed by a man she'd met only two days ago. And yet, it felt incredibly right.

As Magnus peeled the comforter off her, she expected him to fumble in the dark, but he seemed to know exactly where everything was. He hadn't kissed or caressed her as he took off her clothes. In moments, he had her fully naked, which again, should have felt awkward and yet didn't.

"So beautiful," he whispered.

It was sweet of him to say, but there was no way he could see her. And yet, even though her eyes were closed, she could feel his gaze upon her, and it sent shivers of desire up her spine.

"You're cold." Magnus covered her with his body—his fully nude and very aroused body.

When did he take off his clothes?

Propping himself on his forearms, he wasn't giving her his full weight. Vivian wrapped her arms around him and brought him closer to her. Smooth skin, warmth, and a manly scent to trump all others.

"I'm too heavy."

"No, you're not. You're just right."

Even though he was a foot taller and outweighed her by at least a hundred pounds, Magnus felt perfect to her.

Except, she hadn't been with a man in years, and what she'd felt between her legs was proportionate in size to the rest of him. It might hurt, but she was okay with that too.

More than okay.

Not because she was a masochist, far from it, but because the physical pain just might overshadow the ache in her heart.

Anything was better than that.

45

MAGNUS

*M*agnus's conscience and his self-respect were a tangle of contradicting emotions.

On the one hand, he felt like an ass for taking advantage of Vivian and accepting what she was offering. Emotionally, she was in a bad place, and her offer hadn't been the result of some great desire for him, but an escape from reality. What seemed to her like a good idea now, might seem like a mistake later.

But on the other hand, how could he deny her?

Regardless of her motives, Vivian needed him right now, and there was little else he could give her to make her feel better. So what if she was using him?

Magnus didn't mind.

Well, not exactly. He would take her any way he could, but that didn't mean he was satisfied with that.

Even though he had no right, what Magnus wanted was for Vivian to fall for him and crave him with the same intensity that he craved her. Not out of desperation, but out of a sense of connection, of undeniable attraction.

The attraction had been there from the start, but it

seemed like he was the only one feeling the connection. Which, again, given the circumstances, was not a big surprise. If Vivian's head was not focused on her daughter, she might have been more attuned to that special something that was blooming between them.

But this wasn't about him and what he wanted. This was about Vivian and what she needed. Besides, he had no right to even think about connection. All he could ever give her was precisely what she was asking for.

Great sex.

He'd better make it count.

Stretched out over her, he captured her lips in a tender kiss. As he slipped his tongue inside her mouth, Vivian arched beneath him, her tight nipples rubbing against his chest. The thought of sucking on one of those buds had Magnus's mouth water, but he didn't want to rush things.

Besides, her slender neck was calling to him too, and it definitely deserved his attention.

All of her did.

By the time he was done with her, Magnus intended to kiss every little bit of her petite body and find all of her erogenous spots, so he could come back later and tease them individually.

Learning all about a woman's body was as important as learning all about her likes and dislikes and quirks. Maybe even more.

It was certainly easier and more useful.

Men thought that women were complicated and hard to please. But that was a load of crap. A well-pleasured woman would let her man get away with many small misdeeds and mishaps, especially if he remembered to compliment her regularly and tell her how beautiful and desirable he found her.

It was as simple as that.

The problem was, that in order to test his theory, more than occasional hookups were required. He would need to be in a relationship.

A pang of sorrow pierced Magnus's heart as he thought of having it with Vivian. His perfect woman.

That didn't mean he couldn't fulfill the first part of the experiment, though. He could still learn how to pleasure her into oblivion. And oblivion was exactly what she needed now.

Kissing her neck, he flicked his tongue over the spot he was later going to bite, but it was a dangerous place to linger on, so he kept going down, kissing and licking her collarbone on his way to those perky peaks that he was dying to taste.

But as he got closer, Vivian tensed and pushed her hands between them to cover her breasts.

"What's the matter, *leannan*? I'm not going to bite." Not yet, anyway.

"I don't want you to be disappointed," she said in a barely audible whisper.

"Nothing about you can ever do that." He pulled her hands away from her breasts, up over her head, and then gripped both wrists in one of his.

"Why were you trying to hide such sweet berries from me?" He dipped his head and licked one turgid nub, and then the other. "Sweet as can be." He sucked one into his mouth.

If she had a retort on the ready, it had died on her lips the moment his tongue touched her nipple. Her breasts might be small, but they were highly responsive. Just the way he liked them. "You're perfect in every possible way."

Her breasts were worthy of prolonged worship, but they would have to wait for the second round of the night. There was more to making a woman ready than stimulating her nipples, and by the way his erection was throbbing, Magnus wasn't going to last.

It wasn't as if he were huge, maybe only a little larger than the average male because he was also taller than average, but Vivian was so small in comparison that he might as well be. On top of that, it had been a while for her.

With so much pent-up craving, Magnus knew that once he got inside her, he wasn't going to be gentle.

She needed plenty of preparation.

Releasing his grip on her wrists, he slid further down, kissing a trail all the way to her soft petals.

"Oh, my God." Vivian arched up sharply.

He put a hand on her belly and pressed another soft kiss to the top of her slit. The feminine scent of her arousal was like a drug to him, making him dizzy and inducing a euphoric elation like what he imagined his venom did to a female.

"So lovely." He nuzzled between her folds.

She tried to scoot back, but he would have none of that. He wasn't hurting her, and there was no place for shame or embarrassment in this intimate moment between them.

Except, perhaps Vivian was apprehensive and needed reassurance that she smelled terrific to him?

He lifted his head and looked at her, checking to see if she was still following his command and keeping her eyes closed.

She was. Apparently, Vivian was a woman of her word.

Fates, it was just one more reason to fall for her.

Right, as if he needed to be convinced.

"I just love your scent. If I could, I would bottle it up and carry it around with me, but then I would be perpetually hard, and I'd have trouble walking straight."

Her eyes still closed, a small smile lifted one corner of Vivian's lips.

Pushing a hand under her small bottom and cupping both cheeks at once, Magnus darted his tongue out to taste her, and as he'd expected, the taste was just as intoxicating as the scent.

As he sucked and kissed and licked, Vivian moaned softly, turning her head sideways to muffle her sounds of pleasure in a pillow.

Magnus was willing to bet that when free to do so, she would be much louder.

He wondered how she would respond to him when the sex was about the joy of living, and the pleasure of the two becoming one, and not about dispelling sadness and seeking respite from desperation.

When he felt Vivian's bottom clench in his palm, Magnus knew that she was getting close, but so was he. This time around, there would be no prolonging the pleasure until she could stand it no more.

Pushing two fingers inside her tight sheath, he drew her clit into his mouth and sucked.

Vivian came so beautifully, her entire body arching up and her blond hair spilling over the pillow, that he just had to give her another one even though fighting his own need was becoming nearly impossible.

46

VIVIAN

*O*ne moment Vivian was coming down from her second orgasm, and the next Magnus was on top of her, his shaft poised at her entrance.

After seeing to her pleasure so selflessly, she expected him to spear into her right away, but he didn't, even though it must've been torture for him.

He was such a giving lover, so attuned to her needs.

What was he waiting for, though?

She was beyond ready.

Then it dawned on her that Magnus might be waiting for her to tell him that she was, or at least give him a sign.

If she could only see his expression.

It was so tempting to open her eyes and look at him. But first of all she'd promised she wouldn't, and secondly, it was too dark to see. For some reason, it had seemed important to him. Maybe he had some deformities he didn't want her to see? Old injuries?

After all, he was a soldier, and soldiers got hurt.

Silly man. As if she cared about unimportant things like

that. Besides, he had nothing to worry about because it was too dark for her to see anything.

Then again, she'd covered her small breasts because she'd been afraid to disappoint him. That had been silly too. But then Magnus didn't need to see them to know that they were tiny. Touch revealed just as much.

Nevertheless, he'd told her she was beautiful and perfect.

He'd either lied or had an excellent night vision. Since she didn't think he was dishonest, it must have been the vision.

That would explain his request, or rather demand, that she keep her eyes closed. Since he could see her, Magnus assumed that she could see him.

Wrapping her arms around his trim waist, she whispered, "I want to feel you inside me."

As soon as the brave words had left her mouth, though, Vivian clenched in anticipation, holding her breath. This was going to hurt.

Except, as his erection slid into place, sheathing itself inside her in one powerful thrust, the fit was perfect. It was as if they were custom made for each other.

"Oh," she groaned.

Magnus stilled, his face hovering a couple of inches above hers, and his harsh breaths fanning over her cheeks.

"Don't stop. It was a good *oh*."

As his breath came out in a whoosh, he drew his hips back, pulling almost all the way out, before slamming back. Again, and again, and again.

Vivian could do little more than fist her hands in the sheet and hold on for dear life as he pounded into her.

Bracing one hand against the headboard, Magnus pushed the other one under her bottom, the same way he'd done when he'd pleasured her with his tongue, and kept going. She liked the feel of his big hand cupping her like that, this time holding her for his pleasure.

She was like a rag doll in the hands of this powerful man, completely possessed in a way she'd never been possessed before. And it was a possession, not lovemaking, not sex, but a taking that could've been brutal if not for how carefully he'd prepared her.

Building up momentum, another orgasm was about to explode over her, which was a total surprise since Vivian had never come from penetration alone before.

She was about to now.

When Magnus's shaft thickened inside her, and he let out a harsh groan, the impulse to see this magnificent man climaxing was just too overwhelming to deny.

Not expecting to see anything, Vivian opened her eyes, but what she saw could not have been real.

Magnus's eyes were glowing from the inside. This time she had no doubt about it because they cast light on his entire face, illuminating a pair of huge fangs.

It must have been a hallucination. Her mind had finally snapped under pressure. But even as a hallucination it was terrifying.

Faint with fear, Vivian quickly closed her eyes, and listening to instinct, she offered her neck to the predator hovering above her.

A loud hiss preceded the twin pinpricks of his fangs, and the searing pain they inflicted was certainly no hallucination. But just as soon as the pain registered, it dissipated, replaced by a feeling of unimaginable bliss.

When he'd bitten her, Vivian hadn't cried out, but she did when the mother of all orgasms came barreling down on her with the force of a nuclear-powered torpedo.

Through the haze, she heard Magnus calling out her name as his climax shot out of him, but his voice got drowned by another explosion rocking her body, and then another, and another.

Consciousness returned slowly.

It was like drifting down from a fluffy cloud, a piece of it still clinging to her and cushioning her descent.

Even though her body was touching the mattress under it, Vivian felt buoyant, made light by the peace and satisfaction flapping their soft wings inside of her. She didn't want to open her eyes, she didn't want to come down from whatever high she was soaring on. She wanted to stay in this peaceful nowhere world where she had no worries.

"Hello, *mo leannan.*" Strong fingers traced her nose, moved to her cheek, and then feathered over her lips. "Did you sleep well?"

"Uhm. I don't want to wake up."

"Then keep on sleeping. I'll keep you safe."

She lifted a hand toward his voice, putting it on his hard chest. "You're so warm. Come closer."

His arms wrapped around her and pulled her to him. "Better?"

"Yes."

She had a hazy recollection of what had happened between them. Magnus, as his name implied, had been magnificent. Before him, Vivian had had only three lovers, so she wasn't an authority on male prowess, but the way he'd made her feel was like nothing she'd ever experienced before.

Except, she couldn't remember how it ended.

Had she orgasmed again?

The only two she remembered had been the ones he'd given her with his mouth. She also remembered how amazing he'd felt inside her, but she couldn't remember him climaxing, and whether she had climaxed again or not.

Though, given the languid drunk feeling, she must've. It was like being intoxicated but with none of the unpleasant side effects. Everything was fuzzy, but nothing ached.

"I didn't think it was possible to pass out from sexual bliss, but apparently I was wrong."

His mouth came down on her, his lips warm and soft as he gave her the gentlest of kisses. "My beauty."

Did that mean he was her beast?

The thought made her chuckle. He'd certainly pounded into her like one, but Magnus was no beast. He was her prince.

47

TURNER

*N*ight had fallen by the time Turner was done going over the tapes. The most difficult part had been watching Ella's viewing. Not wanting to add insult to injury, he'd averted his eyes when she'd removed her robe, but he'd still had to listen to the proxy's cultured voice as she coldly took part in the humiliation of a young girl.

For the first time since turning immortal, his venom glands had filled up and his fangs had elongated in aggression and not in arousal. The sensation was very different. He wondered if the other immortal males felt it so acutely.

Probably not.

Transitioning as young teenagers, they were bombarded with so many hormonal changes that the lines between aggression and sexual desire were probably blurred for them.

He was pretty sure, though, that Julian would've reacted the same way he had. In fact, it was good that the guy hadn't come with them. He would've lost his shit if he saw that tape.

Once the mission was over, Turner planned on erasing it and then destroying the hard drive so no trace of it remained.

In fact, he could erase it now. Throughout the viewing, the proxy had been sitting in a dark room and all the cameras had been turned on Ella. There was nothing in that portion of the recording he needed. Except, it was bad protocol to erase even seemingly irrelevant evidence before the victim was retrieved, the perpetrators punished, and the case closed.

"Arwel, I need the hard drives of all the computers removed, except for that one." He pointed at the one he was sitting in front of. That was going to be left for the police to use as evidence against the people running the auction house.

He'd copied the information already. What was on the other computers, he was going to destroy after the mission was completed. "We are taking them with us. Have your guys on it."

"Consider it done."

Turner pulled out his phone and dialed Bridget.

She picked up on the first ring. "What's up, Victor? Did you find anything?"

"I have the proxy's face. I found a good close-up that I've already sent to William to run through his facial recognition program."

"Didn't she give her name to whoever was in charge there when she came in? Don't they keep records of their customers?"

"She did. The very imaginative Madame X. None of the names are real. All the buyers and their proxies use pseudonyms. All I know for now is that she is in her mid-forties, has a Bostonian accent, and sounds well-educated."

"That's not giving us much. I'm glad William can find her using her picture."

"By the looks of her, she's had some work done. I just hope none of it was done since she'd applied for her last driver's license. I also sent William a recording of her voice. Maybe it can help in some way."

"I don't think he has a program for that, although he might want to look into it. Between YouTube and Facebook and all the blogging channels and podcasts, there are a lot of voice signatures out there."

"My thoughts exactly. But that's a discussion for another day. I thought we would be coming home tonight and I made no overnight arrangements. I need hotel rooms for the girls and for the Guardians."

"What are you going to do with the employees of the auction house?"

He leaned back in the office chair he'd been sitting in for the past several hours. "Scramble their memories and have them wait patiently for the police to arrive. Hopefully, they will confess their crimes and sing the names of their bosses."

"Arwel's work?"

"Not yet, but he's going to do that before we leave, so the thrall will be fresh once the police arrive. Can you book the hotel rooms for us?"

"Sure. Give me a few moments. I want to check with Kian if we can use any of the clan's properties in New York."

"Thanks."

Turner got up and headed for the kitchen, where he'd left the girls a couple of hours ago. The sound of their excited conversation died out the moment he entered.

"Is there a problem?" he asked.

"When are we leaving?" Rose asked. "We've been waiting here for hours."

"I'm having hotel rooms reserved for tonight. I suggest you pack your belongings and whatever else you want to take with you."

Rose lifted a brow. "Are we allowed to loot?"

"The way I see it, these people owe you much more than whatever you can take from here."

"I don't want anything. It has bad juju," one of the other girls said.

Two of the others nodded in agreement.

Rose didn't share their superstitions. "There isn't much to take anyway. I only want the pillow from my room. I like it."

When his phone buzzed in his pocket, Turner excused himself and stepped out into the corridor.

"What do you have for me?"

Bridget chuckled. "I love you too. Anyway, we have vacancies in one of our hotels, and the good news is that since it's new, the transition team is headed by a clan member. His name is Ragnar Bowen. I already spoke with him and he is reserving an entire floor for you."

"I only need five rooms with double beds. One of the Guardians is going to stay with the prisoners in the jet."

"Prisoners? I thought you had only one."

"For now. I intend to collect the uncle as well."

"Good thinking. Get the perspective of the ringleaders. But back to the hotel. An entire floor is only eight rooms. It's one of the small boutique ones Kian is into lately. Ragnar said he can program the elevator to stop on the thirty-sixth floor only for those who have keycards to the rooms on it."

"What about room service? I don't want to take the girls out to a restaurant."

"I'm sure it can be arranged."

"Thanks. I appreciate it." He hesitated for a moment. "I love you, Bridget. I know I don't say it enough."

She chuckled. "That's okay. I don't expect you to. I was just teasing. Call me when you're in bed?"

"If I get a chance to get to bed, I will. Once William has something for me, I'll get moving no matter what time it is."

"I understand. Good luck."

48

MAGNUS

*M*agnus hadn't slept much. How could he close his eyes with Vivian snuggled up against him, looking so peaceful and relaxed?

By morning, that angelic expression would be gone, replaced by a pinched one, and he hadn't had his fill of that beautiful face yet.

Not that he ever would. He could stare at Vivian for eternity.

The problem was that morning was fast approaching. Outside the window, the sky was getting lighter, which meant that soon he would have to leave her side and tiptoe to his own bedroom.

Parker had played his games well into the night, so it would be some time before the kid got up, but as much as Magnus would've liked to stay and hold Vivian for a little longer, he didn't want to take any chances. It was better to get moving and start his day.

Scooting away as carefully as he could, he got out of bed, picked up his clothes and shoes off the floor, and padded to his bedroom through the connecting bathroom. His clothes went into the dirty pile, and he picked a set of fresh ones from his duffle bag before going back to grab a shower.

As he stood under the spray, he thought about that open duffle bag and the clothes neatly folded inside it. Living out of a suitcase was standard operating procedure when on missions, especially ones that were supposed to be over in a day or two.

Except, even though this was only his third day with Vivian and Parker, it felt like so much more, like this was his life, and what had come before it had somehow faded, feeling less real.

Wishful thinking, that was what it was.

A ready-made family that he could pretend was his but never would be.

Humans and immortals didn't mix.

With a sigh, he went back to thinking about more practical matters. Things hadn't gone as smoothly as they had all anticipated, and the mission was not nearly over. He would need to do laundry.

Showered and dressed, he headed to the kitchen and started the coffee maker. At the sounds of nails skidding on the smooth hardwood floor, he turned around to greet Scarlet.

"Good morning." He crouched in front of her. "Have you been a good girl and didn't pee in Parker's bed?"

Tail wagging, she jumped into his lap and started licking his face.

"Is that a yes, I was a good girl? Or is it look how cute I am and don't get mad at me?"

The dog licked his face again.

"I guess I'll have to check." He pushed up to his feet. "Come on, let me take you outside first."

Holding on to her long leash, Magnus let her roam around while checking his messages. He'd done so several times during the night, but there was a new update from Arwel about William finding the proxy's name by running her photo through the facial recognition program. The hacker team was still working on finding her current whereabouts.

Unfortunately, there was nothing in this or the other messages he'd gotten throughout the night that would be encouraging news for Vivian.

When Scarlet finished doing her business behind her favorite bush, she trotted back, and pushed her head between his legs, which was her way of asking for love.

Magnus put his phone back in his pocket and bent down to scratch behind her ears. "Good girl. Let's go inside."

At some point, he needed to start her training. For now, though, he was just enjoying her company. Scarlet was always happy to see him, gave him unconditional love, and when his roommates were busy, which was most of the time, he had someone to talk to.

Pathetic, but except for the few lucky ones who'd found Dormants, that was life for most immortals. And to think humans coveted immortality. He wondered how many would've chosen it if they knew what they'd be giving up.

When he stepped back inside, Vivian and Parker were still asleep. Scarlet started going up the stairs to the loft, but the moment he opened the bag of puppy chow and refilled her bowl, she reversed direction and came back down.

Maybe the same tactic would work on the other inhabitants of the cabin.

He could make scrambled eggs, hash browns and toast—the classic American breakfast—for Vivian and Parker. For himself, he could open a can of beans and cook them in tomato sauce. He'd forgotten to buy mushrooms, and he wasn't a big fan of sausages, so that was as far as his Scottish breakfast went.

"Good morning." Vivian shuffled into the kitchen and sat on a stool. "What smells so good?"

He wanted to take her into his arms and kiss her, but even though she was smiling, Vivian appeared distant. When he looked at her, she didn't look into his eyes, pretending to observe what he was cooking, and when he moved to come closer, she instinctively leaned away.

He didn't need to be a mind reader to get the hint.

Vivian was acting as if last night hadn't happened.

Planting a smile on his face, Magnus pointed to the three pans he had going. "American and Scottish breakfasts. Scrambled eggs, hash browns, and toast. That's the American part of it. The only Scottish addition is the beans in tomato sauce. Would you like to try some?"

"Sure. It sounds weird to eat beans for breakfast, but I'm willing to give it a try. What else do Scots eat for breakfast?"

"In addition to eggs and toast, many like to eat black pudding or some other type of sausage for breakfast, sometimes both, mushrooms, grilled tomato, and beans in tomato sauce. Also potato cakes. I like to put the beans on my toast."

He poured her a cup of coffee. "Cream. No sugar."

"Thank you. Do you miss Scotland?"

"Sometimes. Mostly I miss my friends and family."

She took a sip. "What made you move to the States?"

"A compelling job offer." He poured himself a second cup. "I guess I have a wee bit of a hero complex. I liked the idea of rescuing girls from bad situations."

She nodded into her cup. "So this is what you do full time?"

"No, not all of the time." He didn't want to get into explaining things that would force him to lie to her.

"I guess you can't talk about the other things."

He flipped the eggs and stirred the beans. "I'd rather not."

"Do you need help in there?"

"You could hand me three plates. That is if Parker is awake."

She got up and pulled two out of the dishwasher. "I don't expect him to get up before noon."

"That's a shame. I was planning on taking you both on a walk through the woods and collecting sticks for arrows." He loaded the two plates and put them on the counter. "Before this is over, I want to teach him how to shoot. And for that we need to make arrows."

As Vivian flinched, he wondered if the reaction was about him teaching her son to shoot, or about the reminder that their time together would soon be coming to an end.

VIVIAN

"What's the matter?" Parker asked as Scarlet stopped and started barking.

A rustle in the bushes was the only warning they got before the dog leaped forward, yanking the leash out of Parker's hand and galloping after the poor creature who'd made the noise.

Vivian hoped the puppy was too young to catch the animal. Nature was brutal, she knew that, but she was in no mood to witness it firsthand.

Magnus, who'd been several steps behind her, dropped the bundle of sticks he'd collected and sprinted after the dog with speed rivaling that of an Olympian champion.

Heck, Vivian had never seen anyone run that fast. His legs and arms were a blur. As she watched with eyes peeled wide, Magnus caught up to the dog, leaped for her, and picked her up while still running.

Vivian was impressed. To perform such feats of athleticism, Magnus must've been a triathlon champion. And if he wasn't, he should enter a competition. It would be an easy win.

Not happy about it, Scarlet growled at him as menacingly as a Golden Retriever puppy could.

"Behave!" His stern voice was enough to turn the growling into a whimper.

"It's okay, girl." He patted her head. "Just don't do that again. There are hungry beasts out here who'd love to have a puppy for a midmorning snack."

The tail started wagging again and she rewarded him with a sloppy lick to his face.

Putting her down, Magnus took hold of the leash and handed it to Parker. "Hold on tight. Wrap it around your wrist. She is not strong enough to yank too hard yet. But when she's fully-grown, don't do that. She might break it."

"I'm sorry," Parker said as he took the leash.

"Nothing to be sorry about. Could have happened to any of us."

Vivian doubted it. Not only were Magnus's responses incredibly fast, but he also wasn't even breathing hard after his sprint. Now that she was watching him more closely, she was noticing things she hadn't before, like the fluidity of every move as he collected the sticks he'd dropped. Everything he did seemed so effortless, so graceful.

Almost unnatural.

Perhaps that was an exaggeration, but Magnus was definitely a rare specimen.

"Is this good?" Parker picked up a stick.

"It's the right thickness, but it's bent wrong. Look for ones that are mostly straight."

As Magnus and Parker kept searching for more right-sized sticks to make arrows from, Vivian pretended to be busy helping them look, when in fact she was falling behind because she wanted to put some distance between them and have a little alone time to think and reflect.

The morning after had been difficult. Most of her female

friends complained about men acting indifferent after hookups and running off as soon as they could.

Vivian had the opposite problem. She would've welcomed indifference. Instead, Magnus had been acting like a besotted teenager who'd fallen in love with his first sex partner.

Well, that was another exaggeration, but he was definitely acting as if the sex was the start of a relationship that he would've very much liked to pursue.

The role of the indifferent morning-after partner had fallen to her, and it had been a tough one to pull off because she was anything but.

The worst, though, was the lost puppy expression on Magnus's big, tough warrior's face. It twisted Vivian's gut and added an extra dose of guilt to an already guilt-ridden conscience.

Not only had she let herself enjoy amazing sex while Ella was going through God knew what kind of torment, but she'd also allowed herself to lead on a good man who didn't deserve to be used and then cast aside.

It was so obvious that he wanted more from her. This morning, when he'd made breakfast for her and Parker, Magnus's inner struggle had been clearly evident even though he'd been making a valiant effort to hide it.

He'd wanted to embrace her, to kiss her, and she'd wanted that too, but it would've been wrong to keep leading him on.

Last night had been a one-time mistake born out of weakness and desperation. In the darkness, she could pretend as if nothing aside from the two of them existed. But in the light of day, reality had come rushing in, and with it shame and guilt, but mostly fear.

Any man she developed feelings for ended up dead.

Magnus could ridicule her conviction all he wanted, but she knew that those seemingly random deaths could not have been a coincidence.

She wasn't the only one to think that.

After Al's death, people at work had stopped introducing her to single men they knew, and she'd overheard the term 'black widow' whispered behind her back more than once.

And those were people who liked her and considered her a friend. Thank God she lived in the age of reason, or as reasonable as human beings could ever get.

Four centuries ago, the consequences of those seemingly random deaths would've been much worse. She would've been accused of witchcraft and burned at the stake.

The regrettable truth was that people were not rational creatures and were ruled by emotions rather than logic.

"Mom, did you find any good sticks?" Parker called.

"I'm still looking."

Magnus turned around with a frown. "Stay close to me, Vivian. Don't wander off."

"Okay."

Closing the distance while keeping her eyes on the ground, she bumped into a solid wall of muscle. "Oh, I'm sorry. I wasn't watching where I was going."

"I'm not," he said quietly. "Any way I can get your hands on me is good."

With a quick glance toward Parker and Scarlet, Vivian took a step back. "We can't," she whispered without looking into his eyes.

"We'll talk later," he said in a tone that brooked no rebuttal.

Ugh, why the hell did she find his assertiveness so sexy?

Up until last night, she'd thought Magnus was easy-going, accommodating, even sweet. But then he'd shown her a different facet of himself, and she would be lying if she claimed it hadn't been a major turn-on.

There was something uber-sexy about a man who was a

fierce protector, good with children and with dogs, polite, kind, attentive, and also assertive in the bedroom.

Except, as amazing as Magnus was, she couldn't allow herself to fall for him. As long as she kept her heart locked up, he was safe from her curse.

Who was she kidding, though?

Vivian could deny it all she wanted, but she already had feelings for him—scary forbidden feelings like seeing him as a life partner and a father figure to Parker and Ella.

Get a grip, Viv.

Those kinds of thoughts were dangerous. They would get this wonderful man killed, and she would never forgive herself if anything happened to him.

"I think we have enough," Magnus said.

Parker looked doubtful. "I have five. How many do you have?"

"Seven."

Vivian lifted the two she'd found. "That makes it fourteen. I think that's plenty of arrows."

"I agree." Magnus took the sticks from her and added them to his bundle. "It will take us the rest of the day to prepare that many, and you're not done with the bow yet. I want us to start practicing before it gets dark."

Parker's face fell. "Maybe we can do only three arrows today and the rest tomorrow? That way we'll have more time to practice shooting."

"Sounds like a plan."

ELLA

It was Ella's second day on the estate, but since she was locked in, all she'd seen were her room, the balcony, and the grounds visible from there.

After spending many hours sitting on the lounger and watching the outdoors, she'd counted five gardeners and eight patrolmen. Every hour or so, two men would walk in front of her balcony. She assumed they circled the house's perimeter, and although they all kind of looked the same, they weren't.

The estate must be so big that it took several hours to complete a full circle on foot, and in order to have every spot patrolled once an hour, several pairs were needed, leaving the starting point in regular one-hour intervals.

The good news was that they were methodical. The patrols arrived like clockwork with no surprises thrown in to mix things up.

If Ella wanted to run, she would have to do it a few minutes after a patrol passed her balcony.

It was a hypothetical escape. A thought exercise. As long as her family was held hostage, she wouldn't dare make a move. But just in case she somehow discovered that they were safe, it would be good to have a plan. Besides, she had nothing better to do.

If she timed it just right, she could have a couple of hours before her escape was discovered.

Since Larissa checked up on her only when delivering meals, after lunch would be a good time. The housekeeper wouldn't be back until dinner.

The problem with that was that Ella didn't know which direction to head in, and whether there were any neighbors nearby who would be willing to call the police for her.

Besides, there were too many holes in that plan and the consequences of failure were terrifying. With the number of guys patrolling the grounds, she wouldn't get far before she was discovered. Larissa might decide to bring her a snack between lunch and dinner and find out that Ella had escaped.

Even if her family's safety was not on the line, the chances of making it out of the grounds were not good enough to take a risk.

Ella was desperate, but not stupid.

As if to prove her right, she heard the door to her room open even though it wasn't lunch time yet. Breakfast had been less than two hours ago.

"Ella, where you are?" Larissa called out.

"Balcony!"

"Come in. The clothes are here."

"And what about me?" said a heavily accented, nasal male voice.

"Pavel is here with the clothes," Larissa added.

Intrigued, Ella got off the lounger and went to see who Pavel was, and what was the deal with the clothes.

As she entered the room, a lanky guy in tight pants that didn't quite reach his bare ankles pushed inside a rolling rack overstuffed with clothes. There were already two like it in the room, with garments in all shapes and colors hanging from them, some still wrapped in the manufacturers' plastic bags, and some not.

"What's all that?" She pointed at the racks.

Pavel sauntered toward her and gave her a critical once-over. "Those, my dear Ella, are your new clothes. I'm here to make you presentable enough to meet the queen." He offered her his hand.

She shook it. "What queen?"

"Any queen." He rolled his eyes. "When I'm done with you, you're going to look elegant, sophisticated, and know how to sit, and how to stand, and which forks to use when. The boss wants you to look and behave like a lady."

Then he should have bought someone older who'd gone to a finishing school.

But of course, Ella didn't say that. Instead, she sat on the couch and leaned forward, bracing her elbows on her knees and her chin on her fists.

Displeased with her slouchy posture, Pavel shook his head. "I see that we have a lot of work to do." He turned to Larissa. "I need a full dinner setup for two, and a five-course meal. How long will it take to make it happen?"

"I need to ask cook. Maybe hour, good?"

"An hour is good." He gave her a light push toward the door. "Chop, chop. I need to get to work."

When Larissa left, he sauntered over and crouched in front of Ella. "Let me see what I have to work with."

As he took her hands in his, his demeanor changed from flamboyant to dead serious. "Listen to me," he whispered. "Drop the teenage games and surly attitude and cooperate to the best of your ability. This is the only way you're going to survive this."

He let go of her hands and leaned back, his expression reverting to the flamboyant fashion diva persona. "Such a gorgeous face. A little mascara, that's all you need." He tilted his head sideways. "And maybe some lip gloss. Anything more and you'll look like a painted doll." He wagged his finger. "A lesser artist might have covered this beauty with unnecessary paints, but not Pavel. I'll make you look fabulous."

And he did.

For the next hour or so, Ella tried outfit after outfit, with Pavel dismissing most, approving some, and clapping his hands in delight for a few.

When they were done, his favorites were hanging on one rack, the maybes on another, and the no ways crowding on the third.

Pavel had good taste, expensive taste, but she would've chosen none of the outfits he had. The Chanel skirt and jacket combos were beautiful but too conservative for her taste. Heck, even the wives of the British princes didn't dress that old. But at least he wasn't dressing her like a bimbo.

"Now shoes." He opened the door, dragged in a large cardboard box, and closed the door behind him.

Apparently, Larissa hadn't thought Ella could slip away with Pavel watching her, and she hadn't locked them in.

The thing was, it would not have made a difference even if the door was unlocked. By now, Ella had figured out that the entire place was swarming with surveillance cameras and patrolmen. She hadn't found one in her room, but Pavel's behavior from before meant that they were hidden somewhere.

Hopefully, there were none in the bathroom, but that was probably wishful thinking.

"Larissa told me your shoe size, but just to be on the safe side, I brought each in half a size smaller and half a size bigger." He pulled out the first box, opened it, and lifted one red-soled black pump.

Ella didn't remember the brand's name, but she'd read about red-soled shoes in one of her mother's billionaire romances. Supposedly, they were insanely pricey.

Not that she gave a damn. Fancy shit didn't impress her.

Pavel made a production of kneeling at her feet and presenting the shoe. "Is Cinderella ready to try on her glass slipper?"

Ella cast him an incredulous look.

This was no fairytale, she was no Cinderella, and Dimitri was no prince.

Using the analogy, though, Ella would have happily traded places with either one of the ugly step-sisters and stayed home with her mom.

TURNER

Out of the eight rooms Ragnar had reserved for the team in the clan-owned hotel, only three were furnished with king beds, and Turner had chosen one for himself. Except, the luxury of single occupancy had been wasted on him. With all the back and forth phone calls between him, William, and Roni, he hadn't done much sleeping.

The two hackers stayed up all night too. But at least they'd snagged a few hours of shuteye during the day. Turner hadn't, and the fatigue was starting to get to him.

He was edgy, impatient, and easily irritable, which was not conducive to leading a rescue operation of any kind.

Mainly, he was angry about having to fly to Boston and losing more precious time. The supposedly simple rescue mission was turning more and more complicated. It seemed like he was always one step behind, and it wasn't even the work of some brilliant adversary.

It was just plain bad luck.

He knocked on Arwel's door. "Ready to go?"

"Yeah, give me a moment."

Arwel was one of the two others who'd gotten a room to themselves, and given the smell wafting from under his door, he'd taken the opportunity to get plastered.

To his credit, though, this was the first time he'd allowed himself to drink on this mission. With his overly receptive mind and the constant bombardment of human emotions, it must've been difficult for him to do without.

Except, when the Guardian opened the door, he looked sober. Apparently, fast metabolism was one more advantage immortals had over humans.

"I wish we could leave the perps behind," Arwel said as they entered the van. "Flying to Boston with them tied up in the jet is ridiculous. I should've thought of that after we got the uncle last night, and had him brought here. Then someone could've gone to bring the nephew. I'm sure Ragnar could've stashed them in the hotel's basement or in some storage room." He eased into traffic.

"Right. As if drugging them for transport twice was not a hassle. It's better to keep them on the jet." Turner glared at the line of cars in front of them, willing it to get moving.

"True," Arwel conceded. "When did you find out where the proxy was?"

"About an hour ago, but I had to call Bridget and have her make flight arrangements. You can't just fly out and land wherever and whenever you want."

"True. So what's the deal with that Eleonora Roberts? Is it even her real name?"

"Probably not. It's one of several names she goes by. Her cover story is that she's an art dealer, and she even participates in a lot of legit auctions, but I had my sources check on her, and she is known to have ties to the Mafia."

"Why was it so difficult to find her address?"

"It wasn't, but I didn't want to fly to Boston and then discover that she was staying in a New York hotel. I had

William check the flights, while my people checked the hotels. Of course, she couldn't make our lives easy, and she used one of her other identities to book the flight. Some serious digging has gone into finding her. William and Roni worked on it most of the night."

Everything was taking too much bloody time, and Turner was starting to realize that he didn't have enough Guardians with him.

Or maybe he was still thinking in human terms.

There was no reason to leave three men to guard five girls on a private floor in a clan-owned hotel that was managed by a clan member.

Liam was going with them to Boston, but he was staying in the jet to guard their prisoners. So that left Turner and Arwel to interrogate the proxy. Hopefully, Eleonora didn't have a bunch of bodyguards on payroll.

It was a shame she was a woman, though.

If the proxy were a guy, Turner would have relished beating the creep up. Regrettably, though, he would have to leave everything to Arwel. If that failed and the lady turned out to be immune or resistant, then he would have no qualms about slapping her around to reveal the buyer's name.

Being a female didn't grant her immunity from justice.

ELLA

"*You* are a fast learner," Pavel said. "You think you can remember all of this?"

"Sure, no problem." As if knowing which fork to use with what dish was rocket science. And to think people wasted time on this in finishing schools.

"When you're not sure what to say, it's always safer to say nothing than blurt something that can get you in trouble."

"Got it. What if someone asks me a question, and I'm not sure how to answer?"

"Take your cues from Dimitri. If he sees that you're confused, he will answer for you. Or just say that you don't know."

"What about if someone asks how we met? It's not like I can tell them that he bought me in an auction."

"No, you'd better not. Again, when in doubt, make an innocent face, look at Dimitri lovingly, and say something like 'Why don't you tell the story, Dimitri? You tell it so much better than me.' Whatever you do, always make him look good, and you'll do fine."

"Got it."

"Watch your posture. That's your biggest failing. Keep your back straight, your legs crossed at the ankles, and your hands in your lap."

"Right. The lady posture." Ella straightened in her chair.

Things were starting to look up. If Dimitri was investing so much effort in making her look like a lady, maybe he needed her mostly as an arm-candy.

Right. She would be his arm-candy all right, and his bed warmer.

"What's the matter?" Pavel asked. "You looked fine until two seconds ago."

"You know what's the matter. I don't need to spell it out for you."

He took her hand and gave it a squeeze. "Courage, girl," he whispered. In a louder voice, he said, "Keep your head up, stay calm, and everything will turn out all right. You'll emerge stronger and smarter on the other side."

Yeah, it was easy for him to say. He wasn't about to get violated by a powerful pervert who could do anything he wanted to him with complete impunity.

Not that Ella could say any of it out loud. Instead, she said, "I'll do my best."

"That's all anyone can do. Now let's choose an outfit for your trip, and pack the rest of your wardrobe."

"What trip?"

"Didn't I tell you?" He frowned. "My bad. Apparently, I forgot in all the excitement. You have no idea what a treat it was to shop for you. It was almost orgasmic." He fanned himself.

Ella still wasn't sure whether Pavel was gay or just dramatic. Not that it mattered. It wasn't as if she was interested in him. Or any guy. She was done with men for good.

"Where am I going, Pavel?"

"First to Boston via helicopter, where you're going to wait

for the boss to pick you up, and then to wherever he is off to next."

Crap, what if he was planning on taking her out of the country?

If he took her to Europe, would she be able to communicate with her mother from across the ocean? They'd never been so far apart. Perhaps she should just open the channel and tell her mom that she was okay and have her promise not to do anything and not tell Parker?

She must be so worried by now.

Except, Ella was not okay, and she knew her mother too well to count on her doing nothing suspicious. Besides, her mom might not believe her that she and Parker were being watched.

The safest thing for everyone involved was to keep quiet and do as she was told. As long as she did that, no one was going to get hurt. Except for her, but that was going to happen either way.

"This is a fabulous travel outfit." Pavel lifted an elegant pantsuit. "Oh, and I almost forgot. I have sexy lingerie for you and some lounge clothes. I know a girl can't stay dressed up all day and needs something comfy and yet sexy to relax in." He pushed to his feet. "Wait here."

As if she could go anywhere.

Several minutes passed before Pavel came back with two fancy suitcases, a carry on and a makeup bag, all matching, of course.

"Only the best for Ella girl." He put the suitcases on the bed and opened one. "Here," he said as he pulled out a pair of panties and a matching bra. "Put those on. The rest I'm going to leave in the suitcase."

"Am I going to wait for him in an airport hotel?"

Pavel chuckled. "The boss doesn't stay in hotels. Think of

his jet as a very fancy motorhome. And I mean fancy." He rolled his eyes. "He spends most of his time on flights."

Great. So she would be stuck with the perv in a small space. If it was the size of a motorhome, it didn't matter how fancy it was. She would have nowhere to hide from him.

Pavel clapped his hands. "Chop, chop. Get in the bathroom and get dressed. I'll pack your things."

53

TURNER

"That's one fancy home," Arwel said as he parked the rental.

Located in one of Boston's most affluent neighborhoods, it was a two-story mansion of at least eight thousand square feet. Just the two acres of land it sat on was probably worth several million.

"She can afford it. If Ms. Roberts takes five percent commission, she just made nearly forty thousand for facilitating Ella's purchase. Including the flight, that's less than one day's worth of work."

Arwel shook his head. "Lucrative business."

"Yeah, if one lacks any kind of morals."

The house was fenced and gated, but the walkway gate wasn't locked.

"How many people are in there?" Turner asked.

"Four women," Arwel answered without a moment's hesitation.

Damn, the guy was good.

The young woman who opened the door wasn't Eleonora, and, hopefully, she wasn't her daughter either.

Turner didn't like to involve the perpetrators' families unless they already were.

Maybe she was an assistant? Or a secretary? She certainly wasn't dressed like a maid or a housekeeper.

"How can I help you, gentlemen?"

"We are here to see Ms. Roberts." Arwel took hold of her mind with a minimal thrall. "She is expecting us."

"You are a little early, but that's fine. I'm sure Ms. Roberts will have no problem seeing you now." She extended her hand. "I'm Stacy, her personal assistant."

"Nice to meet you." Arwel shook her hand but didn't introduce himself or Turner. Another small thrall took care of that.

Apparently Eleonora was expecting visitors, which meant that they needed to conclude their business with her expeditiously.

As they followed behind the assistant, Turner spotted a maid with a stack of laundry hurrying upstairs. So that was the third woman. The fourth was probably another maid or a cook. A house this size required a staff of people to maintain it, and a handyman on call for all the things that went wrong. The bigger the house, the more fixtures and appliances needing repairs.

Stacy knocked on a door and then pushed it open without waiting for a reply. "Your two o'clocks are here."

"Let them in."

Arwel took the young woman's elbow and turned her to face him. "We wish not to be disturbed for the next hour. I suggest you collect the two other ladies and treat them to a cup of coffee at the nearest café. The three of you deserve a break." This time his thrall had been laid on heavier.

Observing a great thraller like Arwel was a treat. He was very precise and delicate, knowing when to trickle and when to push, and careful not to cause damage.

Stacy's eyes were unfocused when she nodded. "Yes, we do. Coffee sounds good."

As they entered the room, Eleonora's eyes widened in fear, but Arwel grabbed hold of her mind before she could reach for her phone or the panic button, or whatever she'd been reaching for.

"Come and sit over here, Eleonora." He pointed to one of the ornate chairs in front of her desk.

Like an automaton, she got up, smoothed her skirt down, walked over to the chair he'd indicated, sat down, and crossed her legs.

"Very good," Arwel praised as he turned the other chair to face her and sat down.

The thrall he'd used hadn't been gentle, but it hadn't been massive either. And yet, the woman was reacting as if it was.

Her susceptibility to thralling surprised Turner. He'd been under the impression that humans with strong minds were less suggestible, which made them more resistant to both hypnosis and thralling. To make as much money as she was obviously making, Ms. Roberts had a strong head on her shoulders, even if it was wired all wrong.

Was it possible that she'd been thralled before? Had someone trained her to obey suggestions? It was a possibility Turner had never considered before. It made sense, though. If it was possible to train a person to respond to hypnosis, the same should be true for thralling.

"Tell me the name of Ella's buyer."

"Dimitri Gorchenco."

"Fuck."

Arwel turned to look at him. "Do you know the guy?"

"Yeah, I do. And this is very bad news."

"Do you want me to ask her anything else?"

"Was Ella taken to Gorchenco's New York estate or flown to meet him abroad?"

"The estate, first," Eleonora said without waiting for Arwel to repeat the question.

"Do you know if he took her somewhere from there?"

"Dimitri was out of the country when the transaction took place. He might have flown her to wherever he was. I don't know."

"Anything else?" Arwel asked Turner.

"No. That's it."

"Well, that was much easier than I expected. What do you want me to do with her?"

"Just make her forget. She is small fry."

Arwel returned his attention to the woman. "You are going to forget you ever saw us. You are going to sit here for the next fifteen minutes and contemplate your choices in life. After that, you will never again assist in trading humans."

Turner rolled his eyes. Eleonora was highly susceptible to thralling, but a rotten soul was a rotten soul. Once the effect wore off, she would be back to her evil deeds.

Not for long, though. Right now he had more urgent matters to take care of, but he would be back for her.

"Who is Dimitri Gorchenco?" Arwel asked as they entered the car.

"A powerful Russian mafia boss. He owns many legitimate businesses, including an executive airline. He is one of the world's biggest arms dealers, but up until now he wasn't involved in human trafficking."

"Buying Ella seems to me like a private matter for him, not part of venturing into a new business," Arwel said. "Remember the picture in that magazine? I think he ordered her delivery."

Turner smoothed his hand over his head. It still surprised him to touch hair and not scalp. "I agree. But that doesn't help us any. If Ella is held at his New York estate, we will need an army to get her out. The place is a fortress and is guarded like a military compound. Other than that one, he also has estates all over the world. If he takes her to the one in Russia, we won't be able to get her out at all."

Arwel snorted. "You still think in human terms. The big bad mafia boss is only a human, and so are the people working for him. The only one we need is Yamanu. He can blanket thrall everyone in that compound. After that, we can stroll in and walk out with the girl. Easy."

"It's not that simple. First of all, we need to scope out the place and find out how many guards he has there. Secondly, some of them might be immune or resistant to thralling. Remember the Russian crew? They were resistant. I don't know if that is because Russians are highly suspicious by nature or if it's something genetic. But we can't count on Yamanu alone. We need reinforcements."

Turner pulled out his phone and dialed Bridget.

54

KIAN

"*D*imitri Gorchenco," Kian repeated the name. "Sounds familiar."

"First time I heard of him," Bridget said. "He must be a big deal because Turner sounded worried, and you know him, Victor never gets worried because he always has a plan."

"Let's find out what we are dealing with." Kian dialed Turner's number and put the call on speaker.

It rang twice. "Hello, Kian. Thank you for calling back right away. I assume you have Bridget with you?"

"I'm here," Bridget said.

"So what's the story with this Gorchenco guy? How bad is he?"

"As bad as they come, but not in the way you think. As far as I know, he's stayed away from human trafficking. His main thing is arms dealing, and I mean the real deal. Nuclear warheads, submarines, you name it, he'll get it for you. Ruthless son of a bitch."

"Bridget tells me you need Yamanu to get the girl out."

"Gorchenco's compound is heavily guarded, and the guy is known to be super paranoid, which doesn't surprise me at all. He owns a fleet of jet planes which he rents out to executives with the crew to fly them, and he uses it extensively for conducting his own international deals. He's rumored to send decoy jets at the same time he flies out so no one knows which plane he is on. Other than his people, that is."

Kian chuckled. "Reminds me of someone."

"Exactly. Which is why I know this is going to be a very difficult extraction operation. If I were him, and it seems that we think alike, I would make that compound impenetrable."

Kian raised an eyebrow. "Even to immortals with thralling and shrouding abilities?"

"That's our only advantage."

"Yeah, but it's a big one."

"True. But we don't want to show our hand either. We need to make it look like something a competitor would do."

"Wouldn't that necessitate taking the compound out?" Bridget asked.

"I don't think we can."

Turner must have been suffering from a lack of sleep to sound so defeatist. "We took out a compound full of immortal warriors. I'm sure we can tackle Gorchenco's."

"Not the same thing. The monastery was in an isolated place, and you basically bombed the place and then invaded it with a large force of what looked like alien invaders. You also got rid of all the enemy soldiers and torched the place. You can't do that with Gorchenco's estate."

"Why not?"

"Because even though it's sprawling, Gorchenco's estate is not in the boonies. Someone will notice what's going on, and not everyone can be thralled. Secondly, many civilians work there, and some of them might get killed in the crossfire. Third, we can't declare war on the Russian mafia. You have to choose your battles, Kian, and you're already fighting on two fronts. You have your enemies to deal with, and you're going after sex traffickers."

He had a point. The good thing about Turner was that he thought with his head and not his heart.

"What's your plan?"

"Arwel and I are on our way back to the airport, and once we get back to New York we will head out to Gorchenco's estate and scope it out. We don't have time for prolonged surveillance, so I have to rely on Arwel to tell me how many people are inside."

"You're overestimating my abilities." Arwel joined the conversation. "I can't get an accurate estimate when dealing with as many people as you think are there, and over long distances."

"I'll take your rough estimate," Turner said. "That's all we got."

"You said you needed Yamanu," Kian interrupted. "Who else?"

"As many Guardians as you can spare without compromising ongoing missions and the village's safety. I don't mind if you pull people off missions that haven't started yet. Those can be rescheduled."

Kian raked his fingers through his hair. What had started as a simple rescue operation was getting more and more complicated by the hour, and required pulling resources from where they were more needed.

Except by now they were committed, and he wasn't going to pull the plug on the operation. If not for any other reason, than for Julian. The guy would never forgive him if he aborted the mission now.

"Let me see how many I can mobilize. There is also the factor of flying everyone to New York. We don't have that many planes. Some will have to fly commercially."

There was a moment of silence, and then Turner voiced

Kian's thoughts. "Do you want to pull the plug? I want to get the girl out, but this operation is getting out of hand. We are contemplating tangling with the Russian mafia for fuck's sake."

Apparently, sometimes Turner also thought with his heart and not just his mind. It was obvious that he wanted to continue with the mission even though it didn't make sense to risk so much for one girl.

"I wish I could. But at this point, I can't. We are committed to this course of action and we need to see it through."

A sigh of relief drifted through the speaker. "Thank you. If it weren't for Julian, I would've voted to abort the mission."

"Would you, really?"

"Frankly? No. Not after seeing what I saw on the surveillance recordings from the auction house. It's easy to make cold-hearted calculated decisions when you don't see the victim's face."

Kian could only imagine. "Once we know how many men are going, Bridget is going to give you an update."

"I appreciate it. I'll give you a call once Arwel and I have more information on the estate." Turner hung up.

"I'd better get on it." Bridget pushed to her feet. "I'm going to have Onegus make a list of Guardians he can spare. Once I know how many are going, I'll get on making flight arrangements for everyone. Should they bring the protective armor with them?"

"I don't see why not. Have the Guardians load their armor and weapons on our planes. After scoping out the Russian's estate, Turner can decide if he wants them to wear the armor or not. I'll also ask William to prepare a couple of the smaller surveillance drones. I'm sure Turner could use them as well."

Bridget grimaced. "I doubt he can. The Doomers didn't expect drones because they are technologically backward.

I'm sure that one of the world's biggest arms dealers is well aware of them and has equipment to monitor the airspace above his estates. If anything, they will only serve to warn him that something is up."

"True. But I believe in being over-prepared rather than under-prepared. I'll send the drones, and Turner will decide if he wants to use them or not."

Bridget shrugged. "As you wish. You're the boss."

55

ELLA

"*K*iss, kiss." Pavel kissed the air next to her cheeks. "Chin up, Ella girl." He chucked her under her chin. "I'll see you the next time your wardrobe needs refreshing."

Given the number of outfits he'd hooked her up with, she wasn't going to see Pavel for a long time.

Unexpectedly, a deep sense of loneliness and despair came crashing down on her.

So far, Pavel had been the only friendly face she'd encountered. He seemed to want to help her. It would've been comforting to have at least one friend she could cry to when things got tough.

Except, Ella seemed to be all out of luck. In fact, everything that could've gone wrong had, including things she'd never imagined.

Her family was cursed.

There was no other explanation for the amount of bad luck that had befallen them.

Ella used to scoff at her mother's conviction that every man who'd ever gotten close to her had ended up dead. She'd argued with Vivian endlessly, trying to convince her mom that it had been a lousy coincidence, and that she should start dating again.

If Ella ever got back home, she would never bring the issue up again because Vivian might have been right.

With tears misting her eyes, Ella got into the back of the limo and waved goodbye to Pavel as Yuri drove off. They were only going to the helipad, but the estate was so vast that it required motorized transport to go from place to place within it.

Not that she could've walked even a short distance in the crazy heels Pavel had had her put on. The shoes were gorgeous, but they were good only for sitting down and looking pretty, which was what she was bought for. Another luxury item the boss could show off. Unfortunately, it wasn't going to be her only job. It was in addition to being Dimitri's bed warmer.

It sounded as if she was talking about a thermal blanket, but Ella couldn't bring herself to call it by any other name. It was just too scary. According to her mother, words had power, and one should choose them carefully even when speaking to oneself.

That was why Ella chose to use the word apprehensive instead of terrified when she saw the helicopter. Jetliners seemed like a safe way to travel. This did not.

She was in no rush to board the thing, which in her opinion looked like a giant bug and provoked similar irrational fear. Logically, she knew that the helicopter was probably safe, just as she knew that cockroaches were disgusting but harmless.

Apparently, her brains and her churning gut were in disagreement.

When Yuri was done transferring her luggage from the

limo to the chopper, he opened the door and wordlessly offered her his pan-sized hand.

Was he mute?

She hadn't heard him talk yet.

Careful on her spiky heels, Ella walked up to the short staircase that Yuri had pushed in front of the craft's door and climbed inside.

The pilot was another expressionless Russian-looking dude, who didn't return her smile. The other guy, who was sitting in the passenger section of the helicopter, was a body-guard—a big dude with bulging muscles and a face that looked like it had been rearranged on more than one occasion.

He made Yuri seem pretty.

But at least he smiled as he pointed her to her seat and then helped her buckle up.

That was the extent of their communication, though.

No one spoke throughout the flight, which was fine with her. The moment the aircraft lifted off the ground, Ella shut her eyes tight, adamant about keeping them closed until the landing.

Hopefully, in one piece.

MAGNUS

"Good shot." Magnus clapped Parker on his back. "Did you see that, Vivian?"

"Uh-huh." She looked up from her book with a forced smile. "Very nice. Good work." She went back to reading.

Obviously, she hadn't been watching.

Sitting on the chair he'd brought for her from inside the cabin, she'd spent the afternoon on the porch. While he and Parker had been working on the bow and arrows, rushing to get them ready for their shooting practice before it got too dark, Vivian had been reading. Or pretending to.

She'd been so distant all day, Magnus was starting to question whether last night had happened at all, or if he had dreamt it.

Either Vivian had the remote and aloof act down to a tee, or he was feeling uncharacteristically needy and clingy.

A first for him, that was for sure.

Usually Magnus had no problem parting with a woman the morning after. And most times the women were okay with that too. He always made it clear that there should be no romantic expectations and that it was only a casual hookup.

But this time, it hadn't been a casual anything.

This was the real deal for him, and he was majorly screwed because he was being stupid about it while Vivian was being smart.

For all the wrong reasons, though.

Vivian believed that she was cursed to be a black widow, and that any man who got close to her died.

It was an absurd notion.

Nevertheless, it was smart of her to keep her heart protected because there was no future for them. As much as he craved her and wanted to be with her, he couldn't.

In fact, she was doing him a favor by distancing herself.

Magnus doubted he would've had what it took to stay away. As long as she ignored him, he wasn't going to make a fool of himself and try to get her to acknowledge him and what they'd shared last night.

He got her full attention, however, when his phone buzzed in his pocket. Tensing, she and Parker watched him with worried expressions on their faces as he read the message from Arwel.

"Do you have news from your team?" Vivian asked.

"Uhm." He kept reading.

"Good or bad?"

"Both." He lifted his eyes to her. "They know who has Ella. That's the good news. The bad news is that he is a powerful mafia boss. Dimitri Gorchenco is a Russian arms dealer, and his estate is more heavily guarded than the White House and the Pentagon put together."

"I've never heard of him."

"Neither have I, but Turner knows all about him."

Emitting a strong scent of despair, Vivian closed her eyes for a moment. "What are we going to do?" she whispered.

"Get her out, of course."

"How? You said his estate is basically impenetrable."

"I didn't say that. I said it was heavily guarded. It makes things more difficult, but not impossible."

"What's Turner's plan? I want my daughter back, but I don't want your people getting killed in the process."

He walked up the stairs, crouched in front of her, and took her trembling hands in his. "Headquarters is sending reinforcements. Turner is going to have a much bigger team. Not only that, they are sending him a very advanced proprietary device that will enable him to get into the compound without a fight."

It wasn't a lie. After all, Yamanu's power was unique, and no one else had access to anything or anyone like him. He was the secret weapon.

Vivian narrowed her eyes at him. "You're not just saying this to calm me down, are you? What kind of a device can do that?"

"I can't disclose that information because it's classified." He put a hand over his heart. "But I can swear to you that all I've said is true."

She let out a breath. "I don't know if I should feel relieved or more worried. Why would a powerful mafia boss need to buy a girl? I'm sure he has no lack of volunteers. There is no shortage of beautiful women who chase rich and powerful men. Is he deformed or something?"

"Not likely. According to Turner, he is elusive and paranoid, but that doesn't mean he is repulsive, only that he is careful."

"Which will make it so much harder to catch him."

"We have no intention of catching him. We just want to get Ella out. Taking the Russian mafia on is not part of the plan."

A mask of determination sliding over her face, Vivian

nodded, pulled her hands out of his grasp, and pushed to her feet. "I'd better get started on dinner."

He let her go. Being busy helped her cope.

It helped Parker too. Spending the day looking for sticks and then fashioning arrows out of them had taken his mind off his sister.

Now, as he sat on the porch's steps with Scarlet in his lap, his shoulders were hunched and his head hung low.

Magnus sat next to the kid and scratched Scarlet's ear. "Ella is going to be okay. My buddies will get her out, and then we'll get her to the best professionals who will help her get over it."

Parker cast him a sidelong glance. "You mean shrinks?"

"Kind of. I know a very good therapist who specializes in trauma cases."

"Ella says that shrinks are worthless. After my dad died, Mom took her to see one. I was a baby, so I don't remember anything, but Ella told me that the shrink didn't help her at all and only made things worse."

Magnus was no expert on the subject of dealing with trauma, but he trusted Vanessa.

"Just like in any other profession, not all therapists are made equal. Some are better than others. I know that ours is the best. She has a lot of experience helping girls in Ella's situation. We wouldn't be much of a rescue organization if we didn't take care of the girls after we got them out."

Parker squared his shoulders. "Can I join your organization when I grow up? I thought I wanted to be a games designer, but I changed my mind. I want to do what you do. I want to be a hero."

Magnus chuckled. "Being a warrior doesn't make me a hero."

"If you save people, you're a hero. And that's what I want to do. Just don't tell my mom. She's gonna freak out."

"I bet. Besides, there is much more money in designing computer games with imaginary heroes fighting evil dudes than in trying to be one for real. It's also less dangerous."

For a long moment, Parker didn't say anything, but the furrow between his eyebrows indicated that he was doing some hard thinking.

"Can I be both?"

"Sure. You can become a famous game-designer billionaire, and then pay schlubs like me to do the saving for you. That's what our boss does."

Parker's eyes widened. "Is he very rich?"

"He's wealthy, but the real money comes from the corporations he manages. He owns stocks in each of them, but so do a lot of other people. I own stocks in them too."

"Are you wealthy?"

"I'm not complaining. I have enough money saved up that I could retire if I wanted to. But I happen to like what I do."

"So your boss, the one who manages all those corporations, he is not a fighter, right?"

"He is, or rather was. He is more valuable with a pen in his hand than a rifle." Catching the dated reference, Magnus corrected, "I mean he is more valuable on the keyboard."

Parker waved a hand. "You see? That's what I want. I want to be like your boss." He squinted. "No, scratch that. I want to be like Bruce Wayne. During the day he is a rich dude who manages big corporations, and at night he's saving people as Batman."

With a chuckle, Magnus ruffled Parker's hair. "An admirable goal, my young apprentice, and there is much to be done in preparation. It is time to resume your training. Pick up the bow."

"Yes, sir."

VIVIAN

*I*n the kitchen, Vivian leaned against the counter and let the tears come.

For her son's sake, she needed to appear strong, but she could allow herself a few moments of crying while Magnus was keeping Parker busy.

Throughout the day, she'd sent countless messages to Ella, hoping for one to slip by her daughter's mental shields.

Why was Ella blocking her?

The one bit of good news was that Ella wasn't dead. Because of the complete lack of communication, this had been Vivian's biggest fear. The one she hadn't dared to voice or even acknowledge in her own mind was that some psychopath had kidnapped Ella, tortured, and murdered her.

Between the two evils, sex traffickers were the lesser ones. They were the scum of the earth, but they weren't psychotic killers. They were in it for profit.

The updates from the team had reassured her that Ella was alive.

Except, with all the bad luck that had befallen her family, Vivian still feared for Ella's life. There was nothing to prevent a psychopathic killer from buying his victims in an auction. In fact, he could keep on killing with impunity and never get caught.

The news of Ella getting bought by a big mafia boss was in fact a relief. That Gorchenco guy might be a killer, but chances were that he wasn't a psychopath. No businessman, even a crooked one who was into illegal trade, paid hundreds of thousands of dollars to buy a girl and then kill her.

Maybe he would even be kind and gentle with Ella.

Yeah, right.

After paying so much money, he would feel entitled, and if Ella resisted, he would take her by force. Maybe he already had.

A cold shiver ran down Vivian's spine.

She'd read about men who thought nothing of forcing a woman. Men who otherwise appeared normal. Luckily for her, she'd never encountered that kind. The three men she'd been romantically involved with had all been good guys who'd always treated her with respect, and the men at the dentists' office were all good people too. None of them had ever tried to take advantage of her or the other women in the office.

What kind of upbringing spawned men who were monsters? Or those who thought of themselves as decent guys, but who objectified women and didn't regard them as people?

At twelve, her son already knew to be respectful and never presume anything. Since Parker didn't have a father to have *the talk* with, she'd done it. There had been a lot of blushing, hers and his, and several eye rolls, his.

As far as the actual act, she hadn't told him anything he hadn't known already, which had been quite a shock. But she'd explained about love, and about respect, and about consent.

Hopefully, the lesson had sunk in. In fact, she was sure it had. She was raising a good man.

Like his father.

Josh would've been proud of his kids.

But that was enough musing. She had work to do. Dinner wasn't going to cook itself. The guys had been working hard all day, and all she'd fed them for lunch were sandwiches.

With a sigh, Vivian wiped the tears away and opened the fridge. In the grocery store, Magnus had bought several trays of steaks with the intention of barbecuing them at some point, but he'd been too busy with Parker.

Such a great guy to come up with a creative way to take Parker's mind off his sister's fate. She wondered what had given him the idea to make a bow and arrows from scratch. Maybe he'd been a Boy Scout. Did they have those in Scotland?

Magnus's mother had done an amazing job raising such a wonderful man, and like Vivian, she'd also done it all on her own.

Well, not exactly. Magnus had mentioned uncles and cousins, so he'd had good male role models growing up.

Parker didn't.

Vivian was an only child to elderly parents who now lived in a retirement home, and Josh had one sister who didn't keep in touch. His father had passed away many years ago.

Bottom line, Parker's male role models were Batman and Superman.

It could've been worse. He could've chosen Deadpool.

Pulling out two trays from the fridge, Vivian unpacked the steaks and went to work. Half an hour later, she had a full meal ready. In addition to the six steaks she'd pan-fried, there was pasta in olive oil, corn on the cob, and a garden salad.

The guys must've smelled the steaks because the door opened before she had the chance to call them.

"I smell steaks." Parker rushed into the kitchen. "Yay, Mom. You're awesome."

"Thank you. Now go wash your hands."

"Yes, ma'am." He ran upstairs.

Tail wagging at a blurring speed, Scarlet bumped her head between Vivian's legs to get her attention.

"Is it okay to give her a steak?"

Magnus shrugged. "Sure. But if you do, get ready to take her home with you. She'll follow you to the ends of the earth in hopes of getting another."

"So maybe you should give it to her. I wouldn't want to break up a family." She'd meant it as a joke, but it had the opposite effect.

On both of them.

His lips pinched in a thin line, Magnus turned his back to her and bent over the kitchen sink to wash his hands.

This little pretend family of theirs would soon have to break apart. As soon as Ella was back, Magnus would leave and take his puppy with him.

Unless, he had a good reason to stick around, as in Vivian showing him how she really felt about him.

She was falling for him.

Heck, who was she kidding?

She already had. If not for her curse, she would have... done what?

Magnus lived and worked in Los Angeles. She had a home and a job in San Diego. Two and a half hours' drive didn't seem like much, but it would make having a relationship impossible.

Besides, her curse hadn't gone anywhere. It was still hovering nearby, waiting for its next victim. Vivian wasn't going to give it one no matter how much it would pain her to say goodbye to Magnus.

His hands still wet, Parker came running down. "Can we eat now? I'm starving."

She pulled him into a quick hug. "Yes, we can eat." She kissed his flushed cheek. It wouldn't stay smooth for long. She had two or three years at the most before her baby started growing facial hair.

"Mom!" He wiggled out of her embrace.

"Don't Mom me. I have the right to those cheeks of yours. Especially when they smell of fresh mountain air."

ELLA

*W*hen Ella had left New York, it was late afternoon, but even though the helicopter flight had taken only a little over an hour, by the time they landed in the private airport in Boston, the sky was already darkening.

A driver with a golf-cart style vehicle was waiting for them next to the landing pad. The bodyguard loaded Ella's luggage onto the cart, and then loaded Ella as well. He simply picked her up and put her in the seat.

"I can walk, you know."

He glanced at her shoes. "I see you walk from limousine to helicopter. It's not safe. If you break a leg, boss break my neck. I bring you to his plane safe." He laughed as if it was a great joke.

Ella had a feeling it wasn't. "Tough boss," she muttered under her breath.

The private airport was apparently smaller than Dimitri's estate. The cart drive took much less time than the one from his house to the landing pad.

"Is that the plane?" Ella gawked.

It was a full-size jumbo jet. How rich was this guy that he could afford that as his motorhome?

"Nice, eh?" the bodyguard said.

"Big, that's for sure. By the way, I'm Ella." She offered him her hand.

If they were going to spend time together, she didn't want to refer to him as the bodyguard.

"I know your name. I'm Misha." He took her hand in two fingers as if afraid to crush it in his hand.

Hey, maybe he was a crusher.

The boss was no doubt mafia. A legitimate businessman didn't go around buying girls, or live in a compound guarded as if it was a top-secret military base.

Hefting her suitcases as if they were empty and not over-stuffed to bursting, Misha jogged up the staircase to the jet's open door.

For a moment, an irrational urge to run rushed through her, but she quashed it with a sneer. There was nowhere to run. Misha would catch up to her in under a minute, and then there would be hell to pay.

Besides, running on high heels was not going to get her far, and barefoot she was going to stumble over her too long pants.

With a heavy sigh, Ella grabbed the railing for balance and climbed after him.

"Are we the only ones here?" she asked as she entered what looked like the living room portion of the plane.

Misha opened a door to a luxurious bedroom. "The cook and the steward are upstairs."

"There is an upstairs?"

"Yes, of course. The kitchen and dining room are there. Also the crew sleeping quarters." He motioned for her to get inside the bedroom. "But you are going to sleep here."

"Wow." She didn't want to sound impressed, but it was impossible not to.

"There is bathroom too." Misha pushed her luggage through the door. "And a closet." He opened the door to one that was bigger than the master closet in her mom's bedroom.

Ella went to investigate the bathroom. There was a sizable shower, double sink vanity, and a separate compartment for the toilet and a bidet, just like the room she'd come from.

"Nice, eh?"

Misha seemed to be proud of his boss's possessions as if they were his. She wondered if he was going to show her off in the same way. *Nice girl, eh? Three quarters of a million the boss paid for her. Nice, eh?*

"You have big TV in here." He pointed to the screen hanging on the wall across from the king-sized bed. "A lot of movies and shows you can choose. It keep you busy until boss comes tomorrow."

That was the best news she'd gotten all day. One more night of freedom.

"Cook is making dinner. But if you are hungry before, you can come up the stairs and he make something for you." Misha smirked. "Or if you want a drink, the steward will make you one or two."

"I'm eighteen."

He waved a dismissive hand. "Eighteen is legal to drink in Russia." He winked. "Sixteen you can get beer in a restaurant."

"We are not in Russia."

"*Da*, but we don't care about American laws. You want a drink, you get a drink, eh?"

Hell, why not. Maybe if she got plastered, she would feel less scared.

Except, she might do something stupid like open a channel to her mom.

"When is dinner?"

"I go ask and come tell you. You want I bring you drink? I can make steward make you a sweet girly cocktail."

"Okay. Just ask him to go easy on the alcohol. I'm not used to it."

"No problem."

When he left, Ella kicked off the torture shoes, lay on the bed, and clicked the television open. The menu of movies and shows that appeared on the screen had all the latest releases, even those that were still playing in movie theaters.

Perhaps watching until her eyes drooped would help her get some sleep.

Except, tomorrow was the big day, and Ella still didn't know much about the man she was going to meet. Larissa hadn't been as talkative as Ella had hoped, and when she had, it was about her family and childhood friends in Russia. It seemed that the housekeeper had been instructed not to divulge any details about her employer.

Perhaps when Misha returned, Ella could ask him some questions about his boss.

She knew his name was Dimitri and that he was rich, and she knew his people feared him but also respected him, but she didn't know how old he was or what he looked like.

For sure he wasn't young.

Unless he'd inherited all that money or was a tech genius, there was no way a young guy could amass so much money and power.

"Keep your head," Pavel had said. "Stay calm," he'd said. "And everything will turn out all right. You'll emerge stronger and smarter on the other side," he'd said.

Maybe if she repeated his words a thousand times, she would also believe them.

JULIAN

"That's a stupid idea, Julian. You are needed here in the clinic. What do you think to accomplish by accompanying Yamanu and the Guardians to New York?"

His mother's famous temper was flaring red hot like her hair. What she hadn't realized, though, was that she'd just given him the perfect excuse to go.

"With so many Guardians taking part in this rescue mission, they will need a doctor to patch them up in case there is actual fighting. If my memory serves me right, you joined the force that attacked the Doomers' stronghold in Ojai."

She waved a dismissive hand. "That was different. We were going to engage the Doomers and take them out. We knew there would be fighting and people would get hurt. I even had Gertrude and Hildegard with me. This time, though, there will be no fighting. Yamanu is going to blanket thrall all the humans in the compound, and the guys are going to get Ella out. That's all. Turner doesn't want to start a war with the Russian mafia."

"If it were that simple, he wouldn't have asked for reinforcements. Yamanu alone would've been enough. But Turner expects trouble, which means that people are going to get injured, and they'll need patching up."

Bridget opened her mouth to argue and then closed it. "Yeah, you're right. They might need you. But you have to promise me that you'll stay a safe distance back. When I went with the Guardians, I wasn't anywhere near the fighting."

"I'll be careful."

She wagged a finger at him. "You're not trained in combat, Julian. If you insist on going with the warriors, you're going to endanger them as well as yourself. You need to listen to Turner and do exactly what he tells you."

Julian liked the guy, but he wasn't his son or his employee or even one of the Guardians. "Turner is not my dad, and I don't have to answer to him."

The glow in Bridget's eyes intensified and she lifted the wagging finger to his face. "First of all, he is in charge of this mission, so everyone who takes part in it answers to him. Secondly, the only reason he is there in person, instead of putting someone else in charge, is you—because this girl who you've never met is important to you for some reason." She lowered the finger to his chest. "Show a little gratitude."

He hadn't thought of it that way. "You're right. I promise to defer to Turner and do whatever he tells me. And I'm sorry about that stupid comment. Ever since I found out Ella had been taken, I can't sleep, I can't eat, and I can't think straight. That's why I have to be there when they get her out. I need to make sure she's okay."

"Come here." His mother pulled him in for a hug. Forcing him to bend nearly in half, she kissed his cheek. "Have faith in Turner. He knows what he is doing."

"Yeah, I know. He is the master, and I am the novice who must listen, obey, and learn."

"Yeah, right. You're good with listening and learning. The

obeying, not so much. That's why I'm so worried about you going and doing something stupid."

He put his hand over his heart. "I promise not to do anything dangerous."

She eyed him suspiciously. "I'm your mother, Julian. You tried to pull the same tricks when you were a kid, and it didn't work then either."

He batted his eyelashes. "I don't know what you're talking about."

"Let's put it this way. Since you and I don't always agree on what's considered dangerous, you must promise me to do exactly what Turner tells you to—without improvisations, or interpretations, or improvements. Am I clear?"

She knew him too well. He was the master of twisting things around to justify his actions. His mother had often joked that he'd missed his calling and should have become a lawyer and not a doctor.

"I swear to do exactly what I'm told without any deviations."

Bridget let out a breath. "Okay. As long as you do that, I'm fine with you going. Now I need to bump another Guardian to a commercial flight."

"I can fly commercial. I don't mind."

A big hand landed on his shoulder. "No way," Yamanu said. "I want you sitting next to me on the flight."

Julian hadn't heard the Guardian walk into Bridget's office. For such a big guy, Yamanu's steps were surprisingly stealthy. Come to think of it, all the Guardians moved like that. It was probably part of their training.

"To what do I owe the honor?" He and Yamanu hadn't exchanged more than two full sentences before.

The big guy shrugged. "Fresh meat. You didn't hear all of my jokes yet."

"Okay…" He didn't know that the Guardian was funny.

The clan's rumor machine whispered that Yamanu was a recluse who didn't like to leave the keep or the village. But that was understandable given his strange pale blue eyes that looked almost white against his dark skin. People probably got creeped out by them and gave him weird looks.

Other than that, the guy was exceedingly tall and embodied male physical perfection. A waste, since the other rumor circulating about Yamanu was that he was celibate. A most unusual choice for an immortal male.

If it were true.

The guy could be keeping his business to himself and being very circumspect with his sexual liaisons.

In any case, sitting next to Yamanu might prove interesting. A five-hour flight was plenty of time to coax the guy into talking about himself and shedding some light on the mystery.

TURNER

*T*urner parked the van as close as he dared to Gorchenco's estate, which was probably too far for Arwel to get anything. What's more, he couldn't stay out there too long without raising suspicion.

Even though the estate was deeply recessed and accessible through a private road, he was sure there were numerous surveillance cameras scattered among the trees lining the way to the gate.

"Are you getting anything?"

Arwel opened his eyes. "Yeah, but it's not much. All I can tell you is that there are a lot of people in there. I would say about forty to fifty."

"Can you differentiate between the males and females? We can assume all the males are security and all the females are domestic help. The Russian mafia is not known for its progressive ideas."

"I can try. But it's too damn far away."

"I'm going to change a tire while you're at it."

"That's the oldest trick in the book. No one is going to fall for it."

"You've got a better idea?"

"No."

"Then I'm going to change the fucking tire."

"Have fun."

The smart thing would've been to wait for Yamanu to arrive and have him thrall the entire compound, so Arwel could get closer and get the emotional signatures of every human in there.

Except, Turner was restless. He had a gut feeling that time was not their friend, and that he couldn't afford to wait until morning, which was when Yamanu and the reinforcements were supposed to arrive.

So here he was, changing a bloody tire in the middle of the night, after nearly forty-eight hours without sleep. He should've gone to the hotel and crashed instead of pushing himself and compromising his clarity.

"Let me help you," Arwel said as he stepped outside.

"I don't need help. You do your thing, and I do mine."

The Guardian leaned against the van and crossed his arms over his chest. "There are only ten people awake in there. All male."

"The night shift."

"Right. Everyone else is either asleep or watching television. Do you know that the brain activity slows down while watching? It's almost the same as during REM sleep."

Turner pulled out the jack from the back and put it in position. "I read that brain activity during REM sleep is not much different than when awake."

"It's different enough for me to differentiate. Anyway, I'm not picking up any distress, which usually is the easiest to perceive."

"Maybe Ella is asleep." Turner started working the jack.

"In her situation, the anxiety would have carried over to

her dreams. She either isn't distressed by her situation, or she's not there."

Turner paused. "What do you mean she is not there? Where could she be?"

"Don't ask me. Maybe he took her out to a nightclub."

"It's two o'clock in the morning."

"Nightclubs are still open."

That gut feeling from before had just gotten stronger. Turner was starting to think that they were already too late. Gorchenco could've had Ella delivered to any of his other estates.

She might have never even been to the New York one. It was possible that Eleonora had assumed Ella had been taken there, when in fact she'd been taken straight to the airport. With Gorchenco's private fleet of executive jets, he could've flown her anywhere, even out of the country.

"Someone's coming," Arwel said.

A couple of moments later, a police car slowed down and then stopped next to them.

"I'll take care of that," Arwel said. He turned to the cops and smiled. "We are just changing a flat tire and we will be on our way. Thank you for stopping by to check on us."

The cop nodded. "You're just changing a flat tire. Carry on." The car drove away.

"Gorchenco's people?" Turner asked.

"On his payroll."

"I thought you couldn't read thoughts."

"I can't without thralling, and even with it I only get recent memories. They got a phone call to check us out. You were right about the surveillance cameras."

"Naturally. Hand me the spare tire."

"Should we get William on it? He can hack into them."

"Not likely. Those don't run through the internet. It's all closed circuit."

"How do you know?"

"Because that's the right way to do it. We are not dealing with amateurs."

"I guess we have no choice but to wait for Yamanu to get here."

"I agree." Turner finished changing the tire and dismounted the jack. "The problem is that I don't think Ella is still there. If she ever was."

He walked around to the passenger side. Even with his new and improved immortal body, Turner knew he shouldn't drive. Besides, he had a few phone calls to make, and people to pull out of bed.

"Who are you calling at this hour of the night?" Arwel asked as he turned on the ignition.

"I want to find out which of Gorchenco's jets flew out of New York yesterday and today and to where. Ella could've been on any of them."

"What about ground transportation? Are you ruling it out?"

"Not Gorchenco's style."

"Helicopters?"

"That's a possibility. I need to find out if his fleet includes any. I don't have an extensive file on him. Just the basics."

In the end, he decided against calling and sent out texts instead. There was no reason to wake up the spouses or significant others. People in his network knew to sleep with their phones nearby.

When he was done with that, Turner fired off another text to Kian. The drones the guy was sending over would be useless because they would get detected right away. The clan's satellite, on the other hand, would not.

The question was whether it was in the right position at this time or would be before morning.

"One hell of an operation this is turning out to be," Arwel

said. "Instead of operation Ella, we should call it operation Helen."

"Like Helen of Troy?"

"The stolen beauty who caused a war."

Turner leaned back against the headrest and closed his eyes. "The beautiful Helen didn't cause the war. The greedy men who lusted after her did."

ELLA

*T*he sound of jet engines revving up woke Ella. She bolted up to a sitting position. They were taking off? Should she buckle up? But how? She was in bed.

"It's okay. You can go back to sleep."

The lightly accented male voice had her whip her head to the right and her heart plunge down.

A man was sitting on a chair next to the bed, gazing at her with the most intense eyes she'd ever seen.

He was terrifying.

Ella didn't need him to introduce himself to know who he was. Even without the fancy slacks and the polished shoes and the gold cufflinks, she would have known it was the boss everyone feared.

Those blue eyes of his were cold and pale, and the soul behind them was rotten and dark.

"You look exactly like her." His tone was calm and contemplative, as if he was examining a rare object. "If I didn't know better, I would've thought you were her daughter."

Ella wanted to ask who he was talking about, but she was

afraid to open her mouth and say something wrong. Pavel's advice had been sound. When in doubt, it was smarter to keep her mouth shut and appear dumb than blurt out something that might get her in trouble.

She didn't want to get in trouble with this man.

He smiled, but it did nothing to soften the harshness of his features. If anything, it made him scarier. "You're a smart girl, Ella. You don't say anything and wait for me to do the talking. She wasn't as smart, just as beautiful. But enough about her. You know who I am, true?"

She nodded.

"Say my name."

"Dimitri," she whispered and then cleared her throat. "I wasn't told your last name," she said a little louder.

"Gorchenco."

His tone implied that she should know who he was, but Ella had never heard of Dimitri Gorchenco. Not all rich and powerful people had stories written about them in magazines.

She nodded again.

"Do you like your new clothes, Ella?"

The way Dimitri had enunciated her name reminded her of a scene from *Breaking Dawn*. That was how the leader of the Volturi vampires had said, "Bella."

The vampire hadn't been half as scary as the human.

"Yes, thank you." What she wanted to say was that he could shove them up his ass, but she was afraid even to think it.

He chuckled. "I see that a new wardrobe worth tens of thousands of dollars does not impress you." He tilted his head as if to take a better look at his new acquisition. "What impresses you, Ella?"

Again, her first instinct was to shrug and tell him that

nothing he had impressed her. But that would only get her in trouble. Besides, she would be lying.

Dimitri Gorchenco was impressive.

She could sense his power as if it was a physical thing. It was tainted, destructive. If Ella ever got to meet the devil, she had a feeling his aura would be very similar to Dimitri's.

"This." She waved a hand at the room she was in. "A bedroom in a jumbo jet. And I'm told that there is a bar and dining area upstairs. That's very impressive."

His thin lips lifted in a smile that didn't reach his eyes. "Smart girl. But you're not as clever as you think."

What did he mean by that? She didn't think herself smart at all. In fact, to fall for Romeo's act she must've been really stupid. The clues had been there. She'd just chosen to ignore them because she'd wanted to buy what he'd been selling.

With a sigh, Gorchenco got out of the chair and sat next to her on the bed.

Instinctively, Ella pulled the comforter up to her chin, even though the silk pajamas she had on were not revealing.

He yanked the comforter down. "Don't hide from me, Ella. As long as you do what you're told, you have nothing to fear from me. But if you don't, the consequences will be dire."

"I didn't do anything," she whispered. "I don't know what you're talking about."

His eyes bored into her. "You sound so sincere that I'm almost inclined to believe you. But the fact remains that someone warned your family and they escaped."

For a split moment, a surge of hope rose in Ella's heart, but it died as soon as Dimitri continued.

"Or rather they thought they did. You see, Ella, the three quarters of a million that I paid for you also bought me the surveillance equipment used to keep an eye on your family. It's no longer in Stefano's hands. It's in mine. I didn't expect to have a use for it so soon, so I only took a look just before coming here to see you. Imagine my surprise when I discovered that they were gone." He pinned her with a terrifying stare.

"I swear I didn't contact them. I couldn't even if I wanted to. I was locked up in one room or another without a phone the whole time. Maybe they went for a vacation?"

For a long moment, he didn't say anything, but his intense eyes seemed to take her apart and reach into her soul.

"A pretty girl like you could've convinced someone to do her a favor."

She shook her head. "I didn't. I swear to God and everything that is holy that I didn't contact my family, and that I didn't ask anyone to do it for me."

After another long moment he nodded. "I believe you. Which is very lucky for you because your punishment would've been quite severe."

Slumping against the pillows, Ella let out a breath. "Thank you."

"Maybe you're right, and they went on a vacation. If your mother intended to run, she would've packed more carefully and wouldn't have taken a tracking device with her. Although it's odd that she left her car at a mall parking lot. So maybe she did try to run but wasn't as smart about it as she thought."

"Maybe she met up with a friend at the mall and they continued together?" Ella couldn't think of anyone her mom would go on a vacation with, but it sounded like a logical explanation.

"Perhaps it's as you say. Nevertheless, I know where they are, and I've sent men to retrieve them. As long as you cooperate, your mother and brother are going to live in the lap of luxury. But if you don't, I'll punish them first and then you. Do you understand?"

Swallowing the bile rising in her throat, Ella nodded.

He caught her chin. "Say it, so I can hear it."

"I understand. I'll cooperate. I promise." She was never as close to peeing herself from fear.

Letting go of her chin, he cupped her cheek. "Good girl." He tucked the comforter around her and pressed a kiss to her forehead. "Get some sleep. I'll wake you up an hour before we land in London. If you need me, I'll be in the front room." With that, he pushed to his feet, collected his suit jacket from the back of the chair, and left the bedroom.

He even closed the door behind him.

For a few moments, all Ella could do was rock back and forth and chant in her head *oh my God, oh my God, oh my God.*

It took several more moments for her to process what Dimitri had said. Her mother and brother had somehow eluded Stefano's watchful equipment, either going on a vacation or running away.

However, Ella found it hard to believe that her mother would take Parker on a vacation at a time like this. Something must've prompted her mother to run and hide.

Whatever it was, though, the result was the same. Right now Gorchenco's people didn't have them, but they were closing in.

Maybe there was still time to warn her mother.

The moment her mom and Parker were caught, it would be game over. The three of them would remain in the devil's clutches until he decided to get rid of them.

There was only one way a man like that got rid of people, and it wasn't by sending them to the Bahamas.

Mom; Ella opened a channel.

There was no answer. At first, she panicked, but then it dawned on her that the sky outside the window was just starting to lighten, and that her mother must be still sleeping.

Mom, wake up!

Ella, oh my God. I thought I was dreaming. Where are you? Are you okay? Why did you block me?

I'm fine. I need you to listen carefully and not interrupt because there is no time.

I'm listening.

Romeo planted surveillance equipment in the house and in some of your things. That's how they ensure my cooperation. If I don't, they are going to hurt you. The guy who bought me just told me that he knows that you've escaped and that he can get you back because there is a tracking device hidden in the things you brought from home. Leave everything behind and run. Do you understand?

I do. I have people helping me, and their friends are going to get you out. We must've missed the tracking device, but we'll find it.

Don't look for it. You have no time. Just run.

Okay. But don't block me again. Leave the channel open.

I can't leave it open. I can't afford for them to suspect anything. But I'll contact you when I'm alone.

Just tell me if you're okay.

I'm fine, Mom. I just need to know you guys are safe.

Same here. Don't despair. Help is on the way.

I doubt it. I'm on a plane heading to London.

Oh my God.

We are wasting time. You need to run. I'll contact you in a few hours.

Okay. I love you.

Love you too. Now run!

VIVIAN

*V*ivian jumped out of bed and ran to Magnus's room through the connecting bathroom.

He opened a pair of sleepy eyes and smiled. "Couldn't stay away after all." Lifting the comforter, he patted the spot next to him. "Get in. I'll warm you up. You're shivering."

God, how was she going to tell him that they needed to run? Claim female intuition? He was never going to believe that Ella and she could communicate telepathically. And she couldn't claim that Ella had called her because her phone was still at the dental office.

Damn it, she didn't have time for a prolonged internal debate.

"We need to run. They know where we are."

He patted the mattress again. "Did you have a bad dream? Come here and I'll make it all better."

"No, damn it." She stamped her foot on the hardwood floor. "Listen to me. Ella and I can communicate telepathically. That's why I went to that psychic convention where I met Julian. She was blocking me for the entire time because they threatened her with harming us, just as you guys said they would. The guy who bought her just told her that he knows Parker and I have escaped, but that he also knows where we are because there is a tracking device hidden in the things we brought from home."

While she talked, Magnus's expression turned from sleepy and amused to serious and concerned.

He threw the comforter off. "I wish you'd told me about you and Ella sooner."

If she weren't so agitated, she might have noticed his nudity in all its magnificence. Instead, she averted her eyes. "It wouldn't have changed a thing. I tried to communicate with her numerous times. But unless she opens the channel, nothing goes through."

Magnus pulled on a pair of exercise pants. "Go wake up Parker."

"Okay."

He'd believed her. Wow. Vivian hadn't expected Magnus to so readily accept what she and Ella could do.

Just one more reason to fall for the guy.

Right. Rushing up the stairs she made enough noise to wake Parker up.

"What's going on, Mom?"

"We need to leave. The bad guys know where we are."

"How?"

"Apparently, we brought a tracker from home. It's hidden somewhere among our things."

Parker rubbed his eyes. "We need to find it."

Vivian pulled the comforter off him. "There is no time. We need to leave everything behind."

His eyes immediately went to his game console. "Everything?"

"I'll buy you everything new. I promise. Now get going. We are leaving in five minutes."

"Okay." He got out of bed and rushed to the bathroom.

Downstairs, Magnus was waiting for her with two folded sets of clothes. "It's good that I did laundry. Take off your clothes and put these on. Give the other ones to Parker."

"Your clothes are going to fall off us both."

"It's only for the car ride. I'm going to stop at the first mall and get you clothes and shoes so you can get out of the car and buy whatever you need."

"Aren't you taking it a bit too far?"

He thrust the clothes at her. "I'm angry with myself for not taking it far enough from the start. I underestimated the scumbag. I should've checked everything you brought with you before heading up here. It's my fault. I'm going to pay for every item you had to leave behind."

Maybe Magnus was right that he should've been more vigilant, but she couldn't accept his generous offer. "No, it's okay. Don't blame yourself."

"I do. I want you to pack everything and then make the beds. I don't want it to look as if you were warned. We are going to drop everything at the nearest donation center."

"Yeah, that's smart. I'll get right to it."

Good thinking on Magnus's part. They needed to stage it to look as if they'd left to continue on their vacation and not run away because they had been warned. God knew what the scum would do to Ella if he suspected her of somehow warning them.

And the idea of donating everything to the Salvation Army was clever too. The goons that Russian mafia boss had sent wouldn't know that everything she'd brought from home was in the donation bags. They would assume that she'd gotten rid of a few things and that the tracker just happened to be among those she'd donated.

Dressed and ready to go, Parker came down the stairs. "You said we are leaving in five minutes."

"Sorry, but Magnus made a few good suggestions. We

need to make it look as if we left to continue on our vacation and not ran away. So we need to pack everything, make the beds, and then take off our clothes and put Magnus's on. His are the only things that are for sure not bugged."

Parker's eyes widened. "Bugged? Can they hear us talk?"

"No. At least I don't think so. I meant a tracker."

From what Ella had told her, the Russian didn't know about Magnus or anyone else helping her. Which meant that no one was listening to what was going on in the cabin. They only knew the location.

"I don't get it. What are we going to do with the things we pack? Drop them in the woods somewhere?"

"No, because then they are going to find them and know that we were warned. That will get Ella in trouble. We are going to take everything to the Salvation Army donation center."

Parker looked at her with narrowed eyes. "I'm going up to pack my stuff. But when we are in the car, I want you to tell me how you know all that." He turned around and took the stairs two at a time.

Vivian sighed. She knew that one day she'd have to tell Parker about the telepathic connection she and Ella shared, but she'd hoped to have more time. He was still an impressionable boy who might feel left out or in some way diminished because he couldn't do what she and Ella could.

While shoving their things back into the trash bags, she tried to come out with a reasonable explanation she could give him for how Ella had warned her. In the end, though, she decided to tell him the truth and trust that he was mature enough to handle it.

As Magnus finished cleaning up the kitchen and took the trash bags out to the car, Vivian ducked into the bathroom to change into the clothes he'd given her.

It was good that the button-down shirt was long enough

to serve as a dress because the slacks were a lost cause. There was no way they would stay up.

"You look good in my shirt," he whispered as she came out.

She felt good in it too. Even though it had been laundered, some of his scent still lingered on the fabric, providing a false sense of security. Ignoring the suggestive comment, she stuffed her things into one of the trash bags.

Holding Magnus's pants up with one hand, Parker came down the stairs with a large trash bag in the other. "You're buying me everything new today."

"I promise," she and Magnus said at the same time.

Parker smiled. "It's okay, guys. You don't need to fight over it. I'm okay with you sharing."

MAGNUS

When everything and everyone was loaded into Turner's SUV—including Scarlet and all of her paraphernalia, all the trash bags containing Vivian and Parker's things, one completed bow, and ten arrows in various states of completion—Magnus locked things up and turned on the alarm.

No reason to make the goons' lives easier.

Getting behind the wheel, he looked at the back seat at Parker who was holding Scarlet on his lap. "Everyone ready?"

"Yep. If she pees, it's going to be on your pants."

He was so proud of the boy. The kid wasn't panicking, he wasn't fussing about having to toss out all of his gaming consoles and his games. When they got to the mall, Magnus was going to treat Parker to every game and console he'd ever dreamt of.

He turned the ignition on. "No problem. As it is, we are going to spend half of the day shopping for clothes and shoes and everything else. I might as well buy myself a couple of pairs of jeans."

Vivian arched a brow. "What happened? The boonies had

such a profound effect on you that you've decided to go native?"

"Not at all. But I can't order custom-made slacks until I get back to civilization." He winked at her.

"You custom order your clothes?"

"It's the only way to go. Ready-made things never fit as well."

"You're a snob, aren't you?"

"Guilty as charged."

She crossed her arms over her chest. "Where are we going? Do you have another safe house somewhere?"

"I'll find us a place to stay. I need to call my boss, but it's too early in the morning."

It was a lie. The sun was up and so was Kian, but he couldn't talk to him with Vivian and Parker listening in.

"We could stay in a hotel."

"That's an option." He hoped Kian would allow him to bring Vivian and Parker to the village.

With the revelation of her paranormal ability, there was a chance that she was a Dormant. And didn't that make him one happy dude. It was too early to get all excited and break out in a song and dance, but he sure as hell felt like doing just that.

Not yet, though. First of all he couldn't be sure, and secondly, Vivian would think he'd lost his marbles.

She uncrossed her arms and shifted to pull on the shirt bottom. "I would give anything for a cup of coffee. But I can't get out of the car dressed like this."

"First, we need to get to the nearest donation center and drop off your stuff. Then I can get us breakfast from a drive-through."

Regrettably, the circumstances demanded some sacrifices. If Vivian and Parker were okay with donating all of their things, he could suffer through eating breakfast in the car.

After all, this was still a mission and he was on duty. His personal preferences should be put aside.

Vivian pulled her phone out of the ziplock bag where she'd put all the things Magnus had deemed safe. The phone was clan issue, so it was good to go.

It took her a minute to find what she was looking for. "The nearest collection center is an hour's drive away."

"It's probably going to be closed this early in the morning."

"I think they have collection bins outside. Are you sure we can't get coffee to go on the way?"

"Keep your eyes open. If you see a drive-through, let me know."

"Thank you." She put her hand on his arm. "You're the best."

If she only knew how right that statement was, and it wasn't because he was full of himself.

Magnus couldn't wait to tell Vivian that he was immortal and that she could be with him without fear. Her so-called curse couldn't kill him.

But again, it was way too early to even think of that. He wasn't sure what steps were required to determine whether someone was a Dormant. Up until now, the possibility of him finding one had been so remote that he hadn't bothered to learn more about the subject.

Would Julian know?

Perhaps it would be better to consult Bridget. She was more experienced.

"What are you thinking about?" Vivian asked.

"This and that."

"Are you thinking about Ella?"

He shook his head. "What else did she tell you?"

"Yeah," Parker said from the back seat. "What I want to know is how Ella called you without having your new number. Did she dial your old one and the call was forwarded to the new one?"

Magnus cast Vivian a sidelong glance. Apparently, Parker was ignorant of the telepathic connection his mom and sister shared. A smart move on Vivian's part. Kids tended to blurt things out without thinking. He would've been laughed at and ridiculed.

Except, it seemed that Vivian and Ella had kept it a secret not only from Parker but from everyone.

Was it out of fear?

Probably.

The most likely outcome would have been disbelief. People would have thought she was delusional and made fun of her. But that was the lesser evil.

Given her history of bad luck, those who believed her might have thought she was a witch. These days it wouldn't have meant death by fire as it had in the past, but it could've resulted in her being shunned.

"Earth calling Mom. I'm still waiting for an answer."

Vivian turned back to look at her son. "Can you accept a raincheck on that?"

"Why? It's either a yes or a no."

"It's more complicated than that. I promise I'll explain. Just not right now."

"Today, though."

"Today. Once we get settled in our new safe house or in a hotel."

Vivian slapped a hand on her forehead. "I'm such an idiot. I almost forgot. Ella said that she's on Gorchenco's plane and that they are on their way to London. You need to tell your boss to cancel the operation. I'm so sorry that I didn't say anything before. In the mad rush to escape, it completely slipped my mind."

Shite. That was really bad news. "No harm done. The reinforcements Turner asked for probably haven't arrived at New York yet, and the extraction was scheduled for much later tonight. I'll text him as soon as I can."

The end...for now...

Dear reader,

Thank you for reading the ***Children of the Gods series.***

If you enjoyed the story, I would be grateful if you could leave a **review** for *Dark Widow's Secret* on Amazon. With a few words, you'll make me very happy. :-)

COMING UP NEXT
THE CHILDREN OF THE GODS BOOK 24
DARK WIDOW'S CURSE
BOOK 2 IN MAGNUS & VIVIAN'S STORY

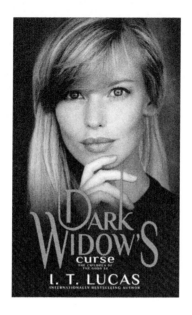

FOR EXCLUSIVE PEEKS AT UPCOMING RELEASES

JOIN MY *VIP CLUB* AND GAIN ACCESS TO THE VIP PORTAL AT

ITLUCAS.COM

CLICK HERE TO JOIN

(OR GO TO: http://eepurl.com/blMTpD)

If you're already a subscriber and forgot the password to the VIP portal, you can find it at the bottom of each of my emails. Or click HERE to retrieve it.

You can also email me at isabell@itlucas.com

DON'T MISS OUT ON

GODDESS'S HOPE

AREANA & NAVUH'S STORY

THE CHILDREN OF THE GODS ORIGINS BOOK 2

IS AVAILABLE ON AMAZON

"I have read all of I. T. Lucas' books in this series and I have loved all of them. I have to be honest, I initially shied away from the Goddess' books because I thought, "Meh. I've heard the backstory so many times in the other books. I'd rather stick to the present." I am so glad I changed my mind! While Goddess's Choice was good, Areana's story in Goddess's Hope surprised me with it's plot twists and kept me on the edge of my seat. Learning about Navuh, the man changed many of my feelings about Navuh, the head of the evil empire. And of course, we're left with many questions that I can't wait for answers to!"

"Wonderful Read!!

No other words but completely captivating! I can't wait for the next book and I feel that way every time I finish reading the latest book in this series! Lucas has created an amazing world! This book provides a lot of background information on Annani and the gods around her when she was younger, her sister, Areana, and the events unfolding to the nuclear bomb that destroyed so much of the world. The story of Navuh and Areana is very interesting and I can't wait to find out what happens to them in a future book!"

skeptical and refuses Amanda's plea to attempt Syssi's activation. But when his enemies learn of the Dormant's existence, he's forced to rush her to the safety of his keep. Inexorably drawn to Syssi, Kian wrestles with his conscience as he is tempted to explore her budding interest in the darker shades of sensuality.

2: Dark Stranger Revealed

While sheltered in the clan's stronghold, Syssi is unaware that Kian and Amanda are not human, and neither are the supposedly religious fanatics that are after her. She feels a powerful connection to Kian, and as he introduces her to a world of pleasure she never dared imagine, his dominant sexuality is a revelation. Considering that she's completely out of her element, Syssi feels comfortable and safe letting go with him. That is, until she begins to suspect that all is not as it seems. Piecing the puzzle together, she draws a scary, yet wrong conclusion...

3: Dark Stranger Immortal

When Kian confesses his true nature, Syssi is not as much shocked by the revelation as she is wounded by what she perceives as his callous plans for her.

If she doesn't turn, he'll be forced to erase her memories and let her go. His family's safety demands secrecy – no one in the mortal world is allowed to know that immortals exist.

Resigned to the cruel reality that even if she stays on to never again leave the keep, she'll get old while Kian won't, Syssi is determined to enjoy what little time she has with him, one day at a time.

Can Kian let go of the mortal woman he loves? Will Syssi turn? And if she does, will she survive the dangerous transition?

4: Dark Enemy Taken

Dalhu can't believe his luck when he stumbles upon the beautiful immortal professor. Presented with a once in a lifetime opportunity to grab an immortal female for himself, he kidnaps her and runs. If he ever gets caught, either by her people or his, his life is forfeit. But for a chance of a loving mate and a family of his own, Dalhu is prepared to do everything in his power to win Amanda's heart, and that includes leaving the Doom brotherhood and his old life behind.

Amanda soon discovers that there is more to the handsome Doomer than his dark past and a hulking, sexy body. But succumbing to her enemy's seduction, or worse, developing feelings for a ruthless killer is out of the question. No man is worth life on the run, not even the one and only immortal male she could claim as her own...

Her clan and her research must come first...

5: Dark Enemy Captive

When the rescue team returns with Amanda and the chained Dalhu to the keep, Amanda is not as thrilled to be back as she thought she'd be. Between Kian's contempt for her and Dalhu's imprisonment, Amanda's budding relationship with Dalhu seems doomed. Things start to look up when Annani offers her help, and together with Syssi they resolve to find a way for Amanda to be with Dalhu. But will she still want him when she realizes that he is responsible for her nephew's murder? Could she? Will she take the easy way out and choose Andrew instead?

6: Dark Enemy Redeemed

Amanda suspects that something fishy is going on onboard the Anna. But when her investigation of the peculiar all-female Russian crew fails to uncover anything other than more speculation, she decides it's time to stop playing detective and face her real problem —a man she shouldn't want but can't live without.

6.5: My Dark Amazon

When Michael and Kri fight off a gang of humans, Michael gets stabbed. The injury to his immortal body recovers fast, but the one to his ego takes longer, putting a strain on his relationship with Kri.

7: Dark Warrior Mine

When Andrew is forced to retire from active duty, he believes that all he has to look forward to is a boring desk job. His glory days in special ops are over. But as it turns out, his thrill ride has just begun. Andrew discovers not only that immortals exist and have been manipulating global affairs since antiquity, but that he and his sister are rare possessors of the immortal genes.

Problem is, Andrew might be too old to attempt the activation process. His sister, who is fourteen years his junior, barely made it through the transition, so the odds of him coming out of it alive, let alone immortal, are slim.

But fate may force his hand.

Helping a friend find his long-lost daughter, Andrew finds a woman who's worth taking the risk for. Nathalie might be a Dormant, but the only way to find out for sure requires fangs and venom.

8: DARK WARRIOR'S PROMISE

Andrew and Nathalie's love flourishes, but the secrets they keep from each other taint their relationship with doubts and suspicions. In the meantime, Sebastian and his men are getting bolder, and the storm that's brewing will shift the balance of power in the millennia-old conflict between Annani's clan and its enemies.

9: DARK WARRIOR'S DESTINY

The new ghost in Nathalie's head remembers who he was in life, providing Andrew and her with indisputable proof that he is real and not a figment of her imagination.

Convinced that she is a Dormant, Andrew decides to go forward with his transition immediately after the rescue mission at the Doomers' HQ.

Fearing for his life, Nathalie pleads with him to reconsider. She'd rather spend the rest of her mortal days with Andrew than risk what they have for the fickle promise of immortality.

While the clan gets ready for battle, Carol gets help from an unlikely ally. Sebastian's second-in-command can no longer ignore the torment she suffers at the hands of his commander and offers to help her, but only if she agrees to his terms.

10: DARK WARRIOR'S LEGACY

Andrew's acclimation to his post-transition body isn't easy. His senses are sharper, he's bigger, stronger, and hungrier. Nathalie fears that the changes in the man she loves are more than physical. Measuring up to this new version of him is going to be a challenge.

Carol and Robert are disillusioned with each other. They are not destined mates, and love is not on the horizon. When Robert's three months are up, he might be left with nothing to show for his sacrifice.

Lana contacts Anandur with disturbing news; the yacht and its human cargo are in Mexico. Kian must find a way to apprehend Alex and rescue the women on board without causing an international incident.

11: Dark Guardian Found

What would you do if you stopped aging?

Eva runs. The ex-DEA agent doesn't know what caused her strange mutation, only that if discovered, she'll be dissected like a lab rat. What Eva doesn't know, though, is that she's a descendant of the gods, and that she is not alone. The man who rocked her world in one life-changing encounter over thirty years ago is an immortal as well.

To keep his people's existence secret, Bhathian was forced to turn his back on the only woman who ever captured his heart, but he's never forgotten and never stopped looking for her.

12: Dark Guardian Craved

Cautious after a lifetime of disappointments, Eva is mistrustful of Bhathian's professed feelings of love. She accepts him as a lover and a confidant but not as a life partner.

Jackson suspects that Tessa is his true love mate, but unless she overcomes her fears, he might never find out.

Carol gets an offer she can't refuse—a chance to prove that there is more to her than meets the eye. Robert believes she's about to commit a deadly mistake, but when he tries to dissuade her, she tells him to leave.

13: Dark Guardian's Mate

Prepare for the heart-warming culmination of Eva and Bhathian's story!

14: Dark Angel's Obsession

The cold and stoic warrior is an enigma even to those closest to him. His secrets are about to unravel...

15: Dark Angel's Seduction

Brundar is fighting a losing battle. Calypso is slowly chipping away his icy armor from the outside, while his need for her is melting it from the inside.

He can't allow it to happen. Calypso is a human with none of the Dormant indicators. There is no way he can keep her for more than a few weeks.

16: Dark Angel's Surrender

Get ready for the heart pounding conclusion to Brundar and Calypso's story.

Callie still couldn't wrap her head around it, nor could she summon even a smidgen of sorrow or regret. After all, she had some memories with him that weren't horrible. She should've felt something. But there was nothing, not even shock. Not even horror at what had transpired over the last couple of hours.

Maybe it was a typical response for survivors--feeling euphoric for the simple reason that they were alive. Especially when that survival was nothing short of miraculous.

Brundar's cold hand closed around hers, reminding her that they weren't out of the woods yet. Her injuries were superficial, and the most she had to worry about was some scarring. But, despite his and Anandur's reassurances, Brundar might never walk again.

If he ended up crippled because of her, she would never forgive herself for getting him involved in her crap.

"Are you okay, sweetling? Are you in pain?" Brundar asked.

Her injuries were nothing compared to his, and yet he was concerned about her. God, she loved this man. The thing was, if she told him that, he would run off, or crawl away as was the case.

Hey, maybe this was the perfect opportunity to spring it on him.

17: Dark Operative: A Shadow of Death

As a brilliant strategist and the only human entrusted with the secret of immortals' existence, Turner is both an asset and a liability to the clan. His request to attempt transition into immortality as an alternative to cancer treatments cannot be denied without risking the clan's exposure. On the other hand, approving it means risking his premature death. In both scenarios, the clan will lose a valuable ally.

When the decision is left to the clan's physician, Turner makes plans to manipulate her by taking advantage of her interest in him.

Will Bridget fall for the cold, calculated operative? Or will Turner fall into his own trap?

18: Dark Operative: A Glimmer of Hope

As Turner and Bridget's relationship deepens, living together seems like the right move, but to make it work both need to make concessions.

Bridget is realistic and keeps her expectations low. Turner could never be the truelove mate she yearns for, but he is as good as she's going to get. Other than his emotional limitations, he's perfect in every way.

Turner's hard shell is starting to show cracks. He wants immortality, he wants to be part of the clan, and he wants Bridget, but he doesn't want to cause her pain.

His options are either abandon his quest for immortality and give Bridget his few remaining decades, or abandon Bridget by going for the transition and most likely dying. His rational mind dictates that he chooses the former, but his gut pulls him toward the latter. Which one is he going to trust?

19: Dark Operative: The Dawn of Love

Get ready for the exciting finale of Bridget and Turner's story!

20: Dark Survivor Awakened

This was a strange new world she had awakened to.

Her memory loss must have been catastrophic because almost nothing was familiar. The language was foreign to her, with only a few words bearing some similarity to the language she thought in. Still, a full moon cycle had passed since her awakening, and little by little she was gaining basic understanding of it--only a few words and phrases, but she was learning more each day.

A week or so ago, a little girl on the street had tugged on her mother's sleeve and pointed at her. "Look, Mama, Wonder Woman!"

The mother smiled apologetically, saying something in the language these people spoke, then scurried away with the child looking behind her shoulder and grinning.

When it happened again with another child on the same day, it was settled.

Wonder Woman must have been the name of someone important in this strange world she had awoken to, and since both times it had been said with a smile it must have been a good one.

Wonder had a nice ring to it.

She just wished she knew what it meant.

21: Dark Survivor Echoes of Love

Wonder's journey continues in *Dark Survivor Echoes of Love*.

22: Dark Survivor Reunited

The exciting finale of Wonder and Anandur's story.

23: Dark Widow's Secret

Vivian and her daughter share a powerful telepathic connection, so when Ella can't be reached by conventional or psychic means, her mother fears the worst.

Help arrives from an unexpected source when Vivian gets a call from the young doctor she met at a psychic convention. Turns out Julian belongs to a private organization specializing in retrieving missing girls.

As Julian's clan mobilizes its considerable resources to rescue the daughter, Magnus is charged with keeping the gorgeous young mother safe.

Worry for Ella and the secrets Vivian and Magnus keep from each other should be enough to prevent the sparks of attraction from kindling a blaze of desire. Except, these pesky sparks have a mind of their own.

24: Dark Widow's Curse

A simple rescue operation turns into mission impossible when the Russian mafia gets involved. Bad things are supposed to come in threes, but in Vivian's case, it seems like there is no limit to bad luck. Her family and everyone who gets close to her is affected by her curse.

Will Magnus and his people prove her wrong?

25: Dark Widow's Blessing

The thrilling finale of the Dark Widow trilogy!

26: Dark Dream's Temptation

Julian has known Ella is the one for him from the moment he saw her picture, but when he finally frees her from captivity, she seems indifferent to him. Could he have been mistaken?

Ella's rescue should've ended that chapter in her life, but it seems like the road back to normalcy has just begun and it's full of obstacles. Between the pitying looks she gets and her mother's attempts to get her into therapy, Ella feels like she's typecast as a victim, when nothing could be further from the truth. She's a tough survivor, and she's going to prove it.

Strangely, the only one who seems to understand is Logan, who keeps popping up in her dreams. But then, he's a figment of her imagination—or is he?

27: Dark Dream's Unraveling

While trying to figure out a way around Logan's silencing compulsion, Ella concocts an ambitious plan. What if instead of trying to keep him out of her dreams, she could pretend to like him and lure him into a trap?

Catching Navuh's son would be a major boon for the clan, as well as for Ella. She will have her revenge, turning the tables on another scumbag out to get her.

28: Dark Dream's Trap

The trap is set, but who is the hunter and who is the prey? Find out in this heart-pounding conclusion to the *Dark Dream* trilogy.

29: Dark Prince's Enigma

As the son of the most dangerous male on the planet, Lokan lives by three rules:

Don't trust a soul.

Don't show emotions.

And don't get attached.

Will one extraordinary woman make him break all three?

30: DARK PRINCE'S DILEMMA

Will Kian decide that the benefits of trusting Lokan outweigh the risks?

Will Lokan betray his father and brothers for the greater good of his people?

Are Carol and Lokan true-love mates, or is one of them playing the other?

So many questions, the path ahead is anything but clear.

31: DARK PRINCE'S AGENDA

While Turner and Kian work out the details of Areana's rescue plan, Carol and Lokan's tumultuous relationship hits another snag. Is it a sign of things to come?

32 : DARK QUEEN'S QUEST

A former beauty queen, a retired undercover agent, and a successful model, Mey is not the typical damsel in distress. But when her sister drops off the radar and then someone starts following her around, she panics.

Following a vague clue that Kalugal might be in New York, Kian sends a team headed by Yamanu to search for him.

As Mey and Yamanu's paths cross, he offers her his help and protection, but will that be all?

33: DARK QUEEN'S KNIGHT

As the only member of his clan with a godlike power over human minds, Yamanu has been shielding his people for centuries, but that power comes at a steep price. When Mey enters his life, he's faced with the most difficult choice.

The safety of his clan or a future with his fated mate.

34: DARK QUEEN'S ARMY

As Mey anxiously waits for her transition to begin and for Yamanu to test whether his godlike powers are gone, the clan sets out to solve two mysteries:

Where is Jin, and is she there voluntarily?

Where is Kalugal, and what is he up to?

35: Dark Spy Conscripted

Jin possesses a unique paranormal ability. Just by touching someone, she can insert a mental hook into their psyche and tie a string of her consciousness to it, creating a tether. That doesn't make her a spy, though, not unless her talent is discovered by those seeking to exploit it.

36: Dark Spy's Mission

Jin's first spying mission is supposed to be easy. Walk into the club, touch Kalugal to tether her consciousness to him, and walk out.

Except, they should have known better.

37: Dark Spy's Resolution

The best-laid plans often go awry...

38: Dark Overlord New Horizon

Jacki has two talents that set her apart from the rest of the human race.

She has unpredictable glimpses of other people's futures, and she is immune to mind manipulation.

Unfortunately, both talents are pretty useless for finding a job other than the one she had in the government's paranormal division.

It seemed like a sweet deal, until she found out that the director planned on producing super babies by compelling the recruits into pairing up. When an opportunity to escape the program presented itself, she took it, only to find out that humans are not at the top of the food chain.

Immortals are real, and at the very top of the hierarchy is Kalugal, the most powerful, arrogant, and sexiest male she has ever met.

With one look, he sets her blood on fire, but Jacki is not a fool. A man like him will never think of her as anything more than a tasty snack, while she will never settle for anything less than his heart.

39: Dark Overlord's Wife

Jacki is still clinging to her all-or-nothing policy, but Kalugal is chipping away at her resistance. Perhaps it's time to ease up on her convictions. A little less than all is still much better than nothing, and a couple of decades with a demigod is probably worth more than a lifetime with a mere mortal.

40: Dark Overlord's Clan

As Jacki and Kalugal prepare to celebrate their union, Kian takes every precaution to safeguard his people. Except, Kalugal and his men are not his only potential adversaries, and compulsion is not the only power he should fear.

41: Dark Choices The Quandary

When Rufsur and Edna meet, the attraction is as unexpected as it is undeniable. Except, she's the clan's judge and councilwoman, and he's Kalugal's second-in-command. Will loyalty and duty to their people keep them apart?

42: Dark Choices Paradigm Shift

Edna and Rufsur are miserable without each other, and their two-week separation seems like an eternity. Long-distance relationships are difficult, but for immortal couples they are impossible. Unless one of them is willing to leave everything behind for the other, things are just going to get worse. Except, the cost of compromise is far greater than giving up their comfortable lives and hard-earned positions. The future of their people is on the line.

43: Dark Choices The Accord

The winds of change blowing over the village demand hard choices. For better or worse, Kian's decisions will alter the trajectory of the clan's future, and he is not ready to take the plunge. But as Edna and Rufsur's plight gains widespread support, his resistance slowly begins to erode.

44: Dark Secrets Resurgence

On a sabbatical from his Stanford teaching position, Professor

David Levinson finally has time to write the sci-fi novel he's been thinking about for years.

The phenomena of past life memories and near-death experiences are too controversial to include in his formal psychiatric research, while fiction is the perfect outlet for his esoteric ideas.

Hoping that a change of pace will provide the inspiration he needs, David accepts a friend's invitation to an old Scottish castle.

45: Dark Secrets Unveiled

When Professor David Levinson accepts a friend's invitation to an old Scottish castle, what he finds there is more fantastical than his most outlandish theories. The castle is home to a clan of immortals, their leader is a stunning demigoddess, and even more shockingly, it might be precisely where he belongs.

Except, the clan founder is hiding a secret that might cast a dark shadow on David's relationship with her daughter.

Nevertheless, when offered a chance at immortality, he agrees to undergo the dangerous induction process.

Will David survive his transition into immortality? And if he does, will his relationship with Sari survive the unveiling of her mother's secret?

46: Dark Secrets Absolved

Absolution.

David had given and received it.

The few short hours since he'd emerged from the coma had felt incredible. He'd finally been free of the guilt and pain, and for the first time since Jonah's death, he had felt truly happy and optimistic about the future.

He'd survived the transition into immortality, had been accepted into the clan, and was about to marry the best woman on the face of the planet, his true love mate, his salvation, his everything.

What could have possibly gone wrong?

Just about everything.

47: Dark haven Illusion

Welcome to Safe Haven, where not everything is what it seems.

On a quest to process personal pain, Anastasia joins the Safe Haven Spiritual Retreat.

Through meditation, self-reflection, and hard work, she hopes to make peace with the voices in her head.

This is where she belongs.

Except, membership comes with a hefty price, doubts are sacrilege, and leaving is not as easy as walking out the front gate.

Is living in utopia worth the sacrifice?

Anastasia believes so until the arrival of a new acolyte changes everything.

Apparently, the gods of old were not a myth, their immortal descendants share the planet with humans, and she might be a carrier of their genes.

48: Dark Haven Unmasked

As Anastasia leaves Safe Haven for a week-long romantic vacation with Leon, she hopes to explore her newly discovered passionate side, their budding relationship, and perhaps also solve the mystery of the voices in her head. What she discovers exceeds her wildest expectations.

In the meantime, Eleanor and Peter hope to solve another mystery. Who is Emmett Haderech, and what is he up to?

TRY THE SERIES ON

AUDIBLE

2 FREE audiobooks with your new Audible subscription!

THE PERFECT MATCH SERIES

Perfect Match 1: Vampire's Consort

When Gabriel's company is ready to start beta testing, he invites his old crush to inspect its medical safety protocol.

Curious about the revolutionary technology of the *Perfect Match Virtual Fantasy-Fulfillment studios*, Brenna agrees.

Neither expects to end up partnering for its first fully immersive test run.

Perfect Match 2: King's Chosen

When Lisa's nutty friends get her a gift certificate to *Perfect Match Virtual Fantasy Studios*, she has no intentions of using it. But since the only way to get a refund is if no partner can be found for her, she makes sure to request a fantasy so girly and over the top that no sane guy will pick it up.

Except, someone does.

Warning: This fantasy contains a hot, domineering crown prince, sweet insta-love, steamy love scenes painted with light shades of gray, a wedding, and a HEA in both the virtual and real worlds.

Intended for mature audience.

PERFECT MATCH 3: CAPTAIN'S CONQUEST

Working as a Starbucks barista, Alicia fends off flirting all day long, but none of the guys are as charming and sexy as Gregg. His frequent visits are the highlight of her day, but since he's never asked her out, she assumes he's taken. Besides, between a day job and a budding music career, she has no time to start a new relationship.

That is until Gregg makes her an offer she can't refuse—a gift certificate to the virtual fantasy fulfillment service everyone is talking about. As a huge Star Trek fan, Alicia has a perfect match in mind—the captain of the Starship Enterprise.

FOR EXCLUSIVE PEEKS AT UPCOMING RELEASES & A FREE COMPANION BOOK

Also by I. T. Lucas

THE CHILDREN OF THE GODS ORIGINS

THE CHILDREN OF THE GODS

Dark Stranger

Dark Enemy

Kri & Michael's Story

Dark Warrior

Dark Guardian

Dark Angel

Dark Operative

ALSO BY I. T. LUCAS

45: Dark Secrets Unveiled
46: Dark Secrets Absolved
Dark Haven
47: Dark haven Illusion
48: Dark Haven Unmasked

PERFECT MATCH

Perfect Match 1: Vampire's Consort
Perfect Match 2: King's Chosen
Perfect Match 3: Captain's Conquest

The Children of the Gods Series Sets

Books 1-3: Dark Stranger trilogy—Includes a bonus short story: **The Fates take a Vacation**

Books 4-6: Dark Enemy Trilogy —Includes a bonus short story—**The Fates' Post-Wedding Celebration**

Books 7-10: Dark Warrior Tetralogy

Books 11-13: Dark Guardian Trilogy

Books 14-16: Dark Angel Trilogy

Books 17-19: Dark Operative Trilogy

Books 20-22: Dark Survivor Trilogy

Books 23-25: Dark Widow Trilogy

Books 26-28: Dark Dream Trilogy

Books 29-31: Dark Prince Trilogy

Books 32-34: Dark Queen Trilogy

Books 35-37: Dark Spy Trilogy

Books 38-40: Dark Overlord Trilogy

Books 41-43: Dark Choices Trilogy

Books 44-46: Dark Secrets Trilogy

MEGA SETS

The Children of the Gods: Books 1-6—includes character lists

The Children of the Gods: Books 6.5-10 —includes character lists

———

TRY THE CHILDREN OF THE GODS SERIES ON AUDIBLE

2 FREE audiobooks with your new Audible subscription!

Printed in Great Britain
by Amazon